Austin Dobson

Horace Walpole A Memoir

With an Appendix of Books Printed at the Strawberry Hill Press

Austin Dobson

Horace Walpole A Memoir
With an Appendix of Books Printed at the Strawberry Hill Press

ISBN/EAN: 9783337087463

Printed in Europe, USA, Canada, Australia, Japan

Cover: Foto ©Raphael Reischuk / pixelio.de

More available books at **www.hansebooks.com**

HORACE WALPOLE

A Memoir

*WITH AN APPENDIX OF BOOKS PRINTED AT
THE STRAWBERRY-HILL PRESS*

BY

AUSTIN DOBSON

NEW YORK
DODD, MEAD AND COMPANY
1893

University Press:
John Wilson and Son, Cambridge, U.S.A.

CONTENTS.

CHAPTER I.

CHAPTER II.

CHAPTER VI.

CHAPTER VII.

CHAPTER VIII.

CHAPTER IX.

CHAPTER X.

LIST OF ILLUSTRATIONS.

HORACE WALPOLE:

𝔄 𝔐emoir.

CHAPTER I.

THE Walpoles of Houghton, in Norfolk, ten miles from King's Lynn, were an ancient family, tracing their pedigree to a certain Reginald de Walpole who was living in the time of William the Conqueror. Under Henry II. there was a Sir Henry de Walpol of Houton and Walpol ; and thenceforward an orderly procession of Henrys and Edwards and Johns (all

' of Houghton ') carried on the family name to the coronation of Charles II., when, in return for his vote and interest as a member of the Convention Parliament, one Edward Walpole was made a Knight of the Bath. This Sir Edward was in due time succeeded by his son, Robert, who married well, sat for Castle Rising,[1] one of the two family boroughs (the other being King's Lynn, for which his father had been member), and reputably filled the combined offices of county magnate and colonel of militia. But his chief claim to distinction is that his eldest son, also a Robert, afterwards became the famous statesman and Prime Minister to whose ' admirable prudence, fidelity, and success ' England owes her prosperity under the first Hanoverians. It is not, however, with the life of ' that corrupter of parliaments, that dissolute tipsy cynic, that courageous lover of peace and liberty, that great citizen, patriot, and statesman,' — to borrow a passage from one of Mr. Thackeray's graphic vignettes,—that these pages are concerned. It is more material to their purpose to note that in the year 1700, and on the 30th day of July in that year (being the day of the death of the Duke of Gloucester, heir presump-

---

[1] Another member for Castle Rising was Samuel Pepys, the Diarist.

tive to the crown of England), Robert Walpole, junior, then a young man of three-and-twenty, and late scholar of King's College, Cambridge, took to himself a wife. The lady chosen was Miss Catherine Shorter, eldest daughter of John Shorter, of Bybrook, an old Elizabethan red-brick house near Ashford in Kent. Her grandfather, Sir John Shorter, had been Lord Mayor of London under James II., and her father was a Norway timber merchant, having his wharf and counting-house on the Southwark side of the Thames, and his town residence in Norfolk Street, Strand, where, in all probability, his daughter met her future husband. They had a family of four sons and two daughters. One of the sons, William, died young. The third son, Horatio,[1] or Horace, born, as he himself tells us, on the 24th September, 1717, O. S., is the subject of this memoir.

With the birth of Horace Walpole is connected a scandal so industriously repeated by his later biographers that (although it has

---

[1] The name of *Horatio* I dislike. It is theatrical, and not English. I have, ever since I was a youth, written and subscribed *Horace*, an English name for an Englishman. In all my books (and perhaps you will think of the *numerosus Horatius*) I so spell my name. — *Walpoliana*, i. 62.

received far more attention than it deserves) it can scarcely be left unnoticed here. He had, it is asserted, little in common, either in tastes or appearance, with his elder brothers Robert and Edward, and he was born eleven years after the rest of his father's children. This led to a suggestion which first found definite expression in the *Introductory Anecdotes* supplied by Lady Louisa Stuart to Lord Wharncliffe's edition of the works of her grandmother, Lady Mary Wortley Montagu.[1] It was to the effect that Horace was not the son of Sir Robert Walpole, but of one of his mother's admirers, Carr, Lord Hervey, elder brother of Pope's ' Sporus,' the Hervey of the *Memoirs*. It is advanced in favour of this supposition that his likeness to the Herveys, both physically and mentally, was remarkable ; that the whilom Catherine Shorter was flighty, indiscreet, and fond of admiration ; and that Sir Robert's cynical disregard of his wife's vagaries, as well as his own gallantries (his second wife, Miss Skerret, had been his mistress), were matters of notoriety. On the

---

[1] It is also to be found asserted as a current story in the *Note Books* (unpublished) of the Duchess of Portland, the daughter of Edward Harley, second Earl of Oxford, and the ' noble, lovely little Peggy ' of her father's friend and *protégé*, Matthew Prior.

other hand, there is no indication that any suspicion of his parentage ever crossed the mind of Horace Walpole himself. His devotion to his mother was one of the most consistent traits in a character made up of many contradictions ; and although between the frail and fastidious virtuoso and the boisterous, fox-hunting Prime Minister there could have been but little sympathy, the son seems nevertheless to have sedulously maintained a filial reverence for his father, of whose enemies and detractors he remained, until his dying day, the implacable foe. Moreover, it must be remembered that, admirable as are Lady Louisa Stuart's recollections, in speaking of Horace Walpole she is speaking of one whose caustic pen and satiric tongue had never spared the reputation of the vivacious lady whose granddaughter she was.

With this reference to what can be, at best, but an insoluble question, we may return to the story of Walpole's earlier years. Of his childhood little is known beyond what he has himself told in the *Short Notes of my Life* which he drew up for the use of Mr. Berry, the nominal editor of his works.[1] His godfathers, he

[1] These, hereafter referred to as the *Short Notes*, are the chief authority for three parts of Walpole's not very eventful life. They were first published with the con-

says, were the Duke of Grafton and his father's second brother, Horatio, who afterwards became Baron Walpole of Wolterton. His godmother was his aunt, the beautiful Dorothy Walpole, who, escaping the snares of Lord Wharton, as related by Lady Louisa Stuart, had become the second wife of Charles, second Viscount Townshend. In 1724, he was ' inoculated for the small-pox ; ' and in the following year, was placed with his cousins, Lord Townshend's younger sons, at Bexley, in Kent, under the charge of one Weston, son to the Bishop of Exeter of that name. In 1726, the same course was pursued at Twickenham, and in the winter months he went to Lord Townshend's. Much of his boyhood, however, must have been spent in the house ' next the College ' at Chelsea, of which his father became possessed in 1722. It still exists in part, with but little alteration, as the infirmary of the hospital, and Ward No. 7 is said to have been its dining-room.[1] With this, or with some other reception-chamber at Chelsea, is connected one of the scanty anecdotes of

cluding series of his *Letters to Sir Horace Mann*, 2 vols., 1844, and are reprinted in Mr. Peter Cunningham's edition of the *Correspondence*, vol. i. (1857), pp. lxi–lxxvii.

[1] Martin's *Old Chelsea*, 1889, p. 82 ; Beaver's *Memorials of Old Chelsea*, 1892, p. 291.

this time. Once, when Walpole was a boy, there came to see his mother one of those formerly famous beauties chronicled by Anthony Hamilton, — 'la belle Jennings,' elder sister to the celebrated Duchess of Marlborough, and afterwards Duchess of Tyrconnell. At this date she was a needy Jacobite seeking Lady Walpole's interest in order to obtain a pension. She no longer possessed those radiant charms which under Charles had revealed her even through the disguise of an orange-girl ; and now, says Walpole, annotating his own copy of the *Memoirs of Grammont*, ' her eyes being dim, and she full of flattery, she commended the beauty of the prospect ; but unluckily the room in which they sat looked only against the garden-wall.' [1]

Another of the few events of his boyhood which he records, illustrates the old proverb that ' One half of the world knows not how the

[1] Cunningham, v. 36, and ix. 519. The Duchess of Tyrconnell's portrait, copied by Milbourn from the original at Lord Spencer's, was one of the prominent ornaments of the Great Bedchamber at Strawberry Hill. (See *A Description of the Villa*, etc., 1774, p. 138.) There are some previously unpublished particulars respecting her as ' Mlle. Genins ' in M. Jusserand's extremely interesting *French Ambassador at the Court of Charles the Second*, 1892, pp. 153 *et seq.*, 170, 182.

other half lives,' rather than any particular phase
of his biography. Going with his mother to buy
some bugles (beads), at the time when the opposition to his father was at its highest, he notes
that having made her purchase, — beads were
then out of fashion, and the shop was in some
obscure alley in the City, where lingered un-
fashionable things, — Lady Walpole bade the
shopman send it home. Being asked whither,
she replied, ' To Sir Robert Walpole's.' ' And
who,' rejoined he coolly, ' is Sir Robert Walpole ? '[1] But the most interesting incident of
his youth was the visit he paid to the King,
which he has himself related in Chapter I. of
the *Reminiscences.* How it came about he does
not know, but at ten years old an overmaster-
ing desire seized him to inspect His Majesty.
This childish caprice was so strong that his
mother, who seldom thwarted him, solicited the
Duchess of Kendal (the *maitresse en titre*) to
obtain for her son the honour of kissing King
George's hand before he set out upon that visit
to Hanover from which he was never to return.
It was an unusual request, but being made by
the Prime Minister's wife, could scarcely be re-
fused. To conciliate etiquette and avoid precedent, however, it was arranged that the audience

----

[1] *Walpole to the Miss Berrys,* 5 March, 1791.

Lady Walpole.

CATHERINE
LADY
WALPOLE

should be in private and at night. 'Accordingly, the night but one before the King began his last journey [*i. c.*, on 1 June, 1727], my mother carried me at ten at night to the apartment of the Countess of Walsingham [Melusina de Schulemberg, the Duchess's reputed niece], on the ground floor, towards the garden at St. James's, which opened into that of her aunt, . . . apartments occupied by George II. after his Queen's death, and by his successive mistresses, the Countesses of Suffolk [Mrs. Howard] and Yarmouth [Madame de Walmoden]. Notice being given that the King was come down to supper, Lady Walsingham took me alone into the Duchess's ante-room, where we found alone the King and her. I knelt down, and kissed his hand. He said a few words to me, and my conductress led me back to my mother. The person of the King is as perfect in my memory as if I saw him but yesterday. It was that of an elderly man, rather pale, and exactly like his pictures and coins; not tall; of an aspect rather good than august; with a dark tie-wig, a plain coat, waistcoat, and breeches of snuff-coloured cloth, with stockings of the same colour, and a blue ribband over all. So entirely was he my object that I do not believe I once looked at the Duchess; but as I could not avoid seeing her on entering the room, I remember that just beyond His Majesty stood a very tall, lean, ill-favoured old lady ; but I did not retain the least idea of her features, nor know what the colour of her dress was.'[1]   In the *Walpoliana* (p. 25)[2] Walpole is made to say that his introducer was his father, and that the King took him up in his arms and kissed him. Walpole's own written account is the more probable one.   His audience must have been one of the last the King granted, for, as already stated, it was almost on the eve of his departure ; and ten days later, when his chariot clattered swiftly into the courtyard of his brother's palace at Osnabruck, he lay dead in his seat, and the reign of his successor had begun.

Although Walpole gives us a description of George I., he does not, of course, supply us with any portrait of himself.   But in Mr. Peter

---

[1] *Reminiscences of the Courts of George the First and Second*, in Cunningham's *Corr.*, i. xciii–xciv.

[2] The book referred to is a ' little lounging miscellany ' of notes and anecdotes by John Pinkerton, and was printed, soon after Walpole's death, by Bensley, who lived in Johnson's old house, No. 8 Bolt Court.   It requires to to be used with caution (see *Quarterly Review*, vol. lxxii., No. cxliv.), and must not be confused with Lord Hardwicke's privately printed *Walpoliana*, which relate to Sir Robert Walpole.

Cunningham's excellent edition of the *Correspondence* there is a copy of an oil-painting belonging (1857) to Mrs. Bedford of Kensington, which, upon the faith of a Cupid who points with an arrow to the number ten upon a dial, may be accepted as representing him about the time of the above interview. It is a full length of a slight, effeminate-looking lad in a stiff-skirted coat, knee-breeches, and open-breasted laced waistcoat, standing in a somewhat affected attitude at the side of the afore-mentioned sun-dial. He has dark, intelligent eyes, and a profusion of light hair curling abundantly about his ears and reaching to his neck. If the date given in the *Short Notes* be correct, he must have already become an Eton boy, since he says that he went to that school on the 26th April, 1727, and he adds in the *Reminiscences* that he shed a flood of tears for the King's death, when, ' with the other scholars at Eton College,' he walked in procession to the proclamation of his successor. Of the cause of this emotion he seems rather doubtful, leaving us to attribute it partly to the King's condescension in gratifying his childish loyalty, partly to the feeling that, as the Prime Minister's son, it was incumbent on him to be more concerned than his schoolfellows; while the spectators, it is hinted, placed it to the

credit of a third and not less cogent cause, —
the probability of that Minister's downfall. Of
this, however, as he says, he could not have had
the slightest conception. His tutor at Eton
was Henry Bland, eldest son of the master
of the school. ' I remember,' says Walpole,
writing later to his relative and schoolfellow
Conway, ' when I was at Eton, and Mr. Bland
had set me an extraordinary task, I used sometimes to pique myself upon not getting it,
because it was not immediately my school business. What, learn more than I was absolutely
forced to learn ! I felt the weight of learning
that, for I was a blockhead, and pushed up
above my parts.' That, as the son of the great
Minister, he was pushed, is probably true ; but,
despite his own disclaimer, it is clear that his abilities were by no means to be despised. Indeed,
one of the *pièces justificatives* in the story of
Lady Louisa Stuart, though advanced for another
purpose, is distinctly in favour of something
more than average talent. Supporting her theory
as to his birth by the statement that in his boyhood he was left so entirely in the hands of his
mother as to have little acquaintance with his
father, she goes on to say that ' Sir Robert
Walpole took scarcely any notice of him, till his
proficiency at Eton School, when a lad of some

standing, drew his attention, and proved that whether he had or had not a right to the name he went by, he was likely to do it honour.'[1] Whatever this may be held to prove, it certainly proves that he was not the blockhead he declares himself to have been.

Among his schoolmates he made many friends. For his cousins, Henry (afterwards Marshal) Conway and Lord Hertford, Conway's elder brother, he formed an attachment which lasted through life, and many of his best letters were written to these relatives. Other associates were the later lyrist, Charles Hanbury Williams, and the famous wit, George Augustus Selwyn, both of whom, if the child be father to the man, must be supposed to have had unusual attractions for their equally witty schoolmate. Another contemporary at school, to whom, in after life, he addressed many letters, was William Cole, subsequently to develop into a laborious antiquary, and probably already exhibiting proclivities towards 'tall copies' and black letter. But his chiefest friends, no doubt, were grouped in the two bodies christened

---

[1] This is quoted by Mr. Hayward and others as if the last words were Sir Robert Walpole's. But Lady Louisa Stuart says nothing to indicate this (Lady Mary Wortley Montagu's *Letters*, etc., 1887, i. xciii).

respectively the 'triumvirate' and the 'quadruple alliance.'

Of these the 'triumvirate' was the less important. It consisted of Walpole and the two sons of Brigadier-General Edward Montagu. George, the elder, afterwards M.P. for Northampton, and the recipient of some of the most genuine specimens of his friend's correspondence, is described in advanced age as 'a gentleman-like body of the *vieille cour*,' usually attended by a younger brother, who was still a midshipman at the mature age of sixty, and whose chief occupation consisted in carrying about his elder's snuff-box. Charles Montagu, the remaining member of the 'triumvirate,' became a Lieut.-General and Knight of the Bath. But it was George, who had 'a fine sense of humour, and much curious information,' who was Walpole's favourite. 'Dear George,'—he writes to him from Cambridge, — 'were not the playing fields at Eton food for all manner of flights? No old maid's gown, though it had been tormented into all the fashions from King James to King George, ever underwent so many transformations as those poor plains have in my idea. At first I was contented with tending a visionary flock, and sighing some pastoral name to the echo of the cascade under the bridge. How happy should I have been to have had a kingdom only for the pleasure of being driven from it, and living disguised in an humble vale! As I got further into Virgil and Clelia, I found myself transported from Arcadia to the garden of Italy; and saw Windsor Castle in no other view than the *Capitoli immobile saxum.*' Further on he makes an admission which need scarcely surprise us. ' I can't say I am sorry I was never quite a schoolboy: an expedition against bargemen, or a match at cricket, may be very pretty things to recollect; but, thank my stars, I can remember things that are very near as pretty. The beginning of my Roman history was spent in the asylum, or conversing in Egeria's hallowed grove; not in thumping and pummelling King Amulius's herdsmen.'[1] The description seems to indicate a schoolboy of a rather refined and effeminate type, who would probably fare ill with robuster spirits. But Walpole's social position doubtless preserved him from the persecution which that variety generally experiences at the hands — literally the hands — of the tyrants of the playground.

The same delicacy of organisation seems to have been a main connecting link in the second or ' quadruple alliance ' already referred to, — an

[1] *Letter to Montagu,* 6 May, 1736.

alliance, it may be, less intrinsically intimate, but more obviously cultivated. The most important figure in this quartet was a boy as frail and delicate as Walpole himself, ' with a broad, pale brow, sharp nose and chin, large eyes, and a pert expression,' who was afterwards to become famous as the author of one of the most popular poems in the language, the *Elegy written in a Country Church Yard.* Thomas Gray was at this time about thirteen, and consequently somewhat older than his schoolmate. Another member of the association was Richard West, also slightly older, a grandson of the Bishop Burnet who wrote the *History of My Own Time*, and son of the Lord Chancellor of Ireland. West, a slim, thoughtful lad, was the most precocious genius of the party, already making verses in Latin and English, and making them even in his sleep. The fourth member was Thomas Ashton, afterwards Fellow of Eton College and Rector of St. Botolph, Bishopsgate. Such was the group which may be pictured sauntering arm in arm through the Eton meadows, or threading the avenue which is still known as the ' Poet's Walk.' Each of the four had his nickname, either conferred by himself or by his schoolmates. Ashton, for example, was Plato ; Gray was Orosmades.

On 27 May, 1731, Walpole was entered at Lincoln's Inn, his father intending him for the law. 'But'—he says in the *Short Notes*—'I never went thither, not caring for the profession.' On 23 September, 1734, he left Eton for good, and no further particulars of his school-days remain. That they were not without their pleasant memories may, however, be inferred from the letters already quoted, and especially from one to George Montagu written some time afterwards upon the occasion of a visit to the once familiar scenes. It is dated from the Christopher Inn, a famous old hostelry, well known to Eton boys,—'The Christopher. How great I used to think anybody just landed at the Christopher! But here are no boys for me to send for; there I am, like Noah, just returned into his old world again, with all sorts of queer feels about me. By the way, the clock strikes the old cracked sound; I recollect so much, and remember so little; and want to play about; and am so afraid of my playfellows; and am ready to shirk Ashton; and can't help *making fun* of myself; and envy a dame over the way, that has just locked in her boarders, and is going to sit down in a little hot parlour to a very bad supper, so comfortably! And I could be so jolly a dog if I did not *fat*,—

which, by the way, is the first time the word was
ever applicable to me.   In short, I should be
out of all *bounds* if I was to tell you half I
feel, — how young again I am one minute, and
how old the next.   But do come and feel with
me, when you will, — to-morrow.   Adieu !   If
I don't compose myself a little more before
Sunday morning, when Ashton is to preach
[' Plato ' at the date of this letter had evidently
taken orders], I shall certainly *be in a bill for
laughing at church ;* but how to help it, to see
him in the pulpit, when the last time I saw him
here was standing up funking over against a
conduit to be catechised.' [1]

This letter, of which the date is not given,
but which Cunningham places after March,
1737, must have been written some time after
the writer had taken up his residence at Cambridge in his father's college of King's.[2]   This
he did in March, 1735, following an interval of
residence in London.   By this time the ' quad-

---

[1] *Walpole to Montagu.*   Cunningham, 1857, i. 15.

[2] Mr. D. C. Tovey (*Gray and his Friends*, 1890, 3 n.)
thinks that Ashton probably never preached at Eton
before he was made Fellow, in December, 1745, — which
would greatly advance the date of Walpole's communication.   But it is cited here solely for its reminiscences of
his school-days.

ruple alliance ' had been broken up by the defection of West, who, much against his will, had gone to Christ Church, Oxford. Ashton and Gray had, however, been a year at Cambridge, the latter as a fellow-commoner of Peterhouse, the former at Walpole's own college, King's. Cole and the Conways were also at Cambridge, so that much of the old intercourse must have been continued. Walpole's record of his university studies is of the most scanty kind. He does little more than give us the names of his tutors, public and private. In civil law he attended the lectures of Dr. Dickens of Trinity Hall ; in anatomy, those of Dr. Battie. French, he says, he had learnt at Eton. His Italian master at Cambridge was Signor Piazza (who had at least an Italian name !), and his instructor in drawing was the miniaturist Bernard Lens, the teacher of the Duke of Cumberland and the Princesses Mary and Louisa. Lens was the author of a *New and Complete Drawing Book for curious young Gentlemen and Ladies that study and practice the noble and commendable Art of Drawing, Colouring. etc.*, and is kindly referred to in the later *Anecdotes of Painting*. In mathematics. which Walpole seems to have hated as cordially as Swift and Goldsmith and Gray did, he sat at the feet of the blind

Professor Nicholas Saunderson, author of the
Elements of Algebra.[1]   Years afterwards (*à
propos* of a misguided enthusiast who had put
the forty-seventh proposition of Euclid into
Latin verse) he tells one of his correspondents
the result of these ministrations : ' I . . . was
always so incapable of learning mathematics
that I could not even get by heart the multipli-
cation table, as blind Professor Saunderson hon-
estly told me, above threescore years ago, when
I went to his lectures at Cambridge.   After the
first fortnight he said to me, ' Young man, it
would be cheating you to take your money ; for
you can never learn what I am trying to teach
you.'   I was exceedingly mortified, and cried ;
for, being a Prime Minister's son, I had firmly
believed all the flattery with which I had been
assured that my parts were capable of anything.
I paid a private instructor for a year ; but, at
the year's end, was forced to own Saunderson

---

[1] Saunderson had lost both his eyes in infancy from
small-pox.   This, however, did not prevent him from
lecturing on Newton's *Optics*, and becoming Lucasian
Professor of Mathematics at Cambridge.   Another under-
graduate who attended his lectures was Chesterfield. (See
Letter to Jouneau, 12 Oct., 1712.)   There is an interesting account of Saunderson by a former pupil, together
with an excellent portrait, in the *Gentleman's Magazine*
for September, 1754.

had been in the right.'[1] This private instructor was in all probability Mr. Trevigar, who, Walpole says, read lectures to him in mathematics and philosophy. From other expressions in his letters, it must be inferred that his progress in the dead languages, if respectable, was not brilliant. He confesses, on one occasion, his inability to help Cole in a Latin epitaph, and he tells Pinkerton that he never was a good Greek scholar.

His correspondence at this period, chiefly addressed to West and George Montagu, is not extensive, but it is already characteristic. In one of his letters to Montagu he encloses a translation of a little French dialogue between a turtle-dove and a passer-by. The verses are of no particular merit, but in the comment one recognizes a cast of style soon to be familiar. ' You will excuse this gentle nothing, I mean mine, when I tell you I translated it out of pure good-nature for the use of a disconsolate wood-pigeon in our grove, that was made a widow by the barbarity of a gun. She coos and calls me so movingly, 't would touch your heart to hear her. I protest to you it grieves me to pity her. She is so allicholly [2] as any

---

[1] *Walpole to Miss Berry*, 16 Aug., 1796.

[2] Indeed, she is given too much to allicholly and musing. — *Merry Wives of Windsor*, act i. sc. iv.

thing. I 'll warrant you now she 's as sorry as one of us would be. Well, good man, he 's gone, and he died like a lamb. She 's an unfortunate woman, but she must have patience.'[1] In another letter to West, after expressing his astonishment that Gray should be at Burnham in Buckinghamshire, and yet be too indolent to revisit the old Eton haunts in his vicinity, he goes on to gird at the university curriculum. At Cambridge, he says, they are supposed to betake themselves 'to some trade, as logic, philosophy, or mathematics.' But he has been used to the delicate food of Parnassus, and can never condescend to the grosser studies of Alma Mater. 'Sober cloth of syllogism colour suits me ill ; or, what 's worse, I hate clothes that one must prove to be of no colour at all. If the Muses *cælique vias et sidera monstrent,* and *quâ vi maria alta tumescant ;* why *accipiant :* but 't is thrashing, to study philosophy in the abstruse authors. I am not against cultivating these studies, as they are certainly useful ; but then they quite neglect all polite literature, all knowledge of this world. Indeed, such people have not much occasion for this latter ; for they shut themselves up from it, and study till they know less than any one.

[1] *Walpole to Montagu,* 30 May, 1736.

Great mathematicians have been of great use ;
but the generality of them are quite uncon-
versible : they frequent the stars, *sub pedibus-
que vident nubes*, but they can't see through
them. I tell you what I see ; that by living
amongst them, I write of nothing else : my letters are all parallelograms, two sides equal to
two sides ; and every paragraph an axiom.
that tells you nothing but what every mortal
almost knows.'[1] In an earlier note he has
been on a tour to Oxford, and, with a pre-
monition of the future connoisseur of Strawberry Hill, criticises the gentlemen's seats on
the road. 'Coming back, we saw Easton
Neston [in Northamptonshire]. a seat of Lord
Pomfret, where in an old greenhouse is a
wonderful fine statue of Tully, haranguing a
numerous assemblage of decayed emperors, ves-
tal virgins with new noses, Colossus's, Venus's,
headless carcases and carcaseless heads. pieces
of tombs, and hieroglyphics.'[2] A little later
he has been to his father's seat at Houghton :
' I am return'd again to Cambridge, and can
tell you what I never expected, — that I like
Norfolk. Not any of the ingredients, as Hunt-
ing or Country Gentlemen, for I had nothing to

---

[1] *Walpole to West,* 17 Aug., 1736.
[2] *Walpole to Montagu,* 20 May, 1736.

do with them, but the county; which a little
from Houghton is woody, and full of delight-
full prospects. I went to see Norwich and
Yarmouth, both which I like exceedingly.   I
spent my time at Houghton for the first week
almost alone. We have a charming garden, all
wilderness; much adapted to my Romantick
inclinations.'   In after life the liking for Norfolk here indicated does not seem to have
continued, especially when his father's death
had withdrawn a part of its attractions.   He
'hated Norfolk,' — says Mr. Cunningham.
'He did not care for Norfolk ale, Norfolk
turnips, Norfolk dumplings, or Norfolk turkeys.
Its flat, sandy, aguish scenery was not to his
taste.'   He preferred 'the rich blue prospects' of his mother's county, Kent.

Of literary effort while at Cambridge, Walpole's record is not great.   In 1736, he was one
of the group of university poets — Gray and
West being also of the number — who addressed
congratulatory verses to Frederick, Prince of
Wales, upon his marriage with the Princess
Augusta of Saxe-Gotha; and he wrote a poem
(which is reprinted in vol. i. of his works) to
the memory of the founder of King's College,
Henry VI.   This is dated 2 February, 1738.
In the interim Lady Walpole died.   Her son's

references to his loss display the most genuine regret. In a letter to Charles Lyttelton (afterwards the well-known Dean of Exeter, and Bishop of Carlisle), which is not included in Cunningham's edition, and is apparently dated in error September, 1732, instead of 1737,[1] he dwells with much feeling on 'the surprizing calmness and courage which my dear Mother show'd before her death. I believe few women wou'd behave so well, & I am certain no man cou'd behave better. For three or four days before she dyed, she spoke of it with less indifference than one speaks of a cold ; and while she was sensible, which she was within her two last hours, she discovered no manner of apprehension.' That his warm affection for her was well known to his friends may be inferred from a passage in one of Gray's letters to West : ' While I write to you, I hear the bad news of Lady Walpole's death on Saturday night last [20 Aug., 1737]. Forgive me if the thought of what my poor Horace must feel on that account, obliges me to have done.' [2] Lady Walpole was buried in Westminster Abbey, where, on her monument in Henry VIIth's Chapel, may be read the piously eulogistic

---

[1] *Notes and Queries*, 2 Jan., 1869.
[2] Gray's *Works*, by Gosse, 1884, ii. 9.

inscription which her youngest son composed
to her memory, — an inscription not easy to
reconcile in all its terms with the current
estimate of her character. But in August,
1737, she was considerably over fifty, and had
probably long outlived the scandals of which
she had been the subject in the days when
Kneller and Eckardt painted her as a young
and beautiful woman.

CHAPTER II.

THAT, in those piping days of patronage, when even very young ladies of quality drew pay as cornets of horse, the son of the Prime Minister of England should be left unprovided for, was not to be expected. While he was still resident at Cambridge, lucrative sinecures came to Horace Walpole. Soon after his mother's death, his father appointed him Inspector of Imports and Exports in the Custom House, — a post which he resigned in January. 1738, on succeeding Colonel William Townshend as Usher of the Exchequer. When, later in the year, he came of age (17 September), he ' took possession of two other little patent-places in the Exchequer, called Comptroller of the Pipe, and Clerk of the Estreats,' which had been held for him by a substitute. In 1782, when he still filled them, the two last-mentioned offices produced together about £300 per annum, while the Ushership of the Exchequer, at the date of his obtaining it, was reckoned to be worth £900 a year. 'From that time [he says] I lived on my own income, and travelled at my own expense; nor did I during my father's life receive from him but £250 at different times, — which I say not in derogation of his extreme tenderness and goodness to me, but to show that I was content with what he had given to me, and that from the age of twenty I was no charge to my family.'[1]

He continued at King's College for some time after he had attained his majority, only quitting it formally in March, 1739, not without regretful memories of which his future correspondence was to bear the traces. If he had neglected mathematics, and only moderately courted the classics, he had learnt something of the polite arts and of modern Continental letters, — studies which would naturally lead his inclination in the direction of

[1] *Account of my Conduct*, etc., *Works*, 1798, ii. 363-70.

Thomas Gray.

the inevitable 'Grand Tour.' Two years earlier he had very unwillingly declined an invitation from George Montagu and Lord Conway to join them in a visit to Italy. Since that date his desire for foreign travel, fostered no doubt by long conversations with Gray, had grown stronger, and he resolved to see · the palms and temples of the south' after the orthodox eighteenth-century fashion. To think of Gray in this connection was but natural, and he accordingly invited his friend (who had now quitted Cambridge, and was vegetating rather disconsolately in his father's house on Cornhill) to be his travelling companion. Walpole was to act as paymaster; but Gray was to be independent. Furthermore, Walpole made a will under which, if he died abroad, Gray was to be his sole legatee. Dispositions so advantageous and considerate scarcely admitted of refusal, even if Gray had been backward, which he was not. The two friends accordingly set out for Paris. Walpole makes the date of departure 10 March, 1739; Gray says they left Dover at twelve on the 29th.

The first records of the journey come from Amiens in a letter written by Gray to his mother. After a rough passage across the

Straits, they reached Calais at five.   Next day
they started for Boulogne in the then new-
fangled invention, a post-chaise, — a vehicle
which Gray describes 'as of much greater use
than beauty, resembling an ill-shaped chariot,
only with the door opening before instead of
[at] the side.'   Of Boulogne they see little,
and of Montreuil (where later Sterne engaged
La Fleur) Gray's only record, besides the
indifferent fare, is that ' Madame the hostess
made her appearance in long lappets of bone
lace, and a sack of linsey-woolsey.'   From
Montreuil they go by Abbeville to Amiens,
where they visit the cathedral, and the chapels
of the Jesuits and Ursuline Nuns.   But the
best part of this first letter is the little picture with which it (or rather as much of it as
Mason published) concludes.   'The country
we have passed through hitherto has been
flat, open, but agreeably diversified with vil-
lages, fields well cultivated, and little rivers.
On every hillock is a windmill, a crucifix, or
a Virgin Mary dressed in flowers and a sar-
cenet robe; one sees not many people or
carriages on the road; now and then indeed
you meet a strolling friar, a countryman with
his great muff, or a woman riding astride on a

little ass, with short petticoats, and a great head-dress of blue wool.'[1]

The foregoing letter is dated the 1st April, and it speaks of reaching Paris on the 3rd. But it was only on the evening of Saturday the 9th that they rolled into the French capital, 'driving through the streets a long while before they knew where they were.' Walpole had wisely resolved not to hurry, and they had besides broken down at Luzarches, and lingered at St. Denis over the curiosities of the abbey, particularly a vase of oriental onyx carved with Bacchus and the nymphs, of which they had dreamed ever since. At Paris, they found a warm welcome among the English residents, — notably from Mason's patron, Lord Holdernesse, and Walpole's cousins, the Conways. They seem to have plunged at once into the pleasures of the place, — pleasures in which, according to Walpole, cards and eating played far too absorbing a part. At Lord Holdernesse's they met at supper the famous author of *Manon Lescaut*, M. l'Abbé Antoine-François Prévost d'Exilles, who had just put forth the final volume of his tedious and scandalous *Histoire de M. Cléveland, fils naturel de Cromwel.* They went to the spec-

<hr>

[1] Gray's *Works*, by Gosse, 1884, ii. 18-19.

tacle of *Pandore* at the Salle des Machines of
the Tuileries ; and they went to the opera,
where they saw the successful *Ballet de la Paix*,
— a curious hotchpot, from Gray's description,
of cracked voices and incongruous mythology.
With the Comédie Française they were better
pleased, although Walpole, strange to say, unlike
Goldsmith ten years later, was not able to com-
mend the performance of Molière's *L'Avare*.
They saw Mademoiselle Gaussin (as yet unrivalled by the unrisen Mademoiselle Clairon)
in La Noue's tragedy of *Mahomet Second*, then
recently produced, with Dufresne in the leading
male part ; and they also saw the prince of
petits-maîtres, Grandval, acting with Dufresne's
sister, Mademoiselle Jeanne-Françoise Qui-
nault (an actress ' somewhat in Mrs. Clive's
way,' says Gray), in the *Philosophe marié* of
Nericault Destouches. — a charming comedy
already transferred to the English stage in the
version by John Kelly of *The Universal
Spectator.*

Theatres, however, are not the only amusements which the two travellers chronicle to
the home-keeping West. A great part of
their time is spent in seeing churches and
palaces full of pictures. Then there is the
inevitable visit to Versailles, which, in sum,

they concur in condemning. ‘ The great
front,’ says Walpole, ‘ is a lumber of littleness, composed of black brick, stuck full of
bad old busts, and fringed with gold rails.’
Gray (he says) likes it ; but Gray is scarcely
more complimentary, — at all events is quite
as hard upon the *façade*, using almost the
same phrases of depreciation. It is ‘ a huge
heap of littleness,’ in hue ‘ black, dirty red,
and yellow ; the first proceeding from stone
changed by age ; the second, from a mixture
of brick ; and the last, from a profusion of
tarnished gilding. You cannot see a more
disagreeable *tout ensemble ;* and, to finish the
matter, it is all stuck over in many places
with small busts of a tawny hue between
every two windows.’ The garden, however,
pleases him better ; nothing could be vaster
and more magnificent than the *coup d'œil*, with
its fountains and statues and grand canal. But
the ‘ general taste of the place ’ is petty and
artificial. ‘ All is forced, all is constrained
about you ; statues and vases sowed everywhere without distinction ; sugar-loaves and
minced pies of yew ; scrawl work of box, and
little squirting *jets d'eau*, besides a great same-
ness in the walks, — cannot help striking one at
first sight ; not to mention the silliest of laby-

rinths, and all Æsop's fables in water.'[1] 'The garden is littered with statues and fountains, each of which has its tutelary deity. In particular, the elementary god of fire solaces himself in one. In another, Enceladus, in lieu of a mountain, is overwhelmed with many waters. There are avenues of water-pots, who disport themselves much in squirting up cascadelins. In short, 'tis a garden for a great child.'[2] The day following, being Whitsunday, they witness a grand ceremonial, — the installation of nine Knights of the Saint Esprit : ' high mass celebrated with music, great crowd, much incense, King, Queen, Dauphin, Mesdames, Cardinals, and Court ; Knights arrayed by His Majesty ; reverences before the altar, not bows, but curtsies ; stiff hams ; much tittering among the ladies ; trumpets, kettle-drums, and fifes.'[8]

It is Gray who thus summarises the show. But we must go to Walpole for the account of another expedition, the visit to the Convent of the Chartreux, the uncouth horror of which, with its gloomy chapel and narrow cloisters, seems to have fascinated the Gothic soul of the future author of the *Castle of Otranto*. Here,

---

[1] *Gray to West*, 22 May, 1739.
[2] *Walpole to West*, no date, 1739.
[3] *Gray to West*, 22 May, 1739.

in one of the cells, they make the acquaintance of a fresh initiate into the order, — the account of whose environment suggests retirement rather than solitude. ' He was extremely civil, and called himself Dom Victor. We have promised to visit him often. Their habit is all white : but besides this he was infinitely clean in his person; and his apartment and garden, which he keeps and cultivates without any assistance, was neat to a degree. He has four little rooms, furnished in the prettiest manner, and hung with good prints. One of them is a library, and another a gallery. He has several canary-birds disposed in a pretty manner in breeding-cages. In his garden was a bed of good tulips in bloom, flowers and fruit-trees, and all neatly kept. They are permitted at certain hours to talk to strangers, but never to one another, or to go out of their convent.' In the same institution they saw Le Sueur's history (in pictures) of St. Bruno, the founder of the Chartreux. Walpole had not yet studied Raphael at Rome, but these pictures, he considered, excelled everything he had seen in England and Paris.[1]

' From thence [Paris],' say Walpole's *Short Notes,* ' we went with my cousin, Henry Conway, to Rheims, in Champagne, [and] staid there three

---

[1] *Walpole to West,* no date, 1739.

months.'   One of their chief objects was to improve themselves in French. 'You must not wonder,' he tells West, 'if all my letters resemble dictionaries, with French on one side, and English on t'other; I deal in nothing else at present, and talk a couple of words of each language alternately from morning till night.'[1] But he does not seem to have yet developed his later passion for letter-writing, and the 'account of our situation and proceedings' is still delegated to Gray, some of whose despatches at this time are not preserved.   There is, however, one from Rheims to Gray's mother which gives a vivid idea of the ancient French Cathedral city, slumbering in its vast vine-clad plain, with its picturesque old houses and lonely streets, its long walks under the ramparts, and its monotonous frog-haunted moat.   They have no want of society, for Henry Conway procured them introductions everywhere; but the Rhemois are more constrained, less familiar, less hospitable, than the Parisians.   Quadrille is the almost invariable amusement, interrupted by one entertainment (for the Rhemois as a rule give neither dinners nor suppers); to wit, a five o'clock *goûter*, which is 'a service of wine, fruits, cream, sweetmeats, crawfish, and cheese,'

[1] *Walpole to West*, 18 June, 1739.

after which they sit down to cards again. Occasionally, however, the demon of impromptu flutters these ' set, gray lives,' and (like Dr. Johnson) even Rheims must ' have a frisk.' ' For instance,' says Gray, ' the other evening we happened to be got together in a company of eighteen people, men and women of the best fashion here, at a garden in the town, to walk ; when one of the ladies bethought herself of asking, Why should we not sup here ? Immediately the cloth was laid by the side of a fountain under the trees, and a very elegant supper served up ; after which another said, Come, let us sing ; and directly began herself. From singing we insensibly fell to dancing, and singing in a round ; when somebody mentioned the violins, and immediately a company of them was ordered. Minuets were begun in the open air, and then came country dances, which held till four o'clock next morning ; at which hour the gayest lady there proposed that such as were weary should get into their coaches, and the rest of them should dance before them with the music in the van ; and in this manner we paraded through all the principal streets of the city, and waked everybody in it.' Walpole, adds Gray, would have made this entertainment chronic. But ' the women did not come into it,' and shrank back decorously ' to their dull cards, and usual formalities.' [1]

At Rheims the travellers lingered on in the hope of being joined by Selwyn and George Montagu. In September they left Rheims for Dijon, the superior attractions of which town made them rather regret their comparative rustication of the last three months. From Dijon they passed southward to Lyons, whence Gray sent to West (then drinking the Tunbridge waters) a daintily elaborated conceit touching the junction of the Rhone and the Saône. While at Lyons they made an excursion to Geneva to escort Henry Conway, who had up to this time been their companion, on his way to that place. They took a roundabout route in order to visit the Convent of the Grande Chartreuse, and on the 28th Walpole writes to West from ' a Hamlet among the mountains of Savoy [Echelles].' He is to undergo many transmigrations, he says, before he ends his letter. ' Yesterday I was a shepherd of Dauphiné ; to-day an Alpine savage ; to-morrow a Carthusian monk ; and Friday a Swiss Calvinist.' When he next takes up his pen, he has passed through his third stage, and visited the Chartreuse. With the convent itself neither Gray

____
[1] Gray's *Works,* by Gosse, 1884, ii. 30.

nor his companions seem to have been much impressed, probably because their expectations had been indefinite. For the approach and the situation they had only enthusiasm. Gray is the accredited landscape-painter of the party, but here even Walpole breaks out: 'The road, West, the road! winding round a prodigious mountain, and surrounded with others, all shagged with hanging woods, obscured with pines, or lost in clouds! Below, a torrent breaking through cliffs, and tumbling through fragments of rocks! Sheets of cascades forcing their silver speed down channelled precipices, and hastening into the roughened river at the bottom! Now and then an old foot bridge, with a broken rail, a leaning cross, a cottage, or the ruin of an hermitage! This sounds too bombast and too romantic to one that has not seen it, too cold for one that has. If I could send you my letter post between two lovely tempests that echoed each other's wrath, you might have some idea of this noble roaring scene, as you were reading it. Almost on the summit, upon a fine verdure, but without any prospect, stands the Chartreuse.'[1]

The foregoing passage is dated Aix-in-Savoy, 30 September. Two days later, passing by Annecy, they came to Geneva. Here they

---

[1] *Walpole to West*, Sept. 28–2 Oct., 1739.

stayed a week to see Conway settled, and made a 'solitary journey' back to Lyons, but by a different road, through the spurs of the Jura and across the plains of La Bresse. At Lyons they found letters awaiting them from Sir Robert Walpole, desiring his son to go to Italy, — a proposal with which Gray, only too glad to exchange the over-commercial city of Lyons for 'the place in the world that best deserves seeing,' was highly delighted. Accordingly, we speedily find them duly equipped with 'beaver bonnets, beaver gloves, beaver stockings, muffs, and bear-skins' *en route* for the Alps. At the foot of Mont Cenis their chaise was taken to pieces and loaded on mules, and they themselves were transferred to low matted legless chairs carried on poles, — a not unperilous mode of progression, when, as in this case, quarrels took place among the bearers. But the tragedy of the journey happened before they had quitted the chaise. Walpole had a fat little black spaniel of King Charles's breed, named Tory, and he had let the little creature out of the carriage for the air. While it was waddling along contentedly at the horses' heads, a gaunt wolf rushed out of a fir wood, and exit poor Tory before any one had time to snap a pistol. In later years, Gray would perhaps have celebrated this mishap as elegantly as he sang the death of his friend's favourite cat ; but in these pre-poetic days he restricts himself to calling it an ' odd accident enough.'[1]

' After eight days' journey through Greenland,' — as Gray puts it to West, — they reached Turin, where among other English they found Pope's friend, Joseph Spence, Professor of Poetry at Oxford. Beyond Walpole's going to Court, and their visiting an extraordinary play called *La Rappresentazione dell' Anima Dannata* (for the benefit of an Hospital), a full and particular account of which is contained in one of Spence's letters to his mother,[2] nothing remarkable seems to have happened to them in the Piedmontese capital. From Turin they went on to Genoa, — ' the happy country where huge lemons grow ' (as Gray quotes, not textually, from Waller), — whose blue sea and vine-trellises they quit reluctantly

---

[1] Tory, however, was not *illachrymabilis*. He found his *vates sacer* in one Edward Burnaby Greene, once of Bennet College ; and in referring to this, thirty-five years later, Walpole explains how Tory got his name. ' His godmother was the widow of Alderman Parsons [Humphrey Parsons, of Goldsmith's ' black champagne '], who gave him at Paris to Lord Conway, and he to me ' (*Walpole to Cole*, 10 Dec., 1775).

[2] Spence's *Anecdotes*, by Singer, 2d ed., 1858, pp. 305-8.

for Bologna, by way of Tortona, Piacenza,
Parma (where they inspect the Correggios in
the Duomo), Reggio, and Modena.   At Bologna, in the absence of introductions, picture-
seeing is their main occupation.   'Except
pictures and statues,' writes Walpole, 'we
are not very fond of sights. . . . Now and then
we drop in at a procession, or a high mass,
hear the music, enjoy a strange attire, and hate
the foul monkhood.   Last week was the feast
of the Immaculate Conception.   On the eve
we went to the Franciscans' church to hear the
academical exercises.   There were moult and
moult clergy, about two dozen dames, that
treated one another with *illustrissima* and brown
kisses, the vice-legate, the gonfalonier, and
some senate.   The vice-legate . . . is a young
personable person of about twenty, and had on
a mighty pretty cardinal-kind of habit ; 't wou'd
make a delightful masquerade dress.   We asked
his name : Spinola.   What, a nephew of the
cardinal-legate ?   *Signor, no ; ma credo che gli
sia qualche cosa.*   He sat on the right hand
with the gonfalonier in two purple fauteuils.
Opposite was a throne of crimson damask,
with the device of the Academy, the Gelati ; [1]

______

[1] Jarchius has taken the trouble to give us a list of
those clubs, or academies [i. e., *the academies of Italy*],

and trimmings of gold. Here sat at a table, in black, the head of the Academy, between the orator and the first poet. At two semicircular tables on either hand sat three poets and three; silent among many candles. The chief made a little introduction, the orator a long Italian vile harangue. Then the chief, the poet, the poets, — who were a Franciscan, an Olivetan, an old abbé, and three lay, — read their compositions; and to-day they are pasted up in all parts of the town. As we came out of the church, we found all the convent and neighbouring houses lighted all over with lanthorns of red and yellow paper, and two bonfires.' [1]

In the Christmas of 1739, the friends crossed the Apennines, and entered Florence. If they had wanted introductions at Bologna, there was no lack of them in Tuscany, and they were to find one friend who afterwards figured largely in Walpole's correspondence. This was Mr.

which amount to five hundred and fifty, each distinguished by somewhat whimsical in the name. The academicians of Bologna, for instance, are divided into the Abbandonati, the Ausiosi, Ociosi, Arcadi, Confusi, Dubbiosi, etc. There are few of these who have not published their Transactions, and scarce a member who is not looked upon as the most famous man in the world, at home. — GOLDSMITH, in *The Bee*, No. vi., for 10 November, 1759.

[1] *Walpole to West*, no date, 1739.

(afterwards Sir Horace) Mann, British Minister Plenipotentiary at the Court of Florence. ' He is the best and most obliging person in the world,' says Gray, and his house, with a brief interval, was their residence for fifteen months. Their letters from Florence are less interesting than those from which quotations have already been made, while their amusements seem to have been more independent of each other than before. Gray occupied himself in the galleries taking the notes of pictures and statuary afterwards published by Mitford, and in forming a collection of MS. music ; Walpole, on the other hand, had slightly cooled in his eagerness for the antique, which now 'pleases him calmly.' 'I recollect ' — he says — ' the joy I used to propose if I could but see the Great Duke's gallery ; I walk into it now with as little emotion as I should into St. Paul's. The statues are a congregation of good sort of people that I have a great deal of unruffled regard for.' The fact was, no doubt, that society had now superior attractions. As the son of the English Prime Minister, and with Mann, who was a relation,[1] at his elbow, all

---

[1] Dr. Doran ('*Mann*' *and Manners at the Court of Florence*, 1876, i. 2) describes this connection as 'a distant cousinship.'

doors were open to him. A correct record of his time would probably show an unvaried succession of suppers, balls, and masquerades. In the carnival week, when he snatches 'a little unmasqued moment' to write to West, he says he has done nothing lately 'but slip out of his domino into bed, and out of bed into his domino. The end of the Carnival is frantic, bacchanalian; all the morn one makes parties in masque to the shops and coffee-houses, and all the evening to the operas and balls.' If Gray was of these junketings, his letters do not betray it. He was probably engaged in writing uncomplimentary notes on the Venus de' Medici, or transcribing a score of Pergolesi.

The first interruption to these diversions came in March, when they quitted Florence for Rome in order to witness the coronation of the successor of Clement XII., who had died in the preceding month. On their road from Siena they were passed by a shrill-voiced figure in a red cloak, with a white handkerchief on its head, which they took for a fat old woman, but which afterwards turned out to be Farinelli's rival, Senesino. Rome disappointed them, — especially in its inhabitants and general desolation. 'I am very glad,' writes Walpole, 'that I see it while it yet exists;' and he goes on to

prophesy that before a great number of years it
will cease to exist. ' I am persuaded,' he says
again, ' that in an hundred years Rome will not
be worth seeing ; 't is less so now than one
would believe.   All the public pictures are
decayed or decaying ; the few ruins cannot last
long ; and the statues and private collections
must be sold, from the great poverty of
the families.'   Perhaps this last consideration,
coupled with the depressing character of Roman
hospitality (' Roman conversations are dreadful things ! ' he tells Conway), revived his
virtuoso tastes.   ' I am far gone in medals,
lamps, idols, prints, etc., and all the small com-
modities to the purchase of which I can attain :
I would buy the Coliseum if I could.'   Meanwhile as the cardinals are quarrelling, the
coronation is still deferred ; and they visit
Naples, whence they explore Herculaneum,
then but recently exposed and identified.   But
neither Gray nor Walpole waxes very eloquent
upon this theme, — probably because at this
time the excavations were only partial, while
Pompeii was, of course, as yet under ground.
Walpole's next letter is written from Radico-
fani, — ' a vile little town at the foot of an old
citadel,' which again is at ' the top of a black
barren mountain ; ' the whole reminding the

writer of ' Hamilton's Bawn ' in Swift's verses.
In this place, although the traditional residence
of one of the Three Kings of Cologne, there
is but one pen, the property of the Governor,
who when Walpole borrows it, sends it to him
under ' conduct of a sergeant and two Swiss,'
with special injunctions as to its restoration, —
a precaution which in Walpole's view renders
it worthy to be ranked with the other precious relics of the poor Capuchins of the place,
concerning which he presently makes rather
unkindly fun. A few days later they were
once more in the Casa Ambrosio, Mann's
pleasant house at Florence, with the river
running so close to them that they could fish
out of the windows. ' I have a terreno [ground-
floor] all to myself,' says Walpole, ' with an
open gallery on the Arno, where I am now
writing to you [*i. e.*, Conway]. Over against
me is the famous Gallery ; and, on either hand,
two fair bridges. Is not this charming and
cool ? ' Add to which, on the bridges aforesaid,
in the serene Italian air, one may linger all night
in a dressing-gown, eating iced fruits to the
notes of a guitar. But (what was even better
than music and moonlight) there is the society
that was the writer's ' fitting environment.' Lady
Pomfret, with her daughters, Lady Charlotte,

afterwards governess to the children of George
III., and the beauty Lady Sophia, held a
'charming conversation' once a week; while
the Princess Craon de Beauvau has 'a constant
pharaoh and supper every night, where one is
quite at one's ease.' Another lady-resident,
scarcely so congenial to Walpole, was his
sister-in-law, the wife of his eldest brother,
Robert, who, with Lady Pomfret, made certain
(in Walpole's eyes) wholly preposterous pre-
tentions to the yet uninvented status of
blue-stocking. To Lady Walpole and Lady
Pomfret was speedily added another 'she-
meteor' in the person of the celebrated Lady
Mary Wortley Montagu.

When Lady Mary arrived in Florence in the
summer of 1740, she was a woman of more
than fifty, and was just entering upon that
unexplained exile from her country and husband which was prolonged for two-and-twenty
years. Her brilliant abilities were unimpaired;
but it is probable that the personal eccentricities which had exposed her to the satire
of Pope, had not decreased with years. That
these would be extenuated under Walpole's
malicious pen was not to be expected; still
less, perhaps, that they would be treated justly.
Although, as already intimated, he was not

aware of the scandal respecting himself which her descendants were to revive, he had ample ground for antipathy. Her husband was the bitter foe of Sir Robert Walpole ; and she herself had been the firm friend and protectress of his mother's rival and successor, Miss Skerret.[1] Accordingly, even before her advent, he makes merry over the anticipated issue of this portentous ' triple alliance ' of mysticism and nonsense, and later he writes to Conway : ' Did I tell you Lady Mary Wortley is here ? She laughs at my Lady Walpole, scolds my Lady Pomfret, and is laughed at by the whole town. Her dress, her avarice, and her impudence must amaze any one that never heard her name. She wears a foul mob, that does not cover her greasy black locks, that hang loose, never combed or curled ; an old mazarine blue wrapper. that gaps open and discovers a canvas petticoat. . . . In three words, I will give you her picture as we drew it in the *Sortes Virgilianæ,* — *Insanam vatem aspicies.* I give you my honour we did not choose it ; but Gray, Mr. Coke, Sir Francis Dashwood, and I, with

---

[1] Shortly after Lady Walpole's death, Sir Robert Walpole married his mistress, Maria Skerret, who died 4 June, 1738, leaving a daughter, Horace Walpole's half-sister, subsequently Lady Mary Churchill.

several others, drew it fairly amongst a thousand for different people.'[1]   In justice to Lady Mary it is only fair to say that she seems to have been quite unconscious that she was an object of ridicule, and was perfectly satisfied with her reception at Florence. ' Lord and Lady Pomfret ' — she tells Mr. Wortley — ' take pains to make the place agreeable to me, and I have been visited by the greatest part of the people of quality.'[2]   But although Walpole's portrait is obviously malicious (some of its details are suppressed in the above quotation), it is plain that even unprejudiced spectators could not deny her peculiarities. ' Lady Mary,' said Spence, ' is one of the most shining characters in the world, but shines like a comet ; she is all irregularity, and always wandering ; the most wise, the most imprudent ; loveliest, most disagreeable ; best-natured, cruellest woman in the world : " all things by turns, but nothing long." '[3]

By this time the new pope, Benedict XIV., had been elected. But although the friends were within four days, journey of Rome, the fear of heat and malaria forced them to forego

---

[1] *Walpole to Conway*, 25 September, 1740.
[2] *Letters*, etc., of Lady Mary Wortley Montagu, ii. 325.
[3] *Spence's Anecdotes*, by Singer, 2nd edn., 1858, p. xxiii.

the spectacle of the coronation. They continued to reside with Mann at Florence until May in the following year. Upon Gray the 'violent delights' of the Tuscan capital had already begun to pall. It is, he says, 'an excellent place to employ all one's animal sensations in, but utterly contrary to one's rational powers.' Walpole, on the other hand, is in his element. 'I am so well within and without,' he says in the same letter which sketches Lady Mary, 'that you would scarce know me: I am younger than ever, think of nothing but diverting myself, and live in a round of pleasures. We have operas, concerts, and balls, mornings and evenings. I dare not tell you all of one's idlenesses ; you would look so grave and senatorial at hearing that one rises at eleven in the morning, goes to the opera at nine at night, to supper at one, and to bed at three ! But literally here the evenings and nights are so charming and so warm, one can't avoid 'em.' In a later letter he says he has lost all curiosity, and 'except the towns in the straight road to Great Britain, shall scarce see a jot more of a foreign land.' Indeed, save a sally concerning the humours of ' Moll Worthless ' (Lady Mary) and Lady Walpole, and the record of the purchase of a few pictures, medals, and busts, —

one of the last of which, a Vespasian in basalt, was subsequently among the glories of the Twickenham Gallery, — his remaining letters from Florence contain little of interest. Early in 1741, the homeward journey was mapped out. They were to go to Bologna to hear the Viscontina sing, they were to visit the Fair at Reggio, and so by Venice homewards.

But whether the Viscontina was in voice or not, there is, as far as our travellers are concerned, absence of evidence. No further letter of Gray from Florence has been preserved, nor is there any mention of him in Walpole's next despatch to West from Reggio. At that place a misunderstanding seems to have arisen, and they parted, Gray going forward to Venice with two other travelling companions, Mr. John Chute and Mr. Whitehed. In the rather barren record of Walpole's story, this misunderstanding naturally assumes an exaggerated importance. But it was really a very trifling and a very intelligible affair. They had been too long together; and the first fascination of travel, which formed at the outset so close a bond, had gradually faded with time. As this alteration took place, their natural dispositions began to assert themselves, and Walpole's normal love of pleasure and Gray's retired studiousness became more and more apparent. It is probable too, that, in all the Florentine gaieties, Gray, who was not a great man's son, fell a little into the background. At all events, the separation was imminent, and it needed but a nothing — the alleged opening by Walpole of a letter of Gray [1] — to bring it about. Whatever the proximate cause, both were silent on the subject, although, years after the quarrel had been made up, and Gray was dead, Walpole took the entire blame upon himself. When Mason was preparing Gray's *Memoirs* in 1773, he authorized him to insert a note by which, in general terms, he admitted himself to have been in fault, assigning as his reason for not being more explicit, that while he was living it would not be pleasant to read his private affairs discussed in magazines and newspapers. But to Mason personally he was at the same time thoroughly candid, as well as considerate to his departed friend : ' I am conscious,' he says, ' that in the beginning of

[1] This rests upon the authority of a shadowy Mr. Roberts of the Pell-office, who told it to Isaac Reed in 1799, more than half a century after the event. The subject is discussed at some length, but of necessity inconclusively, by Mr. D. C. Tovey in his interesting *Gray and his Friends*, 1890. Mr. Tovey thinks that Ashton was obscurely connected with the quarrel.

the differences between Gray and me, the fault
was mine. I was too young, too fond of my
own diversions, nay, I do not doubt, too much
intoxicated by indulgence, vanity, and the
insolence of my situation, as a Prime Minister's son, not to have been inattentive and
insensible to the feelings of one I thought
below me ; of one, I blush to say it, that I
knew was obliged to me ; of one whom pre-
sumption and folly perhaps made me deem not
my superior *then* in parts, though I have since
felt my infinite inferiority to him. I treated
him insolently: he loved me, and I did not think
he did. I reproached him with the difference
between us when he acted from conviction of
knowing he was my superior ; I often dis-
regarded his wishes of seeing places, which I
would not quit other amusements to visit,
though I offered to send him to them without
me. Forgive me, if I say that his temper was
not conciliating. At the same time that I will
confess to you that he acted a more friendly
part, had I had the sense to take advantage of
it ; he freely told me of my faults. I declared
I did not desire to hear them, nor would correct
them. You will not wonder that with the
dignity of his spirit, and the obstinate care-

lessness of mine, the breach must have grown wider till we became incompatible.'[1]

'Sir, you have said more than was necessary' was Johnson's reply to a peace-making speech from Topham Beauclerk. It is needless to comment further upon this incident, except to add that Walpole's generous words show that the disagreement was rather the outcome of a sequence of long-strained circumstances than the result of momentary petulance. For a time reconciliation was deferred, but eventually it was effected by a lady, and the intimacy thus renewed continued for the remainder of Gray's life.

Shortly after Gray's departure in May, Walpole fell ill of a quinsy. He did not, at first, recognise the gravity of his ailment, and doctored himself. By a fortunate chance, Joseph Spence, then travelling as governor to the Earl of Lincoln, was in the neighbourhood, and,

---

[1] *Walpole to Mason*, 2 March, 1773. The letters to Mason were first printed in 1851 by Mitford. But Pinkerton, in the *Walpoliana*, i. 95, had reported much the same thing. 'The quarrel between Gray and me [Walpole] arose from his being too serious a companion. I had just broke loose from the restraints of the university, with as much money as I could spend, and I was willing to indulge myself. Gray was for antiquities, etc., while I was for perpetual balls and plays. The fault was mine.'

responding to a message from Walpole, 'found him scarce able to speak.' Spence immediately sent for medical aid, and summoned from Florence one Antonio Cocchi, a physician and author of some eminence. Under Cocchi's advice, Walpole speedily showed signs of inprovement, though, in his own words in the *Short Notes*, he ' was given over for five hours, escaping with great difficulty.' The sequel may be told from the same source. ' I went to Venice with Henry Clinton, Earl of Lincoln, and Mr. Joseph Spence, Professor of Poetry, and after a month's stay there, returned with them by sea from Genoa, landing at Antibes ; and by the way of Toulon, Marseilles, Aix, and through Languedoc to Montpellier, Toulouse, and Orléans, arrived at Paris, where I left the Earl and Mr. Spence, and landed at Dover, September 12th, 1741, O. S., having been chosen Member of Parliament for Kellington [Callington], in Cornwall, at the preceding General Election [of June], which Parliament put a period to my father's administration, which had continued above twenty years.'

CHAPTER III.

ALTHOUGH, during his stay in Italy, Walpole had neglected to accumulate the store of erudition which his friend Gray had been so industriously hiving for home consumption, he can scarcely be said to have learned nothing, especially at an age when much is learned unconsciously. His epistolary style, which, with its peculiar graces and pseudo-graces, had been already formed before he left England, had now acquired a fresh vivacity from his increased familiarity with the French and Italian languages ; and he had carried on, however discursively, something more than a mere flirtation with antiquities. Dr. Conyers Middleton, whose once famous *Life of Cicero* was published early in 1741, and who was him-

self an antiquary of distinction, thought highly
of Walpole's attainments in this way,[1] and indeed more than one passage in a poem written
by Walpole to Ashton at this time could scarcely
have been penned by any one not fairly familiar
with (for example) the science of those ' medals '
upon which Mr. Joseph Addison had discoursed
so learnedly after his Italian tour : —

> ' What scanty precepts ! studies how confin'd !
>   Too mean to fill your comprehensive mind ;
>   Unsatisfy'd with knowing when or where
>   Some Roman bigot rais'd a fane to FEAR ;
>   On what green medal VIRTUE stands express'd,
>   How CONCORD 's pictur'd, LIBERTY how dress'd ;
>   Or with wise ken judiciously define
>   When Pius marks the honorary coin
>   Of CARACALLA, or of ANTONINE.'[2]

The poem from which these lines are taken
—*An Epistle from Florence. To Thomas*

---

[1] Juvenis, non tam generis nobilitate, ac paterni no-
minis gloriâ, quam ingenio, doctrinâ, et virtute propriâ
illustris. Ille vero haud citius fere in patriam reversus
est, quam de studiis meis, ut consuerat, familiariter per
literas quærens, mihi ultro de copiâ suâ, quicquid ad argu-
menti mei rationem, aut libelli ornamentum pertineret,
pro arbitrio meo utendum obtulit. — *Pref. ad Germana
quædam Antiq. Monumenta*, etc., p. 6 (quoted in Mitford's
Corr. of Walpole and Mason, 1851, i. x-xi).

[2] Walpole's *Works*, 1798, i. 6.

Ashton, Esq., Tutor to the Earl of Plimouth —
extends to some four hundred lines, and exhibits
another side of Walpole's activity in Italy.
' You have seen ' — says Gray to West in July,
1740 — ' an Epistle to Mr. Ashton, that seems
to me full of spirit and thought, and a good
deal of poetic fire.' Writing to him ten years
later, Gray seems still to have retained his first
impression. ' Satire ' — he says — ' will be
heard, for all the audience are by nature her
friends ; especially when she appears in the
spirit of Dryden, with his strength, and often
with his versification, such as you have caught in
those lines on the Royal Unction, on the Papal
dominion, and Convents of both Sexes ; on
Henry VIII. and Charles II., for these are to
me the shining parts of your Epistle. There
are many lines I could wish corrected, and some
blotted out, but beauties enough to atone for a
thousand worse faults than these.' [1] Walpole
has never been ranked among the poets ; but
Gray's praise, in which Middleton and others
concurred, justifies a further quotation. This is
the passage on the Royal Unction and the Papal
Dominion : —

> ' When at the altar a new monarch kneels,
> What conjur'd awe upon the people steals !

1 Gray's *Works*, by Gosse, 1884, ii. 221.

The chosen HE adores the precious oil,
Meekly receives the solemn charm, and while
The priest some blessed nothings mutters o'er,
Sucks in the sacred grease at every pore :
He seems at once to shed his mortal skin,
And feels divinity transfus'd within.
The trembling vulgar dread the royal nod,
And worship God's anointed more than God.

' Such sanction gives the prelate to such kings !
So mischief from those hallow'd fountains springs.
But bend your eye to yonder harass'd plains,
Where king and priest in one united reigns ;
See fair Italia mourn her holy state,
And droop oppress'd beneath a papal weight ;
Where fat celibacy usurps the soil,
And sacred sloth consumes the peasant's toil :
The holy drones monopolise the sky,
And plunder by a vow of poverty.
The Christian cause their lewd profession taints,
Unlearn'd, unchaste, uncharitable saints.' [1]

That the refined and fastidious Horace Walpole of later years should have begun as a passable imitator of Dryden is sufficiently piquant. But that the son of the great courtier Prime Minister should have distinguished himself by the vigour of his denunciations of kings and priests, especially when, as his biographers have not failed to remark, he was writing to one about to take orders, is more noticeable still. The

[1] Walpole's *Works*, 1798, i. 8-9.

poem was reprinted in his works, but he makes no mention of it in the *Short Notes*, nor of an *Inscription for the Neglected Column in the Place of St. Mark at Florence*, written at the same time, and characterized by the same anti-monarchical spirit.

His letters to Mann, his chief correspondent at this date, are greatly occupied, during the next few months, with the climax of the catastrophe recorded at the end of the preceding chapter, — the resignation of Sir Robert Walpole. The first of the long series was written on his way home in September, 1741, when he had for his fellow-passengers the Viscontina, Amorevoli, and other Italian singers, then engaged in invading England. He appears to have at once taken up his residence with his father in Downing Street. Into the network of circumstances which had conspired to array against the great peace Minister the formidable opposition of disaffected Whigs, Jacobites, Tories, and adherents of the Prince of Wales, it would here be impossible to enter. But there were already signs that Sir Robert was nodding to his fall ; and that, although the old courage was as high as ever, the old buoyancy was beginning to flag. Failing health added its weight to the scale. In October Walpole tells his correspondent that he had ' been very near sealing his letter with black wax,' for his father had been in danger of his life, but was recovering, though he is no longer the Sir Robert that Mann once knew. He who formerly would snore before they had drawn his curtains, now never slept above an hour without waking ; and ' he who at dinner always forgot that he was Minister,' now sat silent, with eyes fixed for an hour together.   At the opening of Parliament, however, there was an ostensible majority of forty for the Court, and Walpole seems to have regarded this as encouraging.   But one of the first motions was for an inquiry into the state of the nation, and this was followed by a division upon a Cornish petition which reduced the majority to seven, — a variation which sets the writer nervously jesting about apartments in the Tower.   Seven days later, the opposition obtained a majority of four ; and although Sir Robert, still sanguine in the remembrance of past successes, seemed less anxious than his family, matters were growing grave, and his youngest son was reconciling himself to the coming blow.   It came practically on the 21st January, 1742, when Pulteney moved for a secret committee, which (in reality) was to be a committee of accusation against the Prime Minister.   Walpole defeated this manœuvre with his characteristic courage and address, but only by a narrow majority of three. So inconsiderable a victory upon so crucial a question was perilously close to a reverse ; and when, in the succeeding case of the disputed Chippenham Election, the Government were defeated by one, he yielded to the counsels of his advisers, and decided to resign. He was thereupon raised to the peerage as Earl of Orford, with a pension of £4,000 a year,[1] while his daughter by his second wife, Miss Skerret, was created an Earl's daughter in her own right. His fall was mourned by no one more sincerely than by the master he had served so staunchly for so long ; and when he went to kiss hands at St. James's upon taking leave, the old king fell upon his neck, embraced him, and broke into tears.

The new Earl himself seems to have taken his reverses with his customary equanimity, and, like the shrewd ' old Parliamentary hand ' that he was, to have at once devoted himself to the difficult task of breaking the force of the attack which he foresaw would be made upon himself by those in power. He contrived adroitly to

---

[1] He gave this up at first, but afterwards, when his affairs became involved, reclaimed it (Cunningham's *Corr.*, i. 126 n.)

foster dissension and disunion among the heterogeneous body of his opponents ; he secured that the new Ministry should be mainly composed of his old party, the Whigs; and he managed to discredit his most formidable adversary, Pulteney.   One of the first results of these precautionary measures was that a motion by Lord Limerick for a committee to examine into the conduct of the last twenty years was thrown out by a small majority.   A fortnight later the motion was renewed in a fresh form, the scope of the examination being limited to the last ten years.   Upon this occasion Horace Walpole made his maiden speech, — a graceful and modest, if not very forcible, effort on his father's side.   In this instance, however, the Government were successful, and the Committee was appointed.   Yet, despite the efforts to excite the public mind respecting Lord Orford, the case against him seems to have faded away in the hands of his accusers.   The first report of the Committee, issued in May, contained nothing to criminate the person against whom the inquiry had been directly levelled ; and despite the strenuous and even shameless efforts of the Government to obtain evidence inculpating the late Minister, the Committee were obliged to issue a second report in June, of which, — so far as the chief object was concerned, — the gross result was nil. By the middle of July, Walpole was able to tell Mann that the 'long session was over, and the Secret Committee already forgotten,' — as much forgotten, he says in a later letter, 'as if it had happened in the last reign.'

When Sir Robert Walpole had resigned, he had quitted his official residence in Downing Street (which ever since he first occupied it in 1735 has been the official residence of the First Lord of the Treasury), and moved to No. 5, Arlington Street, opposite to, but smaller than, the No. 17 in which his youngest son had been born, and upon the site of which William Kent built a larger house for Mr. Pelham. No. 5 is now distinguished by a tablet erected by the Society of Arts, proclaiming it to have been the house of the ex-Minister. From Arlington Street, or from the other home at Chelsea already mentioned, most of Walpole's letters were dated during the months which succeeded the crisis. But in August, when the House had risen, he migrated with the rest of the family to Houghton, — the great mansion in Norfolk which had now taken the place of the ancient seat of the Walpoles, where during the summer months his father had been accustomed in his free-handed manner to keep open house to all the county. Fond of hospitality, fond of field-sports, fond of gardening, and all out-door occupations, Lord Orford was at home among the flat expanses and Norfolk turnips. But the family seat had no such attractions to his son, fresh from the multi-coloured Continental life, and still bearing about him, in a certain frailty of physique and enervation of spirit, the tokens of a sickly childhood. 'Next post '—he says despairingly to Mann —' I shall not be able to write to you ; and when I am there [at Houghton]. shall scarce find materials to furnish a letter above every other post. I beg, however, that you will write constantly to me ; it will be my only entertainment ; for I neither hunt, brew, drink, nor reap.' 'Consider'—he says again —' I am in the barren land of Norfolk, where news grows as slow as anything green ; and besides, I am in the house of a fallen minister !' Writing letters (in company with the little white dog 'Patapan'[1] which he had brought from

---

[1] Patapan's portrait was painted by John Wootton, who illustrated Gay's *Fables* in 1727 with Kent. It hung in Walpole's bedroom at Strawberry, and now (1892) belongs to Lord Lifford. In 1743 Walpole wrote a Fable in imitation of La Fontaine, to which he gave the title of *Patapan ; or, the Little White Dog.* It was never printed.

Rome as a successor to the defunct Tory), walking, and playing comet with his sister Lady Mary or any chance visitors to the house, seem to have been his chief resources. A year later he pays a second visit to Houghton, and he is still unreconciled to his environment. 'Only imagine that I here every day see men, who are mountains of roast beef, and only just seem roughly hewn out into the outlines of human form, like the giant-rock at Pratolino! I shudder when I see them brandish their knives in act to carve, and look on them as savages that devour one another.' Then there are the enforced civilities to entirely uninteresting people, — the intolerable female relative, who is curious about her cousins to the fortieth remove. ' I have an Aunt here, a family piece of goods, an old remnant of inquisitive hospitality and economy. who, to all intents and purposes, is as beefy as her neighbours. She wore me so down yesterday with interrogatories that I dreamt all night she was at my ear with " who's " and " why's," and " when's " and " where's," till at last in my very sleep I cried out, " For heaven's sake, Madam, ask me no more questions."' And then, in his impatience of bores in general, he goes on to write a little essay upon that ' growth of English root,' that ' awful yawn, which sleep

cannot abate,' as Byron calls it, — Ennui. ' I am
so far from growing used to mankind [he means
' uncongenial mankind '] by living amongst them,
that my natural ferocity and wildness does but
every day grow worse. They tire me, they
fatigue me ; I don't know what to do with them ;
I don't know what to say to them ; I fling open
the windows, and fancy I want air ; and when I
get by myself, I undress myself, and seem to
have had people in my pockets, in my plaits,
and on my shoulders ! I indeed find this fatigue
worse in the country than in town, because one
can avoid it there, and has more resources ; but
it is there too. I fear 't is growing old ; but I
literally seem to have murdered a man whose
name was Ennui, for his ghost is ever before
me. They say there is no English word for
ennui ; I think you may translate it most literally
by what is called " entertaining people " and
" doing the honours : " that is, you sit an hour
with somebody you don't know and don't care
for, talk about the wind and the weather, and
ask a thousand foolish questions, which all begin
with, " I think you live a good deal in the country," or " I think you don't love this thing or
that." Oh, 't is dreadful ! ' [1]

[1] *Walpole to Chute,* 20 August. 1743. Mr. John Chute
was a friend whom Walpole had made at Florence, and

But even Houghton, with its endless 'doing the honours,' must have had its compensations. There was a library, and — what must have had even stronger attractions for Horace Walpole — that magnificent and almost unique collection of pictures which under a later member of the family, the third Earl of Orford, passed to Catherine of Russia. For years Lord Orford, with unwearied diligence and exceptional opportunities, had been accumulating these treasures. Mann in Florence, Vertue in England, and a host of industrious foragers had helped to bring together the priceless canvases which crowded the rooms of the Minister's house next the Treasury at Whitehall. And if he was inexperienced as a critic, he was far too acute a man to be deceived by the shiploads of ' Holy Families, Madonnas, and other dismal dark subjects, neither entertaining nor ornamental,' against which the one great native artist of his time, — the painter of the ' Rake's Progress,' so

with whom, as already stated in Chapter II., Gray had travelled when they parted company. Until, by the death of a brother, he succeeded to the estate called The Vyne, in Hampshire, he lived principally abroad. His portrait by Müntz, after Pompeio Battoni, hung over the door in Walpole's bedchamber at Strawberry Hill. An exhaustive *History of The Vyne* was published in 1888 by the late Mr. Chaloner W. Chute, at that time its possessor.

persistently inveighed.   There was no doubt
about the pedigrees of the Wouvermanns and
Teniers, the Guidos and Rubens, the Vandykes
and Murillos, which decorated the rooms at
Downing Street and Chelsea and Richmond.
From the few records which remain of prices,
it would seem that, in addition to the merit of
authenticity, many of the pictures must have had
the attraction of being 'bargains.'   In days
when £4,000 or £5,000 is no extravagant price
to be given for an old master, it is instructive to
read that £750 was the largest sum ever given
by Lord Orford for any one picture, and Walpole
himself quotes this amount as £630.   For four
great Snyders, which Vertue bought for him, he
only paid £428, and for a portrait of Clement
IX. by Carlo Maratti no more than £200.
Many of the other pictures in his gallery cost
him still less, being donations — no doubt sometimes in gratitude for favours to come — from
his friends and adherents.   The Earl of Pembroke, Lord Waldegrave, the Duke of Montagu, Lord Tyrawley, were among these.   But,
upon the whole, the collection was gathered
mainly from galleries like the Zambecari at
Bologna, the Arnaldi Palace at Florence, the
Pallavicini at Rome, and from the stores of
noble collectors in England.

In 1743, the majority of these had apparently been concentrated at Houghton, where there was special accommodation for them. ' My Lord,' says Horace, groaning over a fresh visit to Norfolk, ' has pressed me so much that I could not with decency refuse : he is going to furnish and hang his picture-gallery, and wants me.' But it is impossible to believe that he really objected to a duty so congenial to his tastes. In fact, he was really greatly interested in it. His letters contain frequent references to a new Domenichino, a Virgin and Child, which Mann is sending from Florence, and he comes up to London to meet this and other pictures, and is not seriously inconsolable to find that owing to the quarantine for the plague on the Continent, he is detained for some days in town. One of the best evidences of his solicitude in connection with the arrangements of the Houghton collection is, however, the discourse which he wrote in the summer of 1742, under the title of a *Sermon on Painting*, and which he himself tells us was actually preached by the Earl's chaplain in the gallery, and afterwards repeated at Stanno, his elder brother's house. The text was taken from Psalm CXV. : ' They have Mouths, but they speak not : Eyes have they, but they see not :

neither is there any Breath in their Nostrils;' and
the writer, illustrating his theme by reference to
the pictures around his audience in the gallery,
or dispersed through the building, manages to
eulogize the painter's art with considerable skill.
He touches upon the pernicious effect which
the closely realized representation of popish
miracles must have upon the illiterate spectator,
and points out how much more commendable
and serviceable is the portraiture of benignity,
piety, and chastity,—how much more instructive the incidents of the Passion, where every
'touch of the pencil is a lesson of contrition,
each figure an apostle to call you to repentance.'
He lays stress, as Lessing and other writers
have done, on the universal language of the
brush, and indicates its abuse when restricted
to the reproduction of inquisitors, visionaries,
imaginary hermits, 'consecrated gluttons,' or
'noted concubines,' after which (as becomes
his father's son) he does not fail to disclose its
more fitting vocation, to perpetuate the likeness
of William the Deliverer, and the benign, the
honest house of Hanover. *The Dives and La-
zarus* of Veronese and the *Prodigal Son* of
Salvator Rosa, both on the walls, are pressed
into his service, and the famous *Usurers* of
Quentin Matsys also prompt their parable.

Then, after adroitly dwelling upon the pictorial honours lavished upon mere asceticism to the prejudice of real heroes, taking Poussin's picture of *Moses Striking the Rock* for his text, he winds into what was probably the ultimate purpose of his discourse, a neatly veiled panegyric of Sir Robert Walpole under guise of the great lawgiver of the Israelites, which may be cited as a favourable sample of this curious oration :

' But it is not necessary to dive into profane history for examples of unregarded merit ; the Scriptures themselves contain instances of the greatest patriots, who lie neglected, while new-fashioned bigots or noisy incendiaries are the reigning objects of public veneration. See the great Moses himself, — the lawgiver, the defender, the preserver of Israel ! Peevish orators are more run after, and artful Jesuits more popular. Examine but the life of that slighted patriot, how boldly in his youth he understood the cause of liberty ! Unknown, without interest, he stood against the face of Pharaoh ! He saved his countrymen from the hand of tyranny, and from the dominion of an idolatrous king. How patiently did he bear for a series of years the clamours and cabals of a factious people, wandering after strange lusts, and exasperated by ambitious ringleaders ! How oft did he

intercede for their pardon, when injured himself ! How tenderly deny them specious favours,
which he knew must turn to their own destruc-
tion ! See him lead them through opposition,
through plots, through enemies, to the enjoy-
ment of peace, and to the possession of *a land
flowing with milk and honey.* Or with more
surprise see him in the barren desert, where
sands and wilds overspread the dreary scene,
where no hopes of moisture, no prospect of
undiscovered springs, could flatter their parching
thirst ; see how with a miraculous hand —

' " He struck the rock, and straight the waters flowed." '

Whoever denies his praises to such evidences
of merit, or with jealous look can scowl on such
benefits, is like the senseless idol, that *has a
mouth that speaks not, and eyes that cannot
see.*'

If, in accordance with some perverse fashion
of the day, the foregoing production had not
been disguised as a sermon, and actually preached
with the orthodox accompaniment of bands and
doxology, there is no reason why it should not
have been regarded as a harmless and not unac-
complished essay on Art. But the objectionable
spirit of parody upon the ritual, engendered by
the strife between ' high ' and ' low ' (Walpole

himself wrote some *Lessons for the Day*, 1742, which are to be found in the works of Sir Charles Hanbury Williams), seems to have dictated the title of what in other respects is a serious *Spectator*, and needed no spice of irreverence to render it palatable. The *Sermon* had, however, one valuable result, namely, that it suggested to its author the expediency of preparing some record of the pictorial riches of Houghton upon the model of the famous *Ædes Barberini* and *Giustinianæ*. As the dedication of the *Ædes Walpolianæ* is dated 24 August, 1743, it must have been written before that date ; but it was not actually published until 1747, and then only to give away. Another enlarged and more accurate edition was issued in 1752, and it was finally reprinted in the second volume of the *Works* of 1798, pp. 221–78, where it is followed by the *Sermon on Painting*. Professing to be more a catalogue of the pictures than a description of them, it nevertheless gives a good idea of a collection which (as its historian says) both in its extent and the condition of its treasures excelled most of the existing collections of Italy. In an ' Introduction,' the characteristics of the various artists are distinguished with much discrimination, although it is naturally more sympathetic than critical. Perhaps one of its

happiest pages is the following excursus upon
a poem of Prior : ' I cannot conclude this topic
of the ancient painters without taking notice of
an extreme pretty instance of Prior's taste, and
which may make an example on that frequent
subject, the resemblance between poetry and
painting, and prove that taste in the one will
influence in the other.　Everybody has read his
tale of Protogenes and Apelles.　If they have
read the story in Pliny they will recollect that
by the latter's account it seemed to have been
a trial between two Dutch performers.　The
Roman author tells you that when Apelles was
to write his name on a board, to let Protogenes
know who had been to inquire for him, he drew
an exactly straight and slender line.　Protogenes
returned, and with his pencil and another colour,
divided his competitor's.　Apelles, on seeing
the ingenious minuteness of the Rhodian master,
took a third colour, and laid on a still finer and
indivisible line.　But the English poet, who
could distinguish the emulation of genius from
nice experiments about splitting hairs, took the
story into his own hands, and in a less number
of trials, and with bolder execution, compre-
hended the whole force of painting, and flung
drawing, colouring, and the doctrine of light
and shade into the noble contention of those two

absolute masters. In Prior, the first wrote his name in a perfect design, and

> ' " —— with one judicious stroke
> On the plain ground Apelles drew
> A circle regularly true." '

Protogenes knew the hand, and showed Apelles that his own knowledge of colouring was as great as the other's skill in drawing.

> ' " Upon the happy line he laid
> Such obvious light and easy shade
> That Paris' apple stood confest,
> Or Leda's egg, or Chloe's breast." ' [1]

Apelles acknowledged his rival's merit, without jealously persisting to refine on the masterly reply : —

> ' " Pugnavere pares, succubuere pares" ' [2]

Among the other efforts of his pen at this time were some squibs in ridicule of the new

[1] Mr. Vertue the engraver made a very ingenious conjecture on this story; he supposes that Apelles did not draw a straight line, but the outline of a human figure, which not being correct, Protogenes drew a more correct figure within his ; but that still not being perfect, Apelles drew a smaller and exactly proportioned one within both the former. — *Walpole's note.*

[2] Walpole's *Works*, 1798, ii. 229-30. The final quotation is from Martial.

Ministry. One was a parody of a scene in *Macbeth*; the other of a scene in Corneille's *Cinna*. He also wrote a paper against Lord Bath in the *Old England Journal*.

In the not very perplexed web of Horace Walpole's life, the next occurrence of importance is his father's death. When, as Sir Robert Walpole, he had ceased to be Prime Minister, he was sixty-five years of age; and though his equanimity and wonderful constitution still seemed to befriend him, he had personally little desire, even if the ways had been open, to recover his ancient power. ' I believe nothing could prevail on him to return to the Treasury,' writes his son to Mann in 1743. ' He says he will keep the 12th of February — the day he resigned — with his family as long as he lives.' He continued. nevertheless. to assist his old master with his counsel. and more than one step of importance by which the King startled his new Ministry owed its origin to a confidential consultation with Lord Orford. When, in January, 1744, the old question of discontinuing the Hanoverian troops was revived with more than ordinary insistence, it was through Lord Orford's timely exertions, and his personal credit with his friends, that the motion was defeated by an overwhelming majority. On

Sir Robert Walpole.

Sʳ ROBERT WALPOLE
EARL of ORFORD.

the other hand, a further attempt to harass him by another Committee of Secret Inquiry was wholly unsuccessful, and signs were not wanting that his old prestige had by no means departed. Towards the close of 1744, however, his son begins to chronicle a definite decline in his health. He is evidently suffering seriously from stone, and is forbidden to take the least exercise by the King's serjeant-surgeon, that famous Mr. Ranby who was the friend of Hogarth and Fielding.[1] In January of the next year, he is trying a famous specific for his complaint, Mrs. Stephens's medicine. Six weeks later, he has been alarmingly ill for about a month ; and although reckoned out of absolute danger, is hardly ever conscious more than four hours out of the four-and-twenty, from the powerful opiates he takes in order to deaden pain. A month later, on the 18th March, 1745, he died at Arlington Street, in his sixty-ninth year. At first his son dares scarcely speak of his loss, but a fortnight afterwards he writes more fully. After showing that the state of his circumstances proved how little truth there had been in the charges of self-enrichment made against him, Walpole goes on to say : ' It is certain, he is dead very poor :

---

[1] Ranby wrote a *Narrative of the last Illness of the Earl of Orford*, 1745, which provoked much controversy.

his debts, with his legacies, which are trifling, amount to fifty thousand pounds. His estate, a nominal eight thousand a year, much mortgaged. In short, his fondness for Houghton has endangered him. If he had not so overdone it, he might have left such an estate to his family as might have secured the glory of the place for many years : another such debt must expose it to sale. If he had lived, his unbounded generosity and contempt of money would have run him into vast difficulties. However irreparable his personal loss may be to his friends, he certainly did critically well for himself : he had lived to stand the rudest trials with honour, to see his character universally cleared, his enemies brought to infamy for their ignorance or villainy, and the world allowing him to be the only man in England fit to be what he had been ; and he died at a time when his age and infirmities prevented his again undertaking the support of a government, which engrossed his whole care, and which he foresaw was falling into the last confusion. In this I hope his judgment failed ! His fortune attended him to the last. for he died of the most painful of all distempers, with little or no pain.' [1]

From the *Short Notes* we learn further:

[1] *Walpole to Mann,* 15 April, 1745.

' He [my father] left me the house in Arling-
ton-street in which he died, £5000 in money,
and £1000 a year from the Collector's place
in the Custom-house, and the surplus to be
divided between my brother Edward and me.'

CHAPTER IV.

DURING the period between Walpole's
return to England and the death of Lord
Orford, his letters, addressed almost exclusively
to Mann, are largely occupied with the occurrences which accompanied and succeeded his
father's downfall. To Lord Orford's *protégé*
and relative these particulars were naturally of
the first importance, and Walpole's function of
' General Intelligencer ' fell proportionately into
the background. Still, there are occasional references to current events of a merely social
character. After the Secret Committee, he is
interested (probably because his friend Conway
was pecuniarily interested) in the Opera, and
the reception by the British public of the
Viscontina, Amorevoli, and the other Italian
singers whom he had known abroad. Of the

stage he says comparatively little. dismissing
poor Mrs. Woffington, who had then just made
her appearance at Covent Garden, as ' a bad
actress.' who. nevertheless, ' has life,' — an
opinion in which he is supported by Conway,
who calls her ' an impudent, Irish-faced girl.'
In the acting of Garrick, after whom all the
town is (as Gray writes) ' horn-mad ' in May,
1742, he sees nothing wonderful, although he
admits that it is heresy to say so, since that
infallible stage critic, the Duke of Argyll, has
declared him superior to Betterton.   But he
praises ' a little simple farce ' at Drury Lane,
Miss Lucy in Town, by Henry Fielding. in
which his future friend, Mrs. Clive. and Beard
mimic Amorevoli and the Muscovita.   The
same letter contains a reference to another
famous stage-queen, now nearing eighty. Anne
Bracegirdle, who should have had the money
that Congreve left to Henrietta, Duchess of
Marlborough.   ' Tell Mr. Chute [he says] that
his friend Bracegirdle breakfasted with me this
morning.   As she went out, and wanted her
clogs, she turned to me, and said, '' I remember
at the playhouse, they used to call, Mrs.
Oldfield's chair ! Mrs. Barry's clogs ! and
Mrs. Bracegirdle's pattens ! " ' [1]   One pictures

<hr>

[1] *Walpole to Mann,* 26 May, 1742.

a handsome old lady, a little bent, and leaning on a crutch stick as she delivers this parting utterance at the door.[1]

Among the occurrences of 1742 which find fitting record in the correspondence, is the opening of that formidable rival to Vauxhall, Ranelagh Gardens. All through the spring the great Rotunda, with its encircling tiers of galleries and supper-boxes, — the *coup d'œil* of which Johnson thought was the finest thing he had ever seen, — had been rising slowly at the side of Chelsea Hospital. In April it was practically completed, and almost ready for visitors. Walpole, of course, breakfasts there, like the rest of the *beau monde*. 'The building is not finished [he says], but they get great sums by people going to see it and breakfasting in the

---

[1] According to Pinkerton, another anecdote connects Mrs. Bracegirdle with the Walpoles. 'Mr. Shorter, my mother's father [he makes Horace say], was walking down Norfolk Street in the Strand, to his house there, just before poor Mountfort the player was killed in that street, by assassins hired by Lord Mohun. This nobleman, lying in wait for his prey, came up and embraced Mr. Shorter by mistake, saying, 'Dear Mountfort!' It was fortunate that he was instantly undeceived, for Mr. Shorter had hardly reached his house before the murder took place' (*Walpoliana*, ii. 96). Mountfort, it will be remembered, owed his death to Mrs. Bracegirdle's liking for him.

house ; there were yesterday no less than three
hundred and eighty persons, at eighteenpence
a-piece. You see how poor we are, when, with
a tax of four shillings in the pound, we are laying out such sums for cakes and ale.'[1] A week
or two later comes the formal inauguration.
' Two nights ago [May 24] Ranelagh-gardens
were opened at Chelsea ; the Prince, Princess,
Duke. much nobility, and much mob besides,
were there. There is a vast amphitheatre, finely
gilt, painted, and illuminated, into which everybody that loves eating, drinking, staring, or
crowding, is admitted for twelvepence. The
building and disposition of the gardens cost
sixteen thousand pounds. Twice a week there
are to be Ridottos at guinea-tickets, for which
you are to have a supper and music. I was
there last night [May 25], ' — the writer adds, —
' but did not find the joy of it,'[2] and, at present,
he prefers Vauxhall, because of the approach by
water, that ' *trajet du fleuve fatal*,' — as it is
styled in the *Vauxhall de Londres* which a
French poet dedicated in 1769 to M. de
Fontenelle. He seems, however, to have taken
Lord Orford to Ranelagh, and he records in
July that they walked with a train at their heels

---

[1] *Walpole to Mann*, 22 April, 1742.
[2] *Walpole to Mann*, 26 May, 1742.

like two chairmen going to fight, — from which
he argues a return of his father's popularity.
Two years later Fashion has declared itself on
the side of the new garden, and Walpole has
gone over to the side of Fashion. ' Every night
constantly [he tells Conway] I go to Ranelagh :
which has totally beat Vauxhall. Nobody goes
anywhere else, — everybody goes there. My
Lord Chesterfield is so fond of it that he says
he has ordered all his letters to be directed
thither. If you had never seen it, I would make
you a most pompous description of it, and tell
you how the floor is all of beaten princes ; that
you can 't set your foot without treading on
a Prince of Wales or Duke of Cumberland.
The company is universal : there is from his
Grace of Grafton down to children out of the
Foundling Hospital ; from my Lady Townshend
to the kitten ; from my Lord Sandys to your
humble cousin and sincere friend.' [1]

After Lord Orford's death, the next landmark
in Horace Walpole's life is his removal to the
house at Twickenham, subsequently known as
Strawberry Hill. To a description of this historical mansion the next chapter will be in part
devoted. In the mean time we may linger for
a moment upon the record which these letters

[1] *Walpole to Conway,* 29 June, 1744.

contain of the famous '45. No better opportunity will probably occur of exhibiting Walpole as the reporter of history in the process of making. Much that he tells Mann and Montagu is no doubt little more than the skimming of the last *Gazette*; but he had always access to trustworthy information, and is seldom a dull reporter, even of newspaper news. Almost the next letter to that in which he dwells at length upon the loss of his father, records the disaster of Tournay, or Fontenoy, in which, he tells Mann, Mr. Conway has highly distinguished himself, magnificently engaging — as appears from a subsequent communication — no less than two French Grenadiers at once. His account of the battle is bare enough ; but what apparently interests him most is the patriotic conduct of the Prince of Wales, who made a *chanson* on the occasion, after the fashion of the Regent Orléans : —

> ' VENEZ, mes chères Déesses,
> Venez calmer mon chagrin ;
> Aidez, mes belles Princesses,
> A le noyer dans le vin.
> Poussons cette douce Ivresse
> Jusqu'au milieu de la nuit,
> Et n'écoutons que la tendresse
> D'un charmant vis-à-vis.
>
> .   .   .

> ' Que m'importe que l'Europe
>   Ait un ou plusieurs tyrans ?
>   Prions seulement Calliope,
>   Qu'elle inspire nos vers, nos chants.
>   Laissons Mars et toute la gloire ;
>   Livrons nous tous à l'amour ;
>   Que Bacchus nous donne à boire ;
>   A ces deux fasions [*sic*] la cour '

The goddesses addressed were Lady Catherine Hanmer, Lady Fauconberg, and Lady Middlesex, who played Congreve's *Judgment of Paris* at Leicester House, with his Royal Highness as Paris, and Prince Lobkowitz for Mercury. Walpole says of the song that it ' miscarried in nothing but the language, the thoughts, and the poetry.' Yet he copies the whole five verses, of which the above are two, for Mann's delectation.

A more logical sequence to Fontenoy than the lyric of Leicester House is the descent of Charles Edward upon Scotland. In August Walpole reports to Mann that there is a proclamation out ' for apprehending the Pretender's son,' who had landed in July ; in September he is marching on Edinburgh. Ten days later the writer is speculating half ruefully upon the possibilities of being turned out of his comfortable sinecures in favour of some forlorn Irish peer. ' I shall wonderfully dislike being a loyal sufferer in a threadbare coat, and shivering in an ante-chamber at Hanover, or reduced to teach Latin and English to the young princes at Copenhagen. The Dowager Strafford has already written cards for my Lady Nithsdale, my Lady Tullibardine, the Duchess of Perth and Berwick, and twenty more revived peeresses, to invite them to play at whisk, Monday three months ; for your part, you will divert yourself with their old taffeties, and tarnished slippers, and their awkwardness, the first day they go to Court in shifts and clean linen. Will you ever write to me in my garret at Herrenhausen ? [1] Then upon this come the contradictions of rumour, the ' general supineness,' the raising of regiments, and the disaster of Preston Pans, with its inevitable condemnation of Cope. ' I pity poor him, who, with no shining abilities, and no experience, and no force, was sent to fight for a crown ! He never saw a battle but that of Dettingen, where he got his red ribbon ; Churchill, whose led-captain he was, and my Lord Harrington, had pushed him up to this misfortune.[2] We

[1] *Walpole to Montagu*, 17 Sept., 1745.

[2] Walpole later revised this verdict: ' General Cope was tried afterwards for his behaviour in this action, and it appeared very clearly that the Ministry, his inferior officers, and his troops, were greatly to blame ; and that

Charles Edward, the Pretender.

it quite out. Once more, on the 23rd February,
it flares fitfully at Falkirk, and then fades as suddenly. The battle that Walpole hourly expects,
not without some trepidation, for Conway is
one of the Duke of Cumberland's aides-de-
camp, is still deferred, and it is April before the
two armies face each other on Culloden Moor.
Then he writes jubilantly to his Florentine correspondent : ' On the 16th, the Duke, by
forced marches, came up with the rebels a little
on this side Inverness, — by the way, the battle
is not christened yet ; I only know that neither
Preston Pans nor Falkirk are to be god-fathers.
The rebels, who had fled from him after their
victory [of Falkirk], and durst not attack him,
when so much exposed to them at his passage
of the Spey, now stood him, they seven thousand, he ten. They broke through Barril's
regiment and killed Lord Robert Kerr, a handsome young gentleman, who was cut to pieces
with about thirty wounds : but they were soon
repulsed, and fled ; the whole engagement not
lasting above a quarter of an hour. The young
Pretender escaped, Mr. Conway says, he
hears, wounded : he certainly was in the rear.
They have lost above a thousand men in the
engagement and pursuit ; and six hundred were
already taken ; among which latter are their

but the first appearance of the prisoners shocked
me! their behaviour melted me.' After going
on to speak of Lord Kilmarnock and Lord
Cromartie (afterwards reprieved), he continues:
' For Lord Balmerino, he is the most natural
brave old fellow I ever saw : the highest intrepidity, even to indifference. At the bar he
behaved like a soldier and a man ; in the intervals of form, with carelessness and humour.
He pressed extremely to have his wife, his
pretty Peggy [Margaret Chalmers], with him in
the Tower, Lady Cromartie only sees her
husband through the grate, not choosing to be
shut up with him, as she thinks she can serve
him better by her intercession without : she is
big with child and very handsome : so are their
daughters. When they were to be brought from
the Tower in separate coaches, there was some
dispute in which the axe must go: old Balmerino cried, ' Come, come, put it with me.'
At the bar he plays with his fingers upon the
axe, while he talks to the gentleman-gaoler ;
and one day somebody coming up to listen, he
took the blade and held it like a fan between
their faces. During the trial, a little boy was
near him, but not tall enough to see ; he made
room for the child, and placed him near himself.' [1]

<hr>

[1] *Walpole to Mann,* 1 Aug., 1746.

Balmerino's gallant demeanour evidently fascinated Walpole. In his next letter he relates how on his way back to the Tower the sturdy old dragoon had stopped the coach at Charing Cross to buy some 'honey-blobs' (gooseberries); and when afterwards he comes to write his account of the execution, although he tells the story of Kilmarnock's death with feeling, the best passage is given to his companion in misfortune. He describes how, on the fatal 15th August, before he left the Tower, Balmerino drank a bumper to King James; how he wore his rebellious regimentals (blue and red) over a flannel waistcoat and his shroud; how, embracing Lord Kilmarnock, he said, 'My Lord, I wish I could suffer for both.' Then followed the beheading of Kilmarnock; and the narrator goes on: 'The scaffold was immediately new-strewed with sawdust, the block new covered, the executioner new-dressed, and a new axe brought. Then came old Balmerino, treading with the air of a general. As soon as he mounted the scaffold, he read the inscription on his coffin, as he did again afterwards: he then surveyed the spectators, who were in amazing numbers. even upon masts upon ships in the river; and pulling out his spectacles, read a treasonable speech, which he delivered to the

Sheriff, and said, the young Pretender was so
sweet a Prince that flesh and blood could not
resist following him ; and lying down to try the
block, he said, ' If I had a thousand lives, I
would lay them all down here in the same
cause.'　He said if he had not taken the sacra-
ment the day before, he would have knocked
down Williamson, the Lieutenant of the Tower.
for his ill-usage of him.　He took the axe and
felt it, and asked the headsman how many blows
he had given Lord Kilmarnock ; and gave him
three guineas.　Two clergymen, who attended
him, coming up, he said, ' No, gentlemen, I
believe you have already done me all the service
you can.'　Then he went to the corner of the
scaffold, and called very loud for the warder, to
give him his perriwig, which he took off, and
put on a night-cap of Scotch plaid, and then
pulled off his coat and waistcoat and lay down ;
but being told he was on the wrong side, vaulted
round, and immediately gave the sign by tossing
up his arm, as if he were giving the signal for
battle.　He received three blows ; but the first
certainly took away all sensation.　He was not
a quarter of an hour on the scaffold ; Lord
Kilmarnock above half a one.　Balmerino certainly died with the intrepidity of a hero. but
the insensibility of one too.　As he walked from

his prison to execution, seeing every window
and top of house filled with spectators, he cried
out, "Look, look, how they are all piled up
like rotten oranges."[1]

In the old print of the execution, the scaffold
on Tower Hill is shown surrounded by a wide
square of dragoons, beyond which the crowd —
'the immense display of human countenances
which surrounded it like a sea,' as Scott has it
— are visible on every side. No. 14 Tower
Hill is said to have been the house from which
the two lords were led to the block, and a trail
of blood along the hall and up the first flight of
stairs was long shown as indicating the route by
which the mutilated bodies were borne to await
interment in St. Peter's Chapel. A few months
later Walpole records the execution in the same
place of Simon Fraser, Lord Lovat, the cunning
old Jacobite, whose characteristic attitude and

---

[1] *Walpole to Mann*, 21 August, 1746. Gray, who was
at the trial, also mentions Balmerino, not so enthusiastically. 'He is an old soldier-like man, of a vulgar manner
and aspect, speaks the broadest Scotch, and shews an
intrepidity, that some ascribe to real courage, and some
to brandy' (*Letter to Wharton*, August). 'Old Balmerino,
when he had read his paper to the people, pulled off his
spectacles, spit upon his handkerchief, and wiped them
clean for the use of his posterity ; and that is the last page
of his history' (*Letter to Wharton*, 11 Sept., 1746).

' pawky ' expression live for ever in the admirable sketch which Hogarth made of him at St. Albans. He died (says Walpole) ' extremely well, without passion, affectation, buffoonery, or timidity.' But he is not so distinguished as either Kilmarnock or Balmerino, and, however Roman his taking-off, the chief memorable thing about it is, that it was happily the last of these sanguinary scenes in this country. The only other incident which it is here needful to chronicle in connection with the ' Forty Five ' is Walpole's verses on the Suppression of the late Rebellion. On the 4th and 5th November, the anniversaries of King William's birth and landing, it was the custom to play Rowe's *Tamerlane*, and this year (1746) the epilogue spoken by Mrs. Pritchard ' in the Character of the Comic Muse ' was from Walpole's pen. According to the writer, special terrors had threatened the stage from the advent of ' Rome's young missionary spark,' the Chevalier, and the Tragic Muse, raising, ' to eyes well-tutor'd in the trade of grief,' ' a small and well-lac'd handkerchief,' is represented by her lighter sister as bewailing the prospect to her ' buskined progeny ' after this fashion : —

> ' Ah ! sons, our dawn is over-cast ; and all
> Theatric glories nodding to their fall.

From foreign realms a bloody chief is come,
Big with the work of slav'ry and of Rome.
A general ruin on his sword he wears,
Fatal alike to audience and to play'rs.
For ah! my sons, what freedom for the stage
When bigotry with sense shall battle wage?
When monkish laureats only wear the bays,
Inquisitors lord chamberlains of plays?
Plays shall be damn'd that 'scap'd the critic's rage,
For priests are still worse tyrants to the stage.
Cato, receiv'd by audiences so gracious,
Shall find ten Cæsars in one St. Ignatius,
And god-like Brutus here shall meet again
His evil genius in a capuchin.
For heresy the fav'rites of the pit
Must burn, and excommunicated wit;
And at one stake, we shall behold expire
My Anna Bullen, and the Spanish Fryar.'[1]

After this the epilogue digresses into a comparison of the Duke of Cumberland with King William. Virgil, Juvenal, Addison, Dryden, and Pope, upon one of whose lines on Cibber Walpole bases his reference to the Lord Chamberlain, are all laid under contribution in this performance. It 'succeeded to flatter me,' he tells Mann a few days later. —a Gallicism from which we must infer an enthusiastic reception.

Walpole's personal and domestic history does not present much interest at this period. His

[1] Walpole's *Works*, 1798, i. 25-7.

sister Mary (Catherine Shorter's daughter), who
had married the third Earl of Cholmondeley,
had died long before her mother. In February,
1746, his half-sister, Lady Mary, his playmate
at comet in the Houghton days, married Mr.
Churchill, — 'a foolish match,' in Horace's
opinion, to which he will have nothing to say.
With his second brother, Sir Edward Walpole,
he seems to have had but little intercourse, and
that scarcely of a fraternal character. In 1857,
Cunningham published for the first time a very
angry letter from Edward to his junior, in which
the latter was bitterly reproached for his inter-
ference in disposing of the family borough of
Castle Rising, and (incidentally) for his assumption of superiority, mental and otherwise. To
this communication Walpole prepared a most
caustic and categorical answer, which, however, he never sent. For his nieces, Edward
Walpole's natural daughters, of whom it will be
more convenient to speak later, Horace seems
always to have felt a sincere regard. But
although his brother had tastes which must have
been akin to his own, for Edward Walpole was
in his way an art patron (Roubillac the sculptor,
for instance, was much indebted to him) and a
respectable musician, no real cordiality ever
existed between them. 'There is nothing in

the world ' — he tells Montagu in May, 1745 —
' the Baron of Englefield has such an aversion
for as for his brother.'[1]

For his eldest brother's wife, the Lady
Walpole who had formed one of the learned
trio at Florence, he entertained no kind of
respect, and his letters are full of flouts at her
Ladyship's manners and morality. Indeed,
between *préciosité* and ' Platonic love,' her
life does not appear to have been a particularly
worshipful one, and her long sojourn under
Italian skies had not improved her. At present
she was Lady Orford, her husband, who is seldom mentioned, and from whom she had been
living apart, having succeeded to the title at his
father's death. From Walpole's letters to Mann.
it seems that in April, 1745, she was, much to
the dismay of her relatives, already preening
her wings for England. In September, she has
arrived, and Walpole is maliciously delighted at
the cold welcome she obtains from the Court
and from society in general, with the exception
of her old colleague, Lady Pomfret, and that
in one sense congenial spirit, Lady Townshend.
Later on, a definite separation from her hus-

---

[1] Englefield, *i. e.* Englefield Green, in Berkshire, on the
summit of Cooper's Hill, near Windsor, where Edward
Walpole lived.

band appears to have been agreed upon, which
Walpole fondly hopes may have the effect of
bringing about her departure for Italy. ' The
Ladies O[rford] and T[ownshend]' — he says
— 'have exhausted scandal both in their persons and conversations.' However much this
may be exaggerated (and Walpole never spares
his antipathies), the last we hear of Lady
Orford is certainly on his side, for she has
retired from town to a villa near Richmond with
a lover for whom she has postponed that
southward flight which her family so ardently
desired. This fortunate Endymion, the Hon.
Sewallis Shirley, son of Robert, first Earl
Ferrers, had already been one of the most
favoured lovers of the notorious ' lady of quality'
whose memoirs were afterwards foisted into
Peregrine Pickle. To Lady Vane now succeeded Lady Orford, as eminent for wealth —
says sarcastic Lady Mary Wortley Montagu — as
her predecessor had been for beauty, and equal
in her ' heroic contempt for shame.' This new
connection was destined to endure. It was in
September, 1746, that Walpole chronicled his
sister-in-law's latest frailty, and in May, 1751,
only a few weeks after her husband's death,[1]

---

[1] Robert Walpole, second Earl of Orford, Horace
Walpole's eldest brother, died in March, 1751.

she married Shirley at the Rev. Alexander Keith's convenient ' little chapel in May Fair.'

In 1744. died Alexander Pope, to be followed a year later by the great Dean of St. Patrick's. Neither of these events leaves any lasting mark in Walpole's correspondence, — indeed of Swift's death there is no mention at all. A nearer bereavement was the premature loss of West, which had taken place two years before, closing sorrowfully with faint accomplishment a life of promise. *Vale, et vive paulisper cum vivis,* — he had written a few days earlier to Gray, — his friend to the last. With Gray, Walpole's friendship, as will be seen presently, had been resumed. His own literary essays still lie chiefly in the domain of squib and *jeu d'esprit.* In April, 1746, over the appropriate signature of ' Descartes,' he printed in No. II. of *The Museum* a ' Scheme for Raising a Large Sum of Money for the Use of the Government, by laying a tax on Message-Cards and Notes,' and in No. V. a pretended Advertisement and Table of Contents for a *History of Good Breeding, from the Creation of the World,* by the Author of the Whole Duty of Man. The wit of this is a little laboured, and scarcely goes beyond the announcement that ' The Eight last Volumes, which relate to *Germany,* may be had separate ; ' nor does that of the other exceed a mild reflection of Fielding's manner in some of his minor pieces. Among other things, we gather that it was the custom of the fine ladies of the day to send open messages on blank playing-cards ; and it is stated as a fact or a fancy that ' after the fatal day of Fontenoy,' persons of quality ' all wrote their notes on Indian paper, which, being red, when inscribed with Japan ink made a melancholy military kind of elegy on the brave youths who occasioned the fashion, and were often the honourable subject of the epistle.' The only remaining effort of any importance at this time is the little poem of *The Beauties,* somewhat recalling Gay's Prologue to the *Shepherd's Week*, and written in July, 1746, to Eckardt the painter. Here is a specimen : —

> In smiling CAPEL's bounteous look
> Rich autumn's goddess is mistook.
> With poppies and with spiky corn,
> Eckardt. her nut-brown curls adorn ;
> And by her side, in decent line,
> Place charming BERKELEY, Proserpine.
> Mild as a summer sea, serene,
> In dimpled beauty next be seen
> AYLESB'RY, like hoary Neptune's queen.
> 　With her the light-dispensing fair,
> Whose beauty gilds the morning air,

And bright as her attendant sun,
The new Aurora, LYTTELTON.
Such Guido's pencil, beauty-tip'd,
And in ethereal colours dip'd,
In measur'd dance to tuneful song
Drew the sweet goddess, as along
Heaven's azure 'neath their light feet spread,
The buxom hours the fairest led.'[1]

' Charming Berkeley,' here mentioned, afterwards became the third wife of Goldsmith's
friend, Earl Nugent, and the mother of the little
girl who played tricks upon the author of *She
Stoops to Conquer* at her father's country seat
of Gosfield ; ' Aylesb'ry, like hoary Neptune's
queen,' married Walpole's friend, Conway, and
' the new Aurora, Lyttelton,' was that engaging
Lucy Fortescue upon whose death in 1747 her
husband wrote the monody so pitilessly parodied
by Smollett.[2] Lady Almeria Carpenter, Lady
Emily Lenox, Miss Chudleigh (afterwards the
notorious Duchess of Kingston), and many
other well-known names, *quos nunc perscribere
longum est*, are also celebrated.

[1] Walpole's *Works*, 1798, i. 21–2.

[2] Writing to Walpole in March, 1751, Gray says : ' In
the last volume [of *Peregrine Pickle*] is a character of Mr.
Lyttleton [*sic*], under the name of " Gosling Scrag," and a
parody of part of his Monody, under the notion of a Pastoral on the death of his grandmother ' (*Works* by Gosse,
1884, ii. 214).

In August, 1746, Walpole announces to Mann that he has taken a pretty house within the precincts of the castle at Windsor, to which he is going for the remainder of the summer. In September he has entered upon residence, for Gray tells Wharton that he sees him 'usually once a week.' 'All is mighty free, and even friendly more than one could expect,' — and one of the first things posted off to Conway, is Gray's *Ode on a Distant Prospect of Eton College*, which the sender desires he 'will please to like excessively.' He is drawn from his retreat by the arrival of a young Florentine friend, the Marquis Rinuncini, to whom he has to do the London honours. ' I stayed literally an entire week with him, carried him to see palaces and Richmond gardens and park, and Chenevix's shop, and talked a great deal to him *alle conversazioni.*[1] 'Chenevix's shop' suggests the main subject of the next chapter, — the purchase and occupation of Strawberry Hill.

---

[1] *Walpole to Mann*, 15 Sept., 1746.

CHAPTER V.

ON the 5th of June, 1747, Walpole announces to Mann that he has taken a little new farm, just out of Twickenham. 'The house is so small that I can send it to you in a letter to look at : the prospect is as delightful as possible, commanding the river, the town [Twickenham], and Richmond Park ; and, being situated on a hill, descends to the Thames through two or three little meadows, where I have some Turkish sheep and two cows, all studied in their colours for becoming the view. This little rural *bijou* was Mrs. Chenevix's, the toy woman *à la mode*,[1]

---

[1] She was the sister of Pope's Mrs. Bertrand, an equally fashionable toy-woman at Bath. Her shop, according to

who in every dry season is to furnish me with
the best rain water from Paris, and now and
then with some Dresden-china cows, who are
to figure like wooden classics in a library ; so I
shall grow as much a shepherd as any swain in
the Astræa.'   Three days later, further details
are added in a letter to Conway, then in
Flanders with the Duke of Cumberland :
' You perceive by my date [Twickenham, 8
June] that I am got into a new camp, and have
left my tub at Windsor.   It is a little play-thing-
house, that I got out of Mrs. Chenevix's shop,
and is the prettiest bauble you ever saw.   It is
set in enamelled meadows, with filagree hedges :

> ' " A small Euphrates through the piece is roll'd,
>   And little finches wave their wings in gold." ' [1]

---

an advertisement in the *Daily Journal* for May 24, 1733,
was then ' against Suffolk Street, Charing Cross.'   It is
mentioned in Fielding's *Amelia*.   When, in Bk. viii , ch. i.,
Mr. Bondum the bailiff contrives to capture Captain
Booth, it is by a false report that his Lady has been ' taken
violently ill, and carried into Mrs. *Chenevix's* Toy-shop.'
It is also mentioned in the Hon. Mrs. Osborne's *Letters*,
1891, p. 73; and again by Walpole himself in the *World*
for 19 Dec., 1754.

[1] This is slightly varied from ll. 29, 30, of Pope's fifth
Moral Essay (' To Mr. Addison : Occasioned by his Dia-
logues on Medals ').

'Two delightful roads, that you would call dusty, supply me continually with coaches and chaises ; barges as solemn as Barons of the Exchequer move under my window ; Richmond Hill and Ham Walks bound my prospect ; . . . Dowagers as plenty as flounders inhabit all around, and Pope's ghost is just now skimming under my window by a most poetical moonlight. I have about land enough to keep such a farm as Noah's, when he set up in the ark with a pair of each kind ; but my cottage is rather cleaner than I believe his was after they had been cooped up together forty days. The Chenevixes had tricked it out for themselves : up two pair of stairs is what they call Mr. Chenevix's library, furnished with three maps, one shelf, a bust of Sir Isaac Newton, and a lame telescope without any glasses. Lord John Sackville *predecessed* me here, and instituted certain games called *crickelalia*, which have been celebrated this very evening in honour of him in a neighbouring meadow.'[1]

The house thus whimsically described, which grew into the Gothic structure afterwards so closely associated with its owner's name, was not, even at this date, without its history. It stood on the left bank of the Thames, at the

[1] *Walpole to Conway*, 8 June, 1747.

corner of the Upper Road to Teddington, not very far from Twickenham itself. It had been built about 1698 as a 'country box' by a retired coachman of the Earl of Bradford, and, from the fact that he was supposed to have acquired his means by starving his master's horses, was known popularly as Chopped-Straw Hall. Its earliest possessor not long afterwards let it out as a lodging-house, and finally, after several improvements, sub-let it altogether. One of its first tenants was Colley Cibber, who found it convenient when he was in attendance for acting at Hampton Court ; and he is said to have written in it the comedy called *The Refusal; or, the Ladies' Philosophy*, produced at Drury Lane in 1721. Then, for eight years, it was rented by the Bishop of Durham, Dr. Talbot, who was reported to have kept in it a better table than the extent of its kitchen seemed, in Walpole's judgment, to justify. After the Bishop came a Marquis, Henry Bridges, son of the Duke of Chandos ; after the Marquis, Mrs. Chenevix, the toy-woman, who, upon her husband's death, let it for two years to the nobleman who *predecessed* Walpole, Lord John Philip Sackville. Before this, Mrs. Chenevix had taken lodgers, one of whom was the celebrated theologian, Père Le Courrayer. At the expiration of Lord John Sackville's tenancy, Walpole took the remainder of Mrs. Chenevix's lease ; and in 1748 had grown to like the situation so much that he obtained a special act to purchase the fee simple from the existing possessors, three minors of the name of Mortimer. The price he paid was £1356 10s. Nothing was then wanting but the name, and in looking over some old deeds this was supplied. He found that the ground on which it stood had been known originally as 'Strawberry-Hill-Shot.' 'You shall hear from me,' he tells Mann in June, 1748, 'from STRAWBERRY HILL, which I have found out in my lease is the old name of my house ; so pray, never call it Twickenham again.'

The transformation of the toy-woman's 'villakin' into a Gothic residence was not, however, the operation of a day. Indeed, at first, the idea of rebuilding does not seem to have entered its new owner's mind. But he speedily set about extending his boundaries, for before 26 December, 1748, he has added nine acres to his original five, making fourteen in all, — a 'territory prodigious in a situation where land is so scarce.' Among the tenants of some of the buildings which he acquired in making these additions was Richard Francklin, the printer

of the *Craftsman*, who, during Sir Robert
Walpole's administration, had been taken up
for printing that paper. He occupied a small
house in what was afterwards known as the
Flower Garden, and Walpole permitted him to
retain it during his lifetime. Walpole's letters
towards the close of 1748 contain numerous
references to his assiduity in planting. ' My
present and sole occupation,' he says in August,
' is planting, in which I have made great
progress, and talk very learnedly with the
nurserymen, except that now and then a lettuce
run to seed overturns all my botany, as I have
more than once taken it for a curious West
Indian flowering shrub. Then the deliberation
with which trees grow is extremely inconve-
nient to my natural impatience.' Two months
later he is ' all plantation, and sprouts away like
any chaste nymph in the *Metamorphosis.*' In
December, we begin to hear of that famous
lawn so well known in the later history of the
house. He is ' making a terrace the whole
breadth of his garden on the brow of a natural
hill, with meadows at the foot, and commanding
the river, the village [Twickenham], Richmond-
hill, and the park, and part of Kingston.' A
year after this (September, 1749), while he is
still ' digging and planting till it is dark,' come

the first dreams of building. At Cheney's, in Buckinghamshire, he has seen some old stained glass, in the windows of an ancient house which had been degraded into a farm, and he thinks he will beg it of the Duke of Bedford (to whom the farm belongs), as it would be 'magnificent for Strawberry-castle.' Evidently he has discussed this (as yet) *château en Espagne* with Montagu. ' Did I tell you [he says] that I have found a text in Deuteronomy to authorise my future battlements ? " When thou buildest a new house, then shalt thou make a battlement for thy roof, that thou bring not blood upon thy house, if any man fall from thence." ' In January, the new building is an established fact, as far as purpose is concerned. In a postscript to Mann he writes : ' I must trouble you with a commission, which I don't know whether you can execute. *I am going to build a little gothic castle at Strawberry Hill.* If you can pick me up any fragments of old painted glass, arms, or anything, I shall be excessively obliged to you. I can't say I remember any such things in Italy ; but out of old chateaus, I imagine, one might get it cheap, if there is any.'

From a subsequent letter it would seem that Mann, as a resident in Italy, had rather expostulated against the style of architecture which his friend was about to adopt, and had suggested the Grecian. But Walpole, rightly or wrongly, knew what he intended. 'The Grecian,' he said, was 'only proper for magnificent and public buildings. Columns and all their beautiful ornaments look ridiculous when crowded into a closet or a cheesecake-house. The variety is little, and admits no charming irregularities. I am almost as fond of the *Sharawaggi*, or Chinese want of symmetry, in buildings, as in grounds or gardens. I am sure, whenever you come to England, you will be pleased with the liberty of taste into which we are struck, and of which you can have no idea.' The passage shows that he himself anticipated some of the ridicule which was levelled by unsympathetic people at the 'oyster-grotto-like profanation' which he gradually erected by the Thames. In the mean time it went on progressing slowly, as its progress was entirely dependent on his savings out of income ; and the references to it in his letters, perhaps because Mann was doubtful, are not abundant. 'The library and refectory, or great parlour,' he says in his description, 'were entirely new built in 1753 ; the gallery, round tower, great cloyster. and cabinet, in 1760 and 1761 ; and the great north bedchamber in 1770.' To speak of these

later alterations would be to anticipate too
much, and the further description of Strawberry
Hill will be best deferred until his own account
of the house and contents was printed in 1774,
four years after the last addition above recorded.
But even before he made the earliest of them,
he must have done much to alter and improve
the aspect of the place, for Gray, more admiring than Mann, praises what has been done.
‘ I am glad,’ he tells Wharton, ‘ that you enter
into the spirit of Strawberry-castle. It has a
purity and propriety of Gothicism in it (with
very few exceptions) that I have not seen elsewhere ; ’ and in an earlier letter he implies that
its ‘ extreme littleness ’ is its chief defect. But
here, before for the moment leaving the subject,
it is only fair to give the proprietor’s own
description of Strawberry Hill at this date, *i. e.*,
in June, 1753. After telling Mann that it is
‘ so monastic ’ that he has ‘ a little hall decked
with long saints in lean arched windows and
with taper columns, which we call the Para-
clete, in memory of Eloisa’s cloister,’ [1] he sends

[1] In the Tribune (see chap. viii.) was a drawing by
Mr. Bentley, representing two lovers in a church looking
at the tombs of Abelard and Eloisa, and illustrating Pope’s
lines :—

> ‘ If ever chance two wand’ring lovers brings
> To Paraclete’s white walls and silver springs,’ etc.

him a sketch of it, and goes on : ' The enclosed
enchanted little landscape, then, is Strawberry
Hill. . . . This view of the castle is what I
have just finished [it was a view of the south
side, towards the north-east], and is the only
side that will be at all regular. Directly before
it is an open grove, through which you see a
field, which is bounded by a serpentine wood
of all kind of trees, and flowering shrubs, and
flowers. The lawn before the house is situated on the top of a small hill, from whence to
the left you see the town and church of Twickenham encircling a turn of the river, that looks
exactly like a sea-port in miniature. The opposite shore is a most delicious meadow, bounded
by Richmond Hill, which loses itself in the
noble woods of the park to the end of the prospect on the right, where is another turn of the
river, and the suburbs of Kingston as luckily
placed as Twickenham is on the left : and a
natural terrace on the brow of my hill, with
meadows of my own down to the river, com-
mands both extremities. Is not this a tolerable
prospect ? You must figure that all this is per-
petually enlivened by a navigation of boats and
barges, and by a road below my terrace, with
coaches, post-chaises, waggons, and horsemen
constantly in motion, and the fields speckled

with cows, horses, and sheep. Now you shall
walk into the house. The bow window below
leads into a little parlour hung with a stone-
colour Gothic paper and Jackson's Venetian
prints,[1] which I could never endure while they
pretended, infamous as they are, to be after
Titian. etc., but when I gave them this air of
barbarous bas-reliefs, they succeeded to a mira-
cle : it is impossible at first sight not to conclude
that they contain the history of Attila or Tottila
done about the very æra. From hence, under
two gloomy arches, you come to the hall and
staircase, which it is impossible to describe to
you, as it is the most particular and chief beauty
of the castle. Imagine the walls covered with
(I call it paper, but it is really paper painted in
perspective to represent) Gothic fretwork : the
lightest Gothic balustrade to the staircase,
adorned with antelopes (our supporters) bearing
shields : lean windows fattened with rich saints
in painted glass, and a vestibule open with three
arches on the landing place, and niches full of
trophies of old coats of mail, Indian shields made
of rhinoceros's hides, broadswords, quivers, long-

---

[1] The chiaroscuros of John Baptist Jackson, published
at Venice in 1742. At this date he had returned to England, and was working in a paper-hanging manufactory
at Battersea.

bows, arrows, and spears, — all *supposed* to be taken by Sir Terry Robsart [an ancestor of Sir Robert Walpole] in the holy wars. But as none of this regards the enclosed drawing, I will pass to that. The room on the ground floor nearest to you is a bedchamber, hung with yellow paper and prints, framed in a new manner, invented by Lord Cardigan ; that is, with black and white borders printed. Over this is Mr. Chute's bed-chamber, hung with red in the same manner. The bow-window room one pair of stairs is not yet finished ; but in the tower beyond it is the charming closet where I am now writing to you. It is hung with green paper and water-colour pictures ; has two windows : the one in the drawing looks to the garden, the other to the beautiful prospect ; and the top of each glutted with the richest painted glass of the arms of England, crimson roses, and twenty other pieces of green, purple, and historic bits. I must tell you, by the way, that the castle, when finished, will have two-and-thirty windows enriched with painted glass. In this closet, which is Mr. Chute's College of Arms, are two presses of books of heraldry and antiquities, Madame Sévigné's Letters, and any French books that relate to her and her acquaintance. Out of this closet is the room where we always live, hung

with a blue and white paper in stripes adorned
with festoons, and a thousand plump chairs,
couches, and luxurious settees covered with
linen of the same pattern, and with a bow
window commanding the prospect, and gloomed
with limes that shade half each window, already
darkened with painted glass in chiaroscuro, set
in deep blue glass. Under this room is a cool
little hall, where we generally dine, hung with
paper to imitate Dutch tiles.

' I have described so much that you will begin
to think that all the accounts I used to give
you of the diminutiveness of our habitation
were fabulous ; but it is really incredible how
small most of the rooms are. The only two
good chambers I shall have are not yet built :
they will be an eating-room and a library, each
twenty by thirty, and the latter fifteen feet
high. For the rest of the house, I could send
it to you in this letter as easily as the drawing,
only that I should have nowhere to live until
the return of the post. The Chinese summer-
house, which you may distinguish in the distant
landscape, belongs to my Lord Radnor.[1] We

[1] Lord Radnor's fantastic house on the river, which
Walpole nicknamed Mabland, came between Strawberry
Hill and Pope's Villa, and is a conspicuous object in old
views of Twickenham, notably in that, dated 1757, by

pique ourselves upon nothing but simplicity, and have no carvings, gildings, paintings, inlayings, or tawdry businesses.'[1]

From this it will appear that in June, 1753, the library and refectory were not yet built, so that when he says, in the printed description, that they were new built in 1753, he must mean no more than that they had been begun. In a later letter, of May, 1754, they were still unfinished. Meanwhile the house is gradually attracting more and more attention. George Montagu comes, and is 'in raptures and screams. and hoops, and hollas, and dances, and crosses himself a thousand times over.' The next visitor is 'Nolkejumskoi,'—otherwise the Duke of Cumberland,—who inspects it much after the fashion of a gracious Gulliver surveying a castle in Lilliput. Afterwards, attracted by the reports of Lady Hervey and Mr. Bristow (brother of the Countess of Buckingham), arrives my Lord Bath, who is stirred into celebrating it to the tune of a song of Bubb Dodington on Mrs. Strawbridge. His Lordship does not seem to have got further than two stanzas ; but Walpole,

Müntz, a Jersey artist for some time domiciled at Strawberry Hill (*see* p. 138). It was in the garden of Radnor House that Pope first met Warburton.

[1] *Walpole to Mann*, 12 June, 1753.

not to leave so complimentary a tribute in the
depressed condition of a fragment, discreetly
revised and completed it himself. The lines
may fairly find a place here as an example of
his lighter muse. The first and third verses are
Lord Bath's, the rest being obviously written
in order to bring in ' Nolkejumskoi ' and some
personal friends : —

> ' Some cry up Gunnersbury,
>   For Sion some declare ;
> And some say that with Chiswick-house
>   No villa can compare :
> But ask the beaux of Middlesex,
>   Who know the county well,
> If Strawb'ry-hill, if Strawb'ry-hill
>   Don't bear away the bell ?

> ' Some love to roll down Greenwich-hill
>   For this thing and for that ;
> And some prefer sweet Marble-hill,
>   Tho' sure 't is somewhat flat :
> Yet Marble-hill and Greenwich hill,
>   If Kitty Clive can tell,
> From Strawb'ry-hill, from Strawb'ry-hill
>   Will never bear the bell.

> ' Tho' Surrey boasts its Oatlands,
>   And Clermont kept so jim,
> And some prefer sweet Southcote's,
>   'T is but a dainty whim ;
> For ask the gallant Bristow,
>   Who does in taste excell,

> If Strawb'ry-hill, if Strawb'ry-hill
>   Don't bear away the bell
>
> 'Since Denham sung of Cooper's,
>   There's scarce a hill around,
>   But what in song or ditty
>   Is turn'd to fairy-ground, —
>   Ah, peace be with their memories!
>   I wish them wond'rous well;
>   But Strawb'ry-hill, but Strawb'ry-hill
>   Must bear away the bell.
>
> 'Great William dwells at Windsor,
>   As Edward did of old;
>   And many a Gaul and many a Scot
>   Have found him full as bold.
>   On lofty hills like Windsor
>   Such heroes ought to dwell;
>   Yet little folks like Strawb'ry-hill,
>   Like Strawb'ry-hill as well.'[1]

Cumberland Lodge, where, say the old guide-books, the hero of Culloden 'reposed after victory,' still stands on the hill at the end of the Long Walk at Windsor; and at 'Gunnersbury' lived the Princess Amelia. All the other houses referred to are in existence. 'Sweet Marble-hill,' which, like Strawberry, was but recently put up for sale, had at this date for mistress the Countess Dowager of Suffolk (Mrs.

---

[1] The version here followed is that given in *A Description of the Villa*, etc., 1774, pp. 117-19.

Mrs. Howard, Countess of Suffolk.

Howard), for whom it had been built by her royal lover, George II. ; and Chiswick House, (now the Marquis of Bute's), that famous structure of Kent which Lord Hervey said was ' too small to inhabit, and too large to hang to one's watch,' was the residence of Richard, Earl of Burlington. Claremont ' kept so jim ' [neat], was the seat of the Duke of Newcastle at Esher ; Oatlands, near Weybridge, belonged to the Duke of York, and Sion House, on the Thames, to the Duke of Northumberland. Walpole and his friends, it will be perceived, did not shrink from comparing small things with great. But perhaps the most notable circumstance about this glorification of Strawberry is that it should have originated with its reputed author. ' Can there be,' says Walpole, ' an odder revolution of things, than that the printer of the *Craftsman* should live in a house of mine, and that the author of the *Craftsman* should write a panegyric on a house of mine ?' The printer was Richard Francklin, already mentioned as his tenant ; and Lord Bath, if not the actual, was at least the putative, writer of most of the *Craftsman's* attacks upon Sir Robert Walpole. It is possible, however, that, as with the poem. part only of this honour really belonged to him.

Strawberry Hill and its improvements have,
however, carried us far from the date at which
this chapter begins, and we must return to
1747. Happily the life of Walpole, though
voluminously chronicled in his correspondence,
is not so crowded with personal incident as to
make a space of six years a serious matter to
recover, especially when tested by the brief
but still very detailed record in the *Short Notes*
of what he held to be its conspicuous occurrences. In 1747–49 his zeal for his father's
memory involved him in a good deal of party
pamphleteering, and in 1749, he had what he
styles ‘ a remarkable quarrel ’ with the Speaker,
of which one may say that, in these days, it
would scarcely deserve its qualifying epithet,
although it produced more paper war. ‘ These
things [he says himself] were only excusable by
the lengths to which party had been carried
against my father ; or rather, were not excusable even then.’ For this reason it is needless
to dwell upon them here, as well as upon certain other papers in *The Remembrancer* for
1749, and a tract called *Delenda est Oxonia*,
prompted by a heinous scheme, which was med-
itated by the Ministry, of attacking the liberties
of that University by vesting in the Crown the
nomination of the Chancellor. This piece [he

says], which I think one of my best, was seized at the printer's and suppressed.' Then in November, 1749, comes something like a really 'moving incident,' — he is robbed in Hyde Park. He was returning by moonlight to Arlington Street from Lord Holland's, when his coach was stopped by two of the most notorious of 'Diana's foresters,'— Plunket and James Maclean; and the adventure had all but a tragic termination. Maclean's pistol went off by accident, sending a bullet so nearly through Walpole's head that it grazed the skin under his eye, stunned him, and passed through the roof of the chariot. His correspondence contains no more than a passing reference to this narrow escape, — probably because it was amply reported (and expanded) in the public prints. But in a paper which he contributed to the *World* a year or two later, under guise of relating what had happened to one of his acquaintance, he reverts to this experience. 'The whole affair [he says] was conducted with the greatest good-breeding on both sides. The robber, who had only taken a purse *this way*, because he had that morning been disappointed of marrying a great fortune, no sooner returned to his lodgings, than he sent the gentleman [*i. e.*, Walpole himself] two letters of excuses, which, with less wit than the epistles of Voiture, had ten times more natural and easy politeness in the turn of their expression. In the postscript, he appointed a meeting at Tyburn at twelve at night, where the gentleman might *purchase again* any trifles he had lost ; and my friend has been blamed for not accepting the rendezvous, as it seemed liable to be construed by ill-natured people into a doubt of the *honour* of a man who had given him all the satisfaction in his power for having *unluckily* been near shooting him through the head.'[1]

The 'fashionable highwayman' (as Mr. Maclean was called) was taken soon afterwards, and hanged. ' I am honourably mentioned in a Grub-street ballad [says Walpole] for not having contributed to his sentence ; ' and he goes on to say that there are as many prints and pamphlets about him as about that other sensation of 1750, the earthquake. Maclean seems nevertheless to have been rather a pinchbeck Macheath ; but for the moment, in default of larger lions, he was the rage. After his condemnation, several thousand people visited him in his cell at Newgate where he is stated to have fainted twice from the heat and pressure of the crowd. And his visitors were not all

1 *World*, 19 Dec., 1754 (*Works*, 1798, i. 177–8).

men. In a note to *The Modern Fine Lady*, Soame Jenyns says that some of the brightest eyes were in tears for him ; and Walpole himself tells us that he excited the warmest commiseration in two distinguished beauties of the day, Lady Caroline Petersham and Miss Ashe.[1]

Miss Ashe, of whom we are told mysteriously by the commentators that she ' was said to have been of very high parentage,' and Lady Caroline Petersham, a daughter of the Duke of Grafton, figure more pleasantly in another letter of Walpole, which gives a glimpse of some of those diversions with which he was wont to relieve the gothicising of his villa by the Thames. In a sentence that proves how well he understood his own qualities, he says he tells the story ' to show the manners of the age, which are always as entertaining to a person fifty miles off as to one born an hundred and fifty years after the time.' We have not yet reached the

[1] Another instance of Maclean's momentary vogue is given by Cunningham. He is hitched into Gray's *Long Story*, which was written at the very time he was taken:

> ' A sudden fit of ague shook him,
> He stood as mute as poor *Macleane*.'

This couplet has been recently explained by Gray's latest editor, Dr. Bradshaw, to be a reference to Maclean's only observation when called to receive sentence. 'My Lord [he said], I *cannot speak.*'

later limit ; but there is little doubt as to the interest of Walpole's account of his visit in the month of June, 1750, to the famous gardens of Mr. Jonathan Tyers. He got a card, he says, from Lady Caroline to go with her to Vauxhall. He repairs accordingly to her house, and finds her ' and the little Ashe, or the Pollard Ashe, as they call her,' having ' just finished their last layer of red, and looking as handsome as crimson could make them.' Others of the party are the Duke of Kingston ; Lord March, of Thackeray's *Virginians ;* Harry Vane, soon to be Earl of Darlington ; Mr. Whitehead ; a ' pretty Miss Beauclerc,' and a ' very foolish Miss Sparre.' As they sail up the Mall, they encounter cross-grained Lord Petersham (my lady's husband) shambling along after his wont,[1] and ' as sulky as a ghost that nobody will speak to first.' He declines to accompany his wife and her friends, who, getting into the best order they can, march to their barge, which has a boat of French horns attending, and ' little Ashe ' sings. After parading up the river, they ' debark ' at Vauxhall, where at the outset they narrowly escape the excitement of a quarrel. For a certain Mrs. Lloyd, of Spring Gardens, afterwards

---

[1] He was popularly known as ' Peter Shamble.' He afterwards became Earl of Harrington.

married to Lord Haddington, observing Miss Beauclerc and her companion following Lady Caroline, says audibly, ' Poor girls, I am sorry to see them in such bad company,'—a remark which the 'foolish Miss Sparre' (she is but fifteen), for the fun of witnessing a duel, endeavours to make Lord March resent. But my Lord, who is not only 'very lively and agreeable,' but also of a nice discretion, laughs her out of 'this charming frolic, with a great deal of humour.' Next they pick up Lord Granby, arriving very drunk from 'Jenny's Whim,' at Chelsea, where he has left a mixed gathering of thirteen persons of quality playing at Brag. He is in the sentimental stage of his malady, and makes love to Miss Beauclerc and Miss Sparre alternately, until the tide of champagne turns, and he remembers that he is married. ' At last,' says Walpole, —and at this point the story may be surrendered to him entirely, — ' we assembled in our booth, Lady Caroline in the front, with the visor of her hat erect, and looking gloriously jolly and handsome. She had fetched my brother Orford from the next box, where he was enjoying himself with his *petite partie*, to help us to mince chickens. We minced seven chickens into a china dish, which Lady Caroline stewed over a lamp with three pats of butter and a flagon of water, stirring and rattling and laughing, and we every minute expecting to have the dish fly about our ears. She had brought Betty, the fruit girl,[1] with hampers of strawberries and cherries from Rogers's, and made her wait upon us, and then made her sup by us at a little table. The conversation was no less lively than the whole transaction. There was a Mr. O'Brien arrived from Ireland, who would get the Duchess of Manchester from Mr. Hussey, if she were still at liberty. I took up the biggest hautboy in the dish, and said to Lady Caroline, " Madam, Miss Ashe desires you would eat this O'Brien strawberry ; " she replied immediately, " I won't, you hussey." You may imagine the laugh this reply occasioned. After the tempest was a little calmed, the Pollard said, " Now, how anybody would spoil this story that was to

[1] Elizabeth Neale, here referred to, was a well-known personage in St. James's Street, where, for many years, she kept a fruit shop. From Lady Mary Coke's *Letters and Journals*, 1889, vol. ii., p. 427, Betty appears to have assiduously attended the debates in the House of Commons, being characterized as a ' violent Politician, & always in the opposition.' In Mason's *Heroic Epistle to Sir William Chambers, Knight*, she is spoken of as ' Patriot Betty.' She survived until 1797, when her death, at the age of 67, is recorded in the *Gentleman's Magazine.*

repeat it, and say, " I won't, you jade." In short, the whole air of our party was sufficient, as you will easily imagine, to take up the whole attention of the garden ; so much so that from eleven o'clock till half an hour after one we had the whole concourse round our booth : at last, they came into the little gardens of each booth on the sides of our's, till Harry Vane took up a bumper, and drank their healths, and was proceeding to treat them with still greater freedom. It was three o'clock before we got home.' He adds a characteristic touch to explain Lord Granby's eccentricities. He had lost eight hundred pounds to the Prince of Wales at Kew the night before, and this had a ' little ruffled ' his lordship's temper.[1]

Early in 1753, Edward Moore, the author of some *Fables for the Female Sex*, once popular enough to figure, between Thomson and Prior, in Goldsmith's *Beauties of English Poesy*, established the periodical paper called *The World*, which, to quote a latter-day definition, might fairly claim to be ' written by gentlemen for gentlemen.' Soame Jenyns, Cambridge of the *Scribleriad* (Walpole's Twickenham neighbour), Hamilton Boyle, Sir Charles Hanbury Williams, and Lord Chesterfield were all contributors.

[1] *Walpole to Montagu*, 23 June, 1750.

That Walpole should also attempt this 'bow of Ulysses, in which it was the fashion for men of rank and genius to try their strength,' goes without saying. His gifts were exactly suited to the work, and his productions in the new journal are by no means its worst. His first essay was a bright little piece of persiflage upon what he calls the return of nature, and proceeds to illustrate by the introduction of ' real water ' on the stage, by Kent's landscape gardening, and by the fauna and flora of the dessert table. A second effort was devoted to that extraordinary adventurer, Baron Neuhoff, otherwise Theodore, King of Corsica, who, with his realm for his only assets, was at this time a tenant of the King's Bench prison. Walpole, with genuine kindness, proposed a subscription for this bankrupt Belisarius, and a sum of fifty pounds was collected. This, however, proved so much below the expectations of His Corsican Majesty that he actually had the effrontery to threaten Dodsley, the printer of the paper, with a prosecution for using his name unjustifiably. 'I have done with countenancing kings,' wrote Walpole to Mann.[1]   Others of his *World* essays are on the Glastonbury Thorn ; on

---

[1] Nevertheless, when this '*Roi en Exil*' shortly afterwards died, Walpole erected a tablet in St. Anne's

Lady Mary Wortley Montagu.

Lady Mary Wortley Montagu.

Letter-Writing, — a subject of which he might claim to speak with authority ; on old women as objects of passion ; and on politeness, wherein occurs the already quoted anecdote of Maclean the highwayman. His light hand and lighter humour made him an almost ideal contributor to Moore's pages, and it is not surprising to find that such judges as Lady Mary approved his performances, or that he himself regarded them with a complacency which peeps out now and again in his letters. ' I met Mrs. Clive two nights ago,' he says, ' and told her I

Churchyard, Soho, to his memory, with the following inscription : —

' Near this place is interred
Theodore, King of Corsica ;
Who died in this parish, Dec. 11, 1756,
Immediately after leaving the King's-Bench-Prison,
By the benefit of the Act of Insolvency ;
In consequence of which he registered
His Kingdom of Corsica
For the use of his Creditors.

' The Grave, great teacher, to a level brings
Heroes and beggars, galley-slaves and Kings.
But Theodore this moral learn'd, ere dead ;
Fate pour'd its lessons on his *living* head,
Bestow'd a kingdom, and denied him bread.'

Theodore's Great Seal, and ' that very curious piece by which he took the benefit of the Act of Insolvency,' and in which he was only styled Theodore Stephen, Baron de Neuhoff, were among the treasures of the Tribune. (See Chapter VIII.)

had been in the meadows, but would walk no
more there, for there was all the world. " Well,"
says she. " and don't you like *The World ?*　I
hear it was very clever last Thursday."'　'Last
Thursday' had appeared Walpole's paper on
elderly ' flames.'

During the period covered by this chapter
the *redintegratio amoris* with Gray, to which
reference has been made, became confirmed.
Whether the attachment was ever quite on the
old basis, may be doubted.　Gray always poses
a little as the aggrieved person who could not
speak first, and to whom unmistakable overtures must be made by the other side.　He as
yet ' neither repents, nor rejoices over much,
but is pleased,' — he tells Chute in 1750.　On
the other hand, Walpole, though he appears
to have proffered his palm-branch with very
genuine geniality, and desire to let by-gones
be by-gones, was not above very candid criticism of his recovered friend.　' I agree with
you most absolutely in your opinion about
Gray,' he writes to Montagu in September,
1748 : ' he is the worst company in the world.
From a melancholy turn, from living reclusely,
and from a little too much dignity, he never
converses easily ;　all his words are measured
and chosen, and formed into sentences ;　his

writings are admirable ; he himself is not agreeable.' Meantime, however, the revived connection went on pleasantly. Gray made flying visits to Strawberry and Arlington Street, and prattled to Walpole from Pembroke between whiles. And certainly, in a measure, it is to Walpole that we owe Gray. It was Walpole who induced Gray to allow Dodsley to print in 1747, as an attenuated *folio* pamphlet, the *Ode on a Distant Prospect of Eton College*; and it was the tragic end of one of Walpole's favourite cats in a china tub of gold-fish (of which, by the way, there was a large pond called Po-yang at Strawberry) which prompted the delightful occasional verses by Gray beginning : —

> ' 'T was on a lofty vase's side,
>> Where china's gayest art had dy'd
>>> The azure flow'rs that blow ;
>> Demurest of the tabby kind,
>> The pensive Selima reclin'd,
>>> Gaz'd on the lake below,' —

a stanza which, with trifling verbal alterations, long served as a label for the ' lofty vase ' in the Strawberry Hill collection. To Walpole's officious circulation in manuscript of the famous *Elegy written in a Country Church-Yard* must indirectly be attributed its publication by Dodsley in February, 1751 ; to Walpole also is due that typical piece of *vers de société*, the *Long Story*, which originated in the interest in the recluse poet of Stoke Poges with which Walpole's well-meaning (if unwelcome) advocacy had inspired Lady Cobham and some other lion-hunters of the neighbourhood. But his chief enterprise in connection with his friend's productions was the edition of them put forth in March, 1753, with illustrations by Richard Bentley, the youngest child of the famous Master of Trinity. Bentley possessed considerable attainments as an amateur artist, and as a scholar and connoisseur had just that virtuoso *finesse* of manner which was most attractive to Walpole, whose guest and counsellor he frequently became during the progress of the Strawberry improvements. Out of this connection, which, in its hot fits, was of the most confidential character, grew the suggestion that Bentley should make, at Walpole's expense, a series of designs for Gray's poems. These, which are still in existence,[1] were engraved with great delicacy by two of the best engravers of that time, Müller and

---

[1] A copy of the poems, 'illustrated with the original designs of Mr. Richard Bentley, . . . and also with Mr. Gray's original sketch of Stoke House, from which Mr. Bentley made his finished pen drawing,' was sold at the Strawberry Hill sale of 1842 to H. G. Bohn for £8 8s.

Charles Grignion; and the *Poemata - Gray-Bentleiana*, as Walpole christened them, became and remains one of the most remarkable of the illustrated books of the last century. Gray, as may be imagined, could scarcely oppose the compliment; and he seems to have grown minutely interested in the enterprise, rewarding the artist by some commendatory verses, in which he certainly does not deny himself — to use a phrase of Mr. Swinburne — ' the noble pleasure of praising.' [1] But even over this book the sensitive ligament that linked him to Walpole was perilously strained. Without consulting him, Walpole had his likeness engraved as a frontispiece, — a step which instantly drew from Gray a wail of nervous expostulation so unmistakably heartfelt that it was impossible to proceed with the plate. Thus it came about that *Designs by Mr. R. Bentley for Six Poems by Mr. T. Gray* made its appearance without the portrait of the poet.

Bentley's ingenious son was not the only person whom the decoration of Strawberry pressed

---

[1] The verses include this magnificent stanza : —

' But not to one in this benighted age
  Is that diviner inspiration giv'n,
That burns in Shakespeare's or in Milton's page,
  The pomp and prodigality of heav'n.'

into the service of its owner.   Selwyn, the wit,
George James (or 'Gilly') Williams, a connoisseur of considerable ability, and Richard, second
Lord Edgecumbe, occasionally sat as a committee of taste, — a function commemorated by
Reynolds in a conversation-piece which afterwards formed one of the chief ornaments of the
Refectory ;[1] and upon Bentley's recommenda-
tion Walpole invited from Jersey a humbler guest
in the person of a German artist named Müntz,
— 'an inoffensive, good creature,' who would
'rather ponder over a foreign gazette than a
palette,' but whose services kept him domiciled
for some time at the Gothic castle.   Müntz
executed many views of the neighbourhood,
which are still, like that of Twickenham already
referred to,[2] preserved in contemporary engravings.   And besides the persons whom Walpole
drew into his immediate circle, the 'village,'
as he called it, was growing steadily in public
favour.   'Mr. Müntz' — writes Walpole in
July, 1755 — 'says we have more coaches than
there are in half France.   Mrs. Pritchard has
bought Ragman's Castle, for which my Lord

---

[1] It is copied in Cunningham, vol iii. p. 475.   It was
sold for £157 10s. at the Strawberry Hill sale, and passed
into the collection of the late Lord Taunton.

[2] See p. 192 n.

Litchfield could not agree. We shall be as celebrated as Baiæ or Tivoli ; and if we have not as sonorous names as they boast, we have very famous people : Clive and Pritchard, actresses ; Scott and Hudson, painters ; my Lady Suffolk, famous in her time ; Mr. H[ickey], the impudent Lawyer, that Tom Hervey wrote against ; Whitehead, the poet ; and Cambridge, the everything.' Cambridge has already been referred to as a contributor to *The World*, and the Whitehead was the one mentioned in Churchill's stinging couplet : —

'May I (can worse disgrace on manhood fall ?)
Be born a Whitehead, and baptiz'd a Paul,'

who then lived on Twickenham Common. Hickey, a jovial Irish attorney, was the legal adviser of Burke and Reynolds, and the ' blunt, pleasant creature ' of Goldsmith's ' Retaliation.' Scott was Samuel Scott, the ' English Canaletto ; ' Hudson, Sir Joshua's master, who had a house on the river near Lord Radnor's. But Walpole's best allies were two of the other sex. One was Lady Suffolk, the whilom friend (as Mrs. Howard) of Pope and Swift and Gay, whose home at Marble Hill is celebrated in the Walpole - cum - Pulteney poem ; the other was red-faced Mrs. Clive, who occupied a house

known familiarly as ' Clive-den,' and officially
as Little Strawberry. She had not yet retired
from the stage. Lady Suffolk's stories of the
Georgian Court and its scandals, and Mrs.
Clive's anecdotes of the green-room, and of their
common neighbour at Hampton, the great
' Roscius ' himself (with whom she was always
at war), must have furnished Walpole with an
inexhaustible supply of just the particular description of gossip which he most appreciated.

CHAPTER VI.

IN order to take up the little-variegated thread of Walpole's life, we must again resort to the *Short Notes,* in which, as already stated, he has recorded what he considered to be its most important occurrences. In 1754, he had been chosen member, in the new Parliament of that year, for Castle Rising, in Norfolk. In March, 1755, he says, he was very ill-used by his nephew, Lord Orford [*i. e.,* the son of his eldest brother, Robert], upon a contested election in the House of Commons, ' on which I wrote him a long letter, with an account of my own conduct in politics.' This letter does not seem to have been preserved, and it is difficult to conceive that its theme could have involved very lengthy explanations. In February, 1757, he vacated his Castle Rising seat for that of Lynn, and about the same time, he tells us, used his best endeavours, although in vain, to save the unfortunate Admiral Byng, who was executed, *pour encourager les autres*, in the following March.   But with the exception of his erection of a tablet to Theodore of Corsica, and the dismissal, in 1759, of Mr. Müntz, with whom his connection seems to have been exceptionally prolonged, his record for the next decade, or until the publication of the *Castle of Otranto*, is almost exclusively literary, and deals with the establishment of his private printing press at Strawberry Hill, his publication thereat of Gray's *Odes* and other works, his *Catalogue of Royal and Noble Authors*, his *Anecdotes of Painting*, and his above-mentioned romance.   This accidental absorption of his chronicle by literary production will serve as a sufficient reason for devoting this chapter to those efforts of his pen which, from the outset, were destined to the permanence of type.

Already, as far back as March, 1751, he had begun the work afterwards known as the *Memoires of the last Ten Years of the Reign of George II.*, to the progress of which there are scattered references in the *Short Notes*.   He had intended at first to confine them to the history of one year, but they grew under his hand. His first definite literary effort in 1757, however, was the clever little squib, after the model of Montesquieu's *Lettres Persanes*, entitled *A Letter from Xo Ho, a Chinese Philosopher at London, to his Friend Lien Chi, at Peking*, in which he ingeniously satirizes the ' late political revolutions ' and the inconstant disposition of the English nation, not forgetting to fire off a few sarcasms *à propos* of the Byng tragedy. The piece, he tells Mann, was written ' in an hour and a half ' (there is always a little of Oronte's *Je n'ai demeuré qu'un quart d'heure à le faire* about Walpole's literary efforts), was sent to press next day, and ran through five editions in a fortnight.[1] Mrs. Clive was of opinion that the rash satirist would be sent to the Tower ; but he himself regarded it as ' perhaps the only political paper ever written, in which no man of any party could dislike or

[1] It may be observed that when Walpole's letter was published, it was briefly noticed in the *Monthly Review*, where at this very date Oliver Goldsmith was working as the hind of Griffiths and his wife. It is also notable that the name of Xo Ho's correspondent, Lien Chi, seems almost a foreshadowing of Goldsmith's Lien Chi Altangi. Can it be possible that Walpole supplied Goldsmith with his first idea of the *Citizen of the World ?*

deny a single fact ; ' and Henry Fox, to whom
he sent a copy, may be held to confirm this
view, since his only objection seems to have
been that it did not hit some of the *other* side
a little harder.   It would be difficult now without long notes to make it intelligible to modern
readers ; but the following outburst of the
Chinese philosopher respecting the variations
of the English climate has the merit of enduring
applicability.   ' The English have no sun, no
summer, as we have, at least their sun does not
scorch like ours.   They content themselves
with names : at a certain time of the year they
leave their capital, and that makes summer ;
they go out of the city, and that makes the
country.   Their monarch, when he goes into
the country, passes in his calash[1] by a row of
high trees, goes along a gravel walk, crosses
one of the chief streets, is driven by the side
of a canal between two rows of lamps, at the
end of which he has a small house [Kensington
Palace], and then he is supposed to be in the
country.   I saw this ceremony yesterday : as
soon as he was gone the men put on under vest-

---

[1] A four-wheeled carriage with a movable hood.   Cf.
Prior's *Down Hall :* ' Then answer'd Squire Morley :
Pray get a *calash*, That in summer may burn, and in
winter may splash,' etc.

ments of white linen, and the women left off those vast draperies, which they call *hoops*, and which I have described to thee ; and then all the men and all the women said *it was hot.* If thou wilt believe me, I am now [in May] writing to thee before a fire.'[1]

In the following June Walpole had betaken himself to the place he ' loved best of all,' and was amusing himself at Strawberry with his pen. The next work which he records is the publication of a Catalogue of the Collection of Pictures, etc., of [*i. e.*, belonging to] Charles the First, for which he prepared ' a little introduction.' This, and the subsequent ' prefaces or advertisements' to the Catalogues of the Collections of James the Second, and the Duke of Buckingham, are to be found in vol. i., pp. 234-41, of his works. But the great event of 1757 is the establishment of the *Officina Arbuteana.* or private printing press, of Strawberry Hill. · Elzevir, Aldus, and Stephens,' he tells Chute in July, ' are the freshest personages in his memory.' and he jestingly threatens to assume as his motto (with a slight variation) Pope's couplet : —

'Some have at first for wits, then poets pass'd ;
Turn'd *printers* next, and proved plain fools at last.'

<hr>

[1] *Works,* 1798, i. 208.

'I am turned printer,' he writes somewhat later, 'and have converted a little cottage into a printing-office. My abbey is a perfect college or academy. I keep a painter [Müntz] in the house, and a printer,—not to mention Mr. Bentley, who is an academy himself.' William Robinson, the printer, an Irishman with noticeable eyes which Garrick envied ('they are more Richard the Third's than Garrick's own,' says Walpole), must have been a rather original personage, to judge by a copy of one of his letters which his patron incloses to Mann. He says he found it in a drawer where it had evidently been placed to attract his attention. After telling his correspondent in bad blank verse that he dates from the 'shady bowers, nodding groves, and amaranthine shades (?) ' of Twickenham,—'Richmond's near neighbour, where great George the King resides,'—Robinson proceeds to describe his employer as 'the Hon. Horatio Walpole, son to the late great Sir Robert Walpole, who is very studious, and an admirer of all the liberal arts and sciences; amongst the rest he admires printing. He has fitted out a complete printing-house at this his country seat, and has done me the favour to make me sole manager and operator (there being no one but myself). All men of genius resorts his house, courts his company, and admires his understanding: what with his own and their writings, I believe I shall be pretty well employed. I have pleased him, and I hope to continue so to do.' Then, after reference to the extreme heat, — a heat by which fowls and quarters of lamb have been roasted in the London Artillery grounds ' by the help of glasses,' so capricious was the climate over which Walpole had made merry in May, — he proceeds to describe Strawberry. ' The place I am now in is all my comfort from the heat ; the situation of it is close to the Thames, and is Richmond Gardens (if you were ever in them) in miniature, surrounded by bowers, groves, cascades, and ponds, and on a rising ground not very common in this part of the country ; the building elegant, and the furniture of a peculiar taste, magnificent and superb.' At this date poor Robinson seems to have been delighted with the place and the fastidious master whom he hoped ' to continue to please.' But Walpole was nothing if not mutable, and two years later he had found out that Robinson of the remarkable eyes was ' a foolish Irishman who took himself for a genius,' and they parted, with the result that the *Officina Arbuteana* was temporarily at a standstill.

For the moment, however, things went

smoothly enough. It had been intended that the maiden effort of the Strawberry types should have been a translation by Bentley of Paul Hentzner's curious account of England in 1598. But Walpole suddenly became aware that Gray had put the penultimate, if not the final, touches to his painfully elaborated Pindaric Odes, the *Bard* and the *Progress of Poesy*, and he pounced upon them forthwith ; Gray, as usual, half expostulating, half overborne. 'You will dislike this as much as I do,' — he writes to Mason, — 'but there is no help.' 'You understand,' he adds, with the air of one resigning himself to the inevitable, 'it is he that prints them, not for me, but for Dodsley.' However, he persisted in refusing Walpole's not entirely unreasonable request for notes. 'If a thing cannot be understood without them,' he said characteristically, 'it had better not be understood at all.' Consequently, while describing them as 'Greek. Pindaric, sublime,' Walpole confesses under his breath that they are a little obscure. Dodsley paid Gray forty guineas for the book, which was a large, thin quarto, entitled *Odes by Mr. Gray ; Printed, at Strawberry Hill, for R. and J. Dodsley in Pall-Mall.* It was published in August, and the price was a shilling. On the title-page was a vignette of the Gothic castle at Twickenham. From a letter of Walpole to Lyttelton it would seem that his apprehensions as to the poems being 'understanded of the people' proved well founded. 'They [the age] have cast their eyes over them, found them obscure, and looked no further ; yet perhaps no compositions ever had more sublime beauties than are in each,' — and he goes on to criticise them minutely in a fashion which shows that his own appreciation of them was by no means unqualified. But Warburton and Garrick and the 'word-picker' Hurd were enthusiastic. Lyttelton and Shenstone followed more moderately. Upon the whole, the success of the first venture was encouraging, and the share in it of ' Elzevir Horace,' as Conway called his friend, was not forgotten.

Gray's *Odes* were succeeded by Hentzner's *Travels*, or, to speak more accurately, by that portion of Hentzner's *Travels* which refers to England. In England Hentzner was little known, and the 220 copies which Walpole printed in October, 1757, were prefaced by an Advertisement from his pen, and a dedication to the Society of Antiquaries, of which he was a member. After this came, in 1758, his *Catalogue of Royal and Noble Authors ;* a collection of *Fugitive Pieces* (which included his essays in the *World*), dedicated to Conway ;[1] and seven hundred copies of Lord Whitworth's *Account of Russia.* Then followed a book by Joseph Spence, the *Parallel of Magliabecchi and Mr. [Robert] Hill,* a learned tailor of Buckingham, the object of which was to benefit Hill, — an end which must have been attained, as six out of seven hundred copies were sold in a fortnight, and the book was reprinted in London. Bentley's *Lucan,* a quarto of five hundred copies, succeeded Spence, and then came three other quartos of *Anecdotes of Painting,* by Walpole himself. The only other notable products of the press during this period are the Autobiography of Lord Herbert of Cherbury, quarto, 1764, and one hundred copies of the *Poems* of Lady Temple. This, however, is a very fair record for seven years' work, when it is remembered that the Strawberry Hill staff never exceeded a man and a boy. As already stated, the first printer, Robinson, was dismissed in 1759. His place, after a short interval of ' occasional hands,' was taken by Thomas Kirgate, whose name thenceforth appears on all the

---

[1] These, though printed in 1758, were not circulated until 1759. See, at end, ' Appendix of Books printed at the Strawberry Hill Press,' which contains ample details of all these publications.

Twickenham issues, with which it is indissolubly connected. Kirgate continued, with greater good fortune than his predecessors, to perform his duties until Walpole's death.

In the above list there are two volumes which, in these pages, deserve a more extended notice than the rest. *The Catalague of Royal and Noble Authors* had at least the merit of novelty, and certainly a better reason for existing than some of the works to which its author refers in his preface. Even the performances of Pulteney, Earl of Bath, and the English rondeaus of Charles of Orleans are more worthy of a chronicler than the lives of physicians who had been poets, of men who had died laughing, or of Frenchmen who had studied Hebrew. Walpole took considerable pains in obtaining information, and his book was exceedingly well received. — indeed, far more favourably than he had any reason to expect. A second edition, which was not printed at Strawberry Hill, speedily followed the first, with no diminution of its prosperity. For an effort which made no pretensions to symmetry, which is often meagre where it might have been expected to be full, and is everywhere prejudiced by a sort of fine-gentleman disdain of exactitude, this was certainly as much as he could anticipate. But he seems to have been more than usually sensitive to criticism, and some of the amplest of his *Short Notes* are devoted to the discussion of the adverse opinions which were expressed. From these we learn that he was abused by the *Critical Review* for disliking the Stuarts, and by the *Monthly* for liking his father. Further, that he found an apologist in Dr. Hill (of the *Inspector*), whose gross adulation was worse than abuse ; and lastly, that he was seriously attacked in a Pamphlet of *Remarks on Mr. Walpole's ' Catalogue of Royal and Noble Authors '* by a certain Carter, concerning whose antecedents his irritation goes on to bring together all the scandals he can collect. As the *Short Notes* were written long after the events, it shows how his soreness against his critics continued. What it was when still fresh may be gathered from the following quotation from a letter to Rev. Henry Zouch, to whom he was indebted for many new facts and corrections, especially in the second edition, and who afterwards helped him in the *Anecdotes of Painting:* ' I am sick of the character of author; I am sick of the consequences of it ; I am weary of seeing my name in the newspapers ; I am tired with read-

Holbein.

HOLBEIN.

ing foolish criticisms on me, and as foolish defences of me ; and I trust my friends will be so good as to let the last abuse of me pass unanswered. It is called " Remarks " on my Catalogue, asperses the Revolution more than it does my book, and, in one word, is written by a non-juring preacher, who was a dog-doctor. Of me, he knows so little that he thinks to punish me by abusing King William ! ' [1]

In a letter of a few months earlier to the same correspondent, he refers to another task, upon which, in despite of the sentence just quoted, he continued to employ himself. ' Last summer ' — he says — ' I bought of Vertue's widow forty volumes of his MS. collections relating to English painters, sculptors, gravers, and architects. He had actually begun their lives : unluckily he had not gone far, and could not write grammar. I propose to digest and complete this work.' [2] The purchases referred to had been made subsequent to 1756, when Mrs. Vertue applied to Walpole, as a connoisseur, to buy from her the voluminous notes and memoranda which her husband had accumulated with respect to art and artists in England. Walpole also acquired at Vertue's sale in May,

[1] *Walpole to Zouch*, 14 May, 1759.
[2] *Walpole to Zouch*, 12 January, 1759.

1757, a number of copies from Holbein and two or three other pictures.   He seems to have almost immediately set about arranging and digesting this unwieldy and chaotic heap of material,[1] much of which, besides being illiterate, was also illegible.   More than once his patience gave way under the drudgery; but he nevertheless persevered in a way that shows a tenacity of purpose foreign, in this case at all events, to his assumption of dilettante indifference.   His progress is thus chronicled.   He began in January, 1760. and finished the first volume on 14 August.   The second volume was begun in September, and completed on the 23rd October.   On the 4th January in the following year he set about the third volume, but laid it aside after the first day, not resuming it until the end of June.   In August, however, he finished it.   Two volumes were published in 1762, and a third, which is dated 1763, in 1764. As usual, he affected more or less to undervalue

---

[1] 'Mr. Vertue's Manuscripts, in 28 vols.,' were sold at the Sale of Rare Prints and Illustrated Works from the Strawberry Hill Collection on Tuesday, 21 June, 1842, for £26 10s.   Walpole says in the *Short Notes* that he paid £100.   The Vertue MSS. are now in the British Museum, which acquired them from the Dawson Turner collection.

his own share in the work ; but he very justly laid stress in his ' Preface ' upon the fact that he was little more than the arranger of data not collected by his own exertions. ' I would not,' he said to Zouch, ' have the materials of forty years, which was Vertue's case, depreciated in compliment to the work of four months, which is almost my whole merit.' Here, again, the tone is a little in the Oronte manner ; but, upon the main point, the interest of the work, his friends did not share his apprehensions, and Gray especially was ' violent about it.' Nor did the public show themselves less appreciative, for there was so much that was new in the dead engraver's memoranda, and so much which was derived from private galleries or drawn from obscure sources, that the work could scarcely have failed of readers even if the style had been hopelessly corrupt, which, under Walpole's revision, it certainly was not. In 1762, he began a *Catalogue of Engravers*, which he finished in about six weeks as a supplementary volume, and in 1765, still from the Strawberry Press, he issued a second edition of the whole.[1]

---

[1] *The Anecdotes of Painting* was enlarged by the Rev. James Dallaway in 1826-8, and again revised, with additional notes, by Ralph N Wornum in 1839. This last, in three volumes, 8vo, is the accepted edition.

After the appearance of the second edition of the *Anecdotes of Painting*, a silence fell upon the *Officina Arbuteana* for three years, during the earlier part of which time Walpole was at Paris, as will be narrated in the next chapter. His press, as may be guessed, was one of the sights of his Gothic castle, and there are several anecdotes showing how his ingenious fancy made it the vehicle of adroit compliment. Once, not long after it had been established, my Lady Rochford, Lady Townshend (the witty Ethelreda, or Audrey, Harrison),[1] and Sir John Bland's sister were carried after dinner into the printing-room to see Mr. Robinson at work. He immediately struck off some verse which was already in type, and presented it to Lady Townshend : —

The Press speaks.

From me wits and poets their glory obtain ;
Without me their wit and their verses were vain.
Stop, Townshend, and let me but paint[2] what you say,
You, the fame I on others bestow, will repay.

[1] She was married to Charles, 3rd Viscount Townshend, in 1723, and was the mother of Charles Townshend, the statesman. She died in 1788. There was an enamel of her by Zincke after Vanloo in the Tribune at Strawberry Hill, which is engraved at p 150 of Cunningham's second volume.

[2] *Sic. in orig.;* but query ' print.'

The visitors then asked, as had been anticipated, to see the actual process of setting up;
and Walpole ostensibly gave the printer four
lines out of Rowe's *Fair Penitent*. But, by
what would now be styled a clever feat of pres-
tidigitation, the forewarned Robinson struck off
the following, this time to Lady Rochford : —

THE PRESS SPEAKS.

In vain from your properest name you have flown,
And exchanged lovely Cupid's for Hymen's dull throne ;
By my art shall your beauties be constantly sung,
And in spite of yourself, you shall ever be *young*.

Lady Rochford's maiden name, it should be
explained, was ' Young.' Such were what their
inventor call *les amusements des eaux de Stra-
berri* in the month of August and the year of
grace 1757.

Beyond the major efforts already mentioned,
the *Short Notes* contain references to various
fugitive pieces which Walpole composed, some
of which he printed, and some others of which
have been published since his death. One of
these, *The Magpie and her Brood*, was a pleasant little fable from the French of Bonaventure
des Periers, rhymed for Miss Hotham, the
youthful niece of his neighbour Lady Suffolk ;
another, a *Dialogue between two Great Ladies.*

In 1761, he wrote a poem on the King, entitled
The Garland, which first saw the light in the
Quarterly for 1852 [No. CLXXX.]. Besides
these were several epigrams, mock sermons.
and occasional verses. But perhaps the most
interesting of his productions in this kind are
the octosyllabics which he wrote in August,
1759, and called *The Parish Register of
Twickenham*. This is a metrical list of all
the remarkable persons who ever lived there.
for which reason a portion of it may find a place
in these pages : —

> ' Where silver Thames round Twit'nam meads
>   His winding current sweetly leads ;
>   Twit'nam, the Muses' fav'rite seat,
>   Twit'nam, the Graces' lov'd retreat;
>   There polish'd Essex wont to sport,
>   The pride and victim of a court !
>   There Bacon tun'd the grateful lyre
>   To soothe Eliza's haughty ire ;
>   — Ah ! happy had no meaner strain
>   Than friendship's dash'd his mighty vein !
>   Twit'nam, where Hyde, majestic sage,
>   Retir'd from folly's frantic stage,
>   While his vast soul was hung on tenters
>   To mend the world, and vex dissenters ·
>   Twit'nam, where frolic Wharton revel'd,
>   Where Montagu, with locks dishevel'd
>   (Conflict of dirt and warmth divine),
>   Invok'd — and scandaliz'd the Nine;

Where Pope in moral music spoke
To th' anguish'd soul of Bolingbroke,
And whisper'd, how true genius errs,
Preferring joys that pow'r confers;
Bliss, never to great minds arising
From ruling worlds, but from despising:
Where Fielding met his bunter Muse,
And, as they quaff'd the fiery juice,
Droll Nature stamp'd each lucky hit
With inimaginable wit:
Where Suffolk sought the peaceful scene,
Resigning Richmond to the queen,
And all the glory, all the teasing,
Of pleasing one not worth the pleasing:
Where Fanny, "ever-blooming fair,"
Ejaculates the graceful pray'r,
And 'scap'd from sense, with nonsense smit,
For Whitefield's cant leaves Stanhope's wit:
Amid this choir of sounding names
Of statesmen, bards, and beauteous dames,
Shall the last trifler of the throng
Enroll his own such names among?
— Oh! no — Enough if I consign
To lasting types their notes divine:
Enough, if Strawberry's humble hill
The title-page of fame shall fill.'[1]

In 1784, Walpole added a few lines to celebrate a new resident and a new favourite, Lady Di. Beauclerk, the widow of Johnson's famous friend.[2]   Most of the other names which occur

---

[1] *Works*, 1798, vol. iv., pp. 382-3.

[2] See chapter ix.

in the *Twickenham Register* are easily identified. ' Fanny, " ever-blooming fair," ' was the
beautiful Lady Fanny Shirley of Phillips' ballad
and Pope's epistle, aunt of that fourth Earl
Ferrers who in 1760 was hanged at Tyburn
for murdering his steward. Miss Hawkins
remembered her as residing at a house now
called Heath Lane Lodge, with her mother,
' a very ancient Countess Ferrers,' widow of
the first Earl. Henry Fielding, to whom Walpole gives a quatrain, the second couplet of
which must excuse the insolence of the first,
had for some time lodgings in Back Lane,
whence was baptised in February, 1748, the
elder of his sons by his second wife, the
William Fielding who, like his father, became
a Westminster magistrate. It is more likely
that *Tom Jones* was written at Twickenham
than at any of the dozen other places for which
that honour is claimed, since the author quitted
Twickenham late in 1748, and his great novel
was published early in the following year.
Walpole had only been resident for a short time
when Fielding left, but even had this been
otherwise, it is not likely that, between the
master of the Comic Epos (who was also Lady
Mary's cousin !) and the dilettante proprietor
of Strawberry, there could ever have been

much cordiality. Indeed, for some of the robuster spirits of his age Walpole shows an extraordinary distaste, which with him generally implies unsympathetic, if not absolutely illiberal, comment. Almost the only important anecdote of Fielding in his correspondence is one of which the distorting bias is demonstrable ;[1] and to Fielding's contemporary, Hogarth, although as a connoisseur he was shrewd enough to collect his works, he scarcely ever refers but to place him in a ridiculous aspect, —a course which contrasts curiously with the extravagant praise he gives to Bentley, Bunbury, Lady Di. Beauclerk, and some other of the very minor artistic lights in his own circle.

It is, however, possible to write too long an excursus upon the *Twickenham Parish Register*, and the last paragraphs of this chapter belong of right to another and more important work, —*The Castle of Otranto*. According to the *Short Notes*, this ' Gothic romance ' was begun in June, 1764, and finished on the 6th August following. From another account we learn that it occupied eight nights of this period from ten o'clock at night until two in the morning, to the accompaniment of coffee. In a letter to Cole,

---

[1] Cf. chapter vi. of *Fielding*, by the present writer, in the *Men of Letters* series, 2nd edition, 1889, pp. 145-7.

the Cambridge antiquary, with whom Walpole commenced to correspond in 1762, he gives some further particulars, which, because they have been so often quoted, can scarcely be omitted here : ' Shall I even confess to you what was the origin of this romance ? I waked one morning, in the beginning of last June, from a dream, of which all I could recover was, that I had thought myself in an ancient castle (a very natural dream for a head filled, like mine, with Gothic story), and that on the uppermost bannister of a great staircase I saw a gigantic hand in armour. In the evening I sat down and began to write, without knowing in the least what I intended to say or relate. The work grew on my hands, and I grew fond of it, — add that I was very glad to think of anything, rather than politics. In short, I was so engrossed with my tale, which I completed in less than two months, that one evening I wrote from the time I had drunk my tea, about six o'clock, till half an hour after one in the morning, when my hand and fingers were so weary that I could not hold the pen to finish the sentence, but left Matilda and Isabella talking, in the middle of a paragraph.'[1]

The work of which the origin is thus de-

---

[1] *Letter to Cole*, 9 March, 1765

scribed was published in a limited edition on the 24th December, 1764, with the title of *The Castle of Otranto, a Story, translated by William Marshal, Gent., from the original Italian of Onuphrio Muralto, Canon of the Church of St. Nicholas at Otranto.* The name of the alleged Italian author is sometimes described as an anagram from Horace Walpole, — a misconception which is easily demonstrated by counting the letters. The book was printed, not for Walpole, but for Lownds, of Fleet Street, and it was prefaced by an introduction in which the author described and criticised the supposed original, which he declared to be a black-letter printed at Naples in 1529. Its success was considerable. It seems at first to have excited no suspicion as to its authenticity, and it is not clear that even Gray, to whom a copy was sent immediately after publication, was in the secret. 'I have received the *Castle of Otranto*,' he says, ' and return you my thanks for it. It engages our attention here [at Cambridge], makes some of us cry a little, and all in general afraid to go to bed o' nights.' In the second edition, which followed in April, 1765, Walpole dropped the mask, disclosing his authorship in a second preface of great ability, which, among other things, contains a vindication of Shakespeare's

mingling of comedy and tragedy against the
strictures of Voltaire, — a piece of temerity
which some of his French friends feared might
prejudice him with that formidable critic.   But
what is even more interesting is his own account
of what he had attempted. He had endeavoured
to blend ancient and modern romance, — to employ the old supernatural agencies of Scudéry
and La Calprenède as the background to the
adventures of personages modelled as closely
upon ordinary life as the personages of *Tom
Jones.* These are not his actual illustrations,
but they express his meaning. ' The actions,
sentiments, conversations, of the heroes and
heroines of ancient days were as unnatural as
the machines employed to put them in motion.'
He would make his heroes and heroines natural
in all these things, only borrowing from the
older school some of that imagination, invention,
and fancy which, in the literal reproduction of
life, he thought too much neglected.

His idea was novel, and the moment a favourable one for its development.   Fluently and
lucidly written, the *Castle of Otranto* set a
fashion in literature.   But, like many other
works produced under similar conditions, it had
its day.   To the pioneer of a movement which
has exhausted itself, there comes often what is

almost worse than oblivion, — discredit and neglect. A generation like the present, for whom fiction has unravelled so many intricate combinations, and whose Gothicism and Mediæ- valism are better instructed than Walpole's, no longer feels its soul harrowed up in the same way as did his hushed and awe-struck readers of the days of the third George. To the critic the book is interesting as the first of a school of romances which had the honour of influencing even the mighty ' Wizard of the North,' who, no doubt in gratitude, wrote for *Ballantyne's Novelist's Library* a most appreciative study of the story. But we doubt if that many-plumed and monstrous helmet, which crashes through stone walls and cellars, could now give a single shiver to the most timorous Cambridge don, while we suspect that the majority of modern students would, like the author, leave Matilda and Isabella talking, in the middle of a para- graph, but from a different kind of weariness. *Autres temps, autres mœurs*, — especially in the matter of Gothic romance.

CHAPTER VII.

State of French Society in 1765. — Walpole at Paris. — The Royal Family and the Bête du Gévaudan. — French Ladies of Quality. — Madame du Deffand — A Letter from Madame de Sévigné. — Rousseau and the King of Prussia. — The Hume-Rousseau Quarrel. — Returns to England, and hears Wesley at Bath. — Paris again. — Madame du Deffand's Vitality. — Her Character. — Minor Literary Efforts. — The *Historic Doubts*. — The *Mysterious Mother*. — Tragedy in England. — Doings of the Strawberry Press. — Walpole and Chatterton.

WHEN, towards the close of 1765, Walpole made the first of several visits to Paris, the society of the French capital, and indeed French society as a whole, was showing signs of that coming *culbute générale* which was not to be long deferred. The upper classes were shamelessly immoral, and, from the King downwards, *liaisons* of the most open character excited neither censure nor comment. It was the era of Voltaire and the Encyclopædists ; it was the era of Rousseau and the Sentimentalists ; it was also the era of confirmed Anglomania. While we, on our side, were beginning to copy the *comédies larmoyantes* of

La Chaussée and Diderot, the French in their turn were acting *Romeo and Juliet*, and raving over Richardson. Richardson's chief rival in their eyes was Hume, then a *chargé d'affaires*, and, in spite of his plain face and bad French, the idol of the freethinkers. He 'is treated here,' writes Walpole, 'with perfect veneration ; ' and we learn from other sources that no lady's toilette was complete without his attendance. 'At the Opera,' — says Lord Charlemont, — ' his broad, unmeaning face was usually seen *entre deux jolis minois;* the ladies in France gave the *ton*, and the *ton* was Deism.' Apart from literature, irreligion, and philosophy, the chief occupation was cards. ' Whisk and Richardson ' is Walpole's later definition of French society ; ' Whisk and disputes,' that of Hume. According to Walpole, a kind of pedantry and solemnity was the characteristic of conversation, and ' laughing was as much out of fashion as pantins or bilboquets. Good folks, they have no time to laugh. There is God and the King to be pulled down first ; and men and women, one and all, are devoutly employed in the demolition.' How that enterprise eventuated, history has recorded.

It is needless, however, to rehearse the origins of the French Revolution, in order to make a

background for the visit of an English gentleman to Paris in 1765. Walpole had been medi-
tating this journey for two or three years ; but
the state of his health, among other things (he
suffered much from gout), had from time to time
postponed it. In 1763, he had been going
next spring ;[1] but when next spring came he
talked of the beginning of 1765. Nevertheless,
in March of that year, Gilly Williams writes to
Selwyn : ' Horry Walpole has now postponed
his journey till May,' and then he goes on to
speak of the *Castle of Otranto* in a way which
shows that all the author's friends were not
equally enthusiastic respecting that ingenious
romance. ' How do you think he has employed
that leisure which his political frenzy has allowed of ? In writing a novel, . . . and such
a novel that no boarding-school miss of thirteen
could get through without yawning. It consists
of ghosts and enchantments ; pictures walk out
of their frames, and are good company for half
an hour together ; helmets drop from the moon,

---

[1] It is curious to note in one of his letters at this date
a *mot* which may be compared with the famous ' Good
Americans, when they die, go to Paris.' Walpole is more
sardonic. ' Paris,' he says, ' . . . like the description
of the grave, is the way of all flesh ' (*Walpole to Mann*,
30 June, 1763).

and cover half a family. He says it was a dream, and I fancy one when he had some feverish disposition in him.'[1] May, however, had arrived and passed, and the *Castle of Otranto* was in its second edition, before Walpole at last set out, on Monday, the 9th September, 1765. After a seven hours' passage, he reached Calais from Dover. Near Amiens he was refreshed by a sight of one of his favourites, Lady Mary Coke,[2] ' in pea-green and silver ; ' at Chantilly he was robbed of his port-

[1] *Gilly Williams to Selwyn*, 19 March, 1765.

[2] Lady Mary Coke, to whom the second edition of the Gothic romance was dedicated, was the youngest daughter of John, Duke of Argyll and Greenwich. At this date, she was a widow, — Lord Coke having died in 1753. Two volumes of her *Letters and Journals*, with an excellent introduction by Lady Louisa Stuart, were printed privately at Edinburgh in 1889 from MSS. in the possession of the Earl of Home. A third volume, which includes a number of epistles addressed to her by Walpole, found among the papers of the late Mr. Drummond Moray of Abercairny, was issued in 1892. Walpole's tone in these documents is one of fantastic adoration ; but the pair ultimately (and inevitably) quarrelled. There is a well-known mezzotint of Lady Mary by McArdell after Allan Ramsay, in which she appears in white satin, holding a tall theorbo. The original painting is at Mount Stuart, and belongs to Lord Bute.

manteau. By the time he reached Paris, on the
13th, he had already 'fallen in love with twenty
things, and in hate with forty.' The dirt of
Paris, the narrowness of the streets, the 'trees
clipped to resemble brooms, and planted on
pedestals of chalk,' disgust him. But he is
enraptured with the *treillage* and fountains,
'and will prove it at Strawberry.' He detests
the French opera, though he loves the French
opéra-comique, with its Italian comedy and his
passion, — 'his dear favourite harlequin.' Upon
the whole, in these first impressions he is disappointed. Society is duller than he expected,
and with the staple topics of its conversation, —
philosophy, literature, and freethinking, — he is
(or says he is) out of sympathy. ' Freethinking
is for one's self, surely not for society. . . . I
dined to-day with half-a-dozen *savans*, and though
all the servants were waiting, the conversation was much more unrestrained, even on the
Old Testament, than I would suffer at my own
table in England if a single footman was present. For literature, it is very amusing when
one has nothing else to do. I think it rather
pedantic in society; tiresome when displayed
professedly ; and, besides, in this country one is
sure it is only the fashion of the day.' And

then he goes on to say that the reigning fashion is Richardson and Hume.[1]

One of his earliest experiences was his presentation at Versailles to the royal family, — a ceremony which luckily involved but one operation instead of several, as in England, where the Princess Dowager of Wales, the Duke of Cumberland, and the Princess Amelia had all their different levees. He gives an account of this to Lady Hervey; but repeats it on the same day with much greater detail in a letter to Chute. ‘You perceive [he says] that I have been presented. The Queen took great notice of me [for which reason, in imitation of Madame de Sévigné, he tells Lady Hervey that she is *le plus grand roi du monde*]; none of the rest said a syllable. You are let into the King's bedchamber just as he has put on his shirt; he dresses, and talks good-humouredly to a few, glares at strangers, goes to mass, to dinner, and a-hunting. The good old Queen, who is like Lady Primrose in the face, and Queen Caroline in the immensity of her cap, is at her dressing-table, attended by two or three old ladies. . . . Thence you go to the Dauphin, for all is done in an hour. He scarce stays a minute; indeed, poor creature, he is a ghost, and cannot possibly

1 *Walpole to Montagu*, 22 September, 1765.

last three months. [He died, in fact, within
this time, on the 20th December.] The
Dauphiness is in her bed-chamber, but dressed
and standing; looks cross, is not civil, and has
the true Westphalian grace and accents. The
four Mesdames [these were the *Graille*, *Chiffe*,
Coche, and *Loque* of history], who are clumsy,
plump old wenches, with a bad likeness to their
father, stand in a bedchamber in a row, with
black cloaks and knotting-bags, looking good-
humoured, [and] not knowing what to say. . . .
This ceremony is very short; then you are carried
to the Dauphin's three boys, who, you may be
sure, only bow and stare. The Duke of Berry
[afterwards Louis XVI.] looks weak and weak-
eyed; the Count de Provence [Louis XVIII.]
is a fine boy; the Count d'Artois [Charles X.]
well enough. The whole concludes with seeing
the Dauphin's little girl dine, who is as round and
as fat as a pudding.'[1] Such is Walpole's account
of the royal family of France on exhibition. In
the Queen's ante-chamber he was treated to a
sight of the famous *bête du Géraudan*, a hugeous
wolf, of which a highly sensational representation had been given in the *St. James's Chronicle*
for June 6-8. It had just been shot, after a
prosperous but nefarious career, and was ex-

---

[1] *Walpole to Chute*, 3 October, 1765.

hibited by two chasseurs ' with as much parade as if it was Mr. Pitt.' [1]

When he had been at Paris little less than a month, he was laid up with the gout in both feet. He was visited during his illness by Wilkes, for whom he expresses no admiration. From another letter it appears that Sterne and Foote were also staying in the French capital at this time. In November he is still limping about, and it is evident that confinement in ' a bedchamber in a *hôtel garni,* . . . when the court is at Fontainebleau,' has not been without its effect upon his views of things in general. In writing to Gray (who replies with all sorts of kindly remedies), he says, ' The charms of Paris have not the least attraction for me, nor

---

[1] Madame de Genlis mentions this fearsome monster in her *Mémoires:* ' Tout le monde a entendu parler de la hyène de Gévaudan, qui a fait tant de ravages.' The point of Walpole's allusion to Pitt is explained in one of his hitherto unpublished letters to Lady Mary Coke at this date: ' I had the fortune to be treated with the sight of what, next to Mr. Pitt, has occasioned most alarm in France, the Beast of the Gévaudan' (*Letters and Journals,* iii. [1892], xvii). In another letter, to Pitt's sister Ann, maid of honour to Queen Caroline, he says: ' It is a very large wolf, to be sure, and they say has twelve teeth more than any of the species, and six less than the Czarina' (*Fortescue Corr., Hist. MSS. Commission,* 13th *Rept., App.* iii., 1892, i. 147).

would keep me an hour on their own account.
For the city itself, I cannot conceive where my
eyes were: it is the ugliest, beastliest town in
the universe. I have not seen a mouthful of
verdure out of it, nor have they anything green
but their *treillage* and window shutters. . . .
Their boasted knowledge of society is reduced
to talking of their suppers, and every malady
they have about them, or know of.' A day or
two later his gout and his stick have left him,
and his good humour is coming back. Before
the month ends, he is growing reconciled to his
environment ; and by January 'France is so
agreeable, and England so much the reverse,' —
he tells Lady Hervey, —' that he does not know
when he shall return.' The great ladies, too,
Madame de Brionne, Madame d'Aiguillon,
Marshal Richelieu's daughter, Madame d'Eg-
mont (with whom he could fall in love if it
would break anybody's heart in England), begin
to flatter and caress him. His ' last new passion ' is the Duchess de Choiseul, who is so
charming that ' you would take her for the
queen of an allegory.' ' One dreads its finish-
ing, as much as a lover, if she would admit one,
would wish it should finish.' There is also a
beautiful Countess de Forcalquier, the ' broken
music ' of whose imperfect English stirs him

into heroics too Arcadian for the matter-of-fact meridian of London, where Lady Hervey is cautioned not to exhibit them to the profane.[1]

In a letter of later date to Gray, he describes some more of these graceful and witty leaders of fashion, whose '*douceur*' he seems to have greatly preferred to the pompous and arrogant fatuity of the men. 'They have taken up gravity,'—he says of these latter,— 'thinking it was philosophy and English, and so have acquired nothing in the room of their natural levity and cheerfulness.' But with the women the case is different. He knows six or seven 'with very superior understandings : some of them with wit, or with softness, or very good sense.' His first portrait is of the famous Madame Geoffrin, to whom he had been recommended by Lady Hervey, and who had visited him when imprisoned in his *chambre garni.* He lays stress upon her knowledge of character, her tact and good sense, and the happy mingling of freedom and severity by

[1] Of Mad. de Forcalquier it is related that, entering a theatre during the performance of Gresset's *Le Méchant,* just as the line was uttered, '*La faute est aux dieux, qui la firent si belle,*' the applause was so great as to interrupt the play. The point of this, in a recent repetition of the anecdote, was a little blunted by the printer's substitution of '*bête*' for '*belle.*'

which she preserved her position as 'an epi-
tome of empire, subsisting by rewards and
punishments.' Then there is the Maréchale
de Mirepoix, a courtier and an *intrigante* of the
first order. 'She is false, artful, and insinu-
ating beyond measure when it is her interest,
but indolent and a coward,' says Walpole,
who does not measure his words even when
speaking of a beauty and a Princess of Lorraine.
Others are the *savante*, Madame de Boufflers,
who visited England and Johnson, and whom
the writer hits off neatly by saying that you
would think she was always sitting for her
picture to her biographer ; a second *savante*,
Madame de Rochfort, 'the *decent* friend' of
Walpole's former guest at Strawberry, the Duc
de Nivernois ;[1] the already mentioned Duchess

[1] Louis-Jules-Barbon-Mancini-Mazarini, Duc de Nivernois (1716–98), who had visited Twickenham three years
earlier, when he was Ambassador to England. He was
a man of fine manners, and tastes so literary that his
works fill eight volumes. They include a translation of
Walpole's *Essay on Modern Gardening* (see appendix at
end). In his letters to Miss Ann Pitt at this date,
Walpole speaks of the Duke's clever fables, by which he
is now best remembered. Lord Chesterfield told his son
in 1749 that Nivernois was 'one of the prettiest men he
had ever known,' and in 1762 his opinion was unaltered.
' *M. de Nivernois est aimé, respecté, et admiré par tout ce qu'*

Madame du Deffand.

de Choiseul, and Madame la Maréchale de Luxembourg, whose youth had been stormy, but who was now softening down into a kind of twilight melancholy which made her rather attractive. This last, with one exception, completes his list.

The one exception is a figure which henceforth played no inconsiderable part in Walpole's correspondence, — that of the brilliant and witty Madame du Deffand. As Marie de Vichy-Chamrond, she had been married at one-and-twenty to the nobleman whose name she bore, and had followed the custom of her day by speedily choosing a lover, who had many successors. For a brief space she had captivated the Regent himself, and at this date, being nearly seventy and hopelessly blind, was continuing, from mere force of habit, a ' decent friendship ' with the deaf President Hénault. At first Walpole was not impressed with her, and speaks of her, disrespectfully, as ' an old blind debauchee of wit.' A little later, although he still refers to her as the ' old lady of the

il y a d'honnêtes gens à la cour et à la ville,' he writes to Madame de Monconseil. The Duke's end was worthy of Chesterfield himself, for he spent some of his last hours in composing valedictory verses to his doctor, which are said to have been '*pleins de sentiments affectueux.*'

house,' he says she is very agreeable.   Later
still, she has completed her conquest by telling
him he has *le fou mocquer ;* and in the letter to
Gray above quoted, it is plain that she has
become an object of absorbing interest to him,
not unmingled with a nervous apprehension of
her undisguised partiality for his society.   In
spite of her affliction (he says) she ' retains all
her vivacity, wit, memory, judgment, passions,
and agreeableness.   She goes to Operas, Plays.
suppers. and Versailles ; gives suppers twice
a week ; has every thing new read to her ;
makes new songs and epigrams, ay, admirably,[1]
and remembers every one that has been made
these fourscore years.   She corresponds with
Voltaire, dictates charming letters to him, contradicts him, is no bigot to him or anybody,
and laughs both at the clergy and the philoso-
phers.   In a dispute, into which she easily falls,
she is very warm, and yet scarce ever in the
wrong ; her judgment on every subject is as
just as possible ; on every point of conduct as

---

[1] One of her *logogriphes,* or enigmas, is as follows : —

> ' *Quoique je forme un corps, je ne suis qu'une idée ;*
> *Plus ma beauté vieillit, plus elle est décidée :*
> *Il faut, pour me trouver, ignorer d'où je viens :*
> *Je tiens tout de lui, qui reduit tout à rien.*'

The answer is *noblesse.*   Lord Chesterfield thought it so
good that he sent it to his godson (Letter 166).

wrong as possible : for she is all love and hatred, passionate for her friends to enthusiasm, still anxious to be loved, I don't mean by lovers, and a vehement enemy, but openly. As she can have no amusement but conversation, the least solitude and ennui are insupportable to her, and put her into the power of several worthless people, who eat her suppers when they can eat nobody's of higher rank ; wink to one another and laugh at her ; hate her because she has forty times more parts, and venture to hate her because she is not rich.'[1] In another letter, to Mr. James Crawford of Auchinames (Hume's *Fish* Crawford, who was also one of Madame du Deffand's admirers, he says, in repeating some of the above details, that he is not ' ashamed of interesting himself exceedingly about her. To say nothing of her extraordinary parts, she is certainly the most generous, friendly being upon earth.' Upon her side, Madame du Deffand seems to have been equally attracted by the strange mixture of independence and effeminacy which went to make up Walpole's character. Her attachment to him rapidly grew into a kind of infatuation. He had no sooner quitted Paris, which he did on the 17th April, than she

[1] *Walpole to Gray,* 25 January, 1766.

began to correspond with him ; and thenceforward, until her death in 1780, her letters, dictated to her faithful secretary. Wiart, continued, except when Walpole was actually visiting her (and she sometimes wrote to him even then), to reach him regularly. Not long after his return to England, she made him the victim of a charming hoax. He had, when in Paris, admired a snuff-box which bore a portrait of Madame de Sévigné, for whom he professed an extravagant admiration. Madame du Deffand procured a similar box, had the portrait copied. and sent it to him with a letter, purporting to come from the dateless Elysian Fields and ' Notre Dame de Livry ' herself, in which he was enjoined to use his present always, and to bring it often to France and the Faubourg St. Germain. Walpole was completely taken in, and imagined that the box had come from Madame de Choiseul ; but he should have known at first that no one living but his blind friend could have written 'that most charming of all letters.' The box itself, the memento of so much old-world ingenuity, was sold (with the pseudo-Sévigné epistle) at the Strawberry Hill sale for £28 7s. When witty Mrs. Clive heard of the last addition to Walpole's list of favourites, she delivered herself of a good-humoured *bon mot.* There was a new resident at Twickenham, — the first Earl of Shelburne's widow. ' If the new Countess is but lame,' quoth Clive (referring to the fact that Lady Suffolk was deaf, and Madame du Deffand blind), ' I shall have no chance of ever seeing you.' But there is nothing to show that he ever relaxed in his attentions to the delightful actress, whom he somewhere styles *dimidium animæ meæ*.[1]

One of the other illustrious visitors to Paris during Walpole's stay there was Rousseau. Being no longer safe in his Swiss asylum, where the curate of Motiers had excited the mob against him, that extraordinary self-tormentor, clad in his Armenian costume, had arrived in December at the French capital, and shortly afterwards left for England, under the safe-conduct of Hume, who had undertaken to procure him a fresh resting-place. He reached London on the 14th January, 1766. Walpole had, to

---

[1] He was malicious enough to add, ' a pretty round half.' In middle life Mrs. Clive, like her Twickenham neighbour, Mrs. Pritchard, grew excessively stout; and there is a pleasant anecdote that, on one occasion, when the pair were acting together in Cibber's *Careless Husband*, the audience were regaled by the spectacle of two leading actresses, neither of whom could manage to pick up a letter which, by ill-luck, had been dropped upon the ground.

use his own phrase, 'a hearty contempt' for the fugitive sentimentalist and his grievances ; and not long before Rousseau's advent in Paris, taking for his pretext an offer made by the King of Prussia, he had woven some of the light mockery at Madame Geoffrin's into a sham letter from Frederick to Jean-Jacques, couched in the true Walpolean spirit of persiflage. It is difficult to summarize, and may be reproduced here as its author transcribed it on the 12th January, for the benefit of Conway : —

Le Roi de Prusse à Monsieur Rousseau.

Mon cher Jean-Jacques, — Vous avez renoncé à Génève votre patrie ; vous vous êtes fait chasser de la Suisse, pays tant vanté dans vos écrits ; la France vous a décrété. Venez donc chez moi ; j'admire vos talens ; je m'amuse de vos rêveries, qui (soit dit en passant) vous occupent trop, et trop longtems. Il faut à la fin être sage et heureux. Vous avez fait assez parler de vous par des singularités peu convenables à un véritable grand homme. Démontrez à vos ennemis que vous pouvez avoir quelquefois le sens commun : cela les fachera, sans vous faire tort. Mes états vous offrent une retraite paisible ; je vous veux du bien, et je vous en ferai, si vous le trouvez bon. Mais si vous vous obstiniez à rejetter mon secours, attendez-vous que je ne le dirai à personne. Si vous persistez à vous creuser l'esprit pour trouver de nouveaux malheurs, choisissez les tels que vous voudrez. Je suis roi, je puis vous en procurer au gré de vos souhaits : et ce qui sûrement ne vous arrivera pas vis à vis de vos ennemis, je cesserai de vous persécuter quand vous cesserez de mettre votre gloire à l'être.

Votre bon ami,

FRÉDÉRIC.

This composition, the French of which was touched up by Helvétius, Hénault, and the Duc de Nivernois, gave extreme satisfaction to all the anti-Rousseau party.[1] While Hume and his *protégé* were still in Paris, Walpole, out of delicacy to Hume, managed to keep the matter

---

[1] In a recently printed letter to Miss Ann Pitt, 19 Jan., 1766, Walpole makes reference to the popularity which this *jeu d'esprit* procured for him. 'Everybody wou'd have a copy [of course he encloses one to his correspondent]; the next thing was, everybody wou'd see the author. . . . I thought at last I shou'd have a box quilted for me, like Gulliver, be set upon the dressing-table of a maid of honour, and fed with bonbons. . . . If, contrary to all precedent, I shou'd exist in vogue a week longer, I will send you the first statue that is cast of me in *berga-motte* or *biscuite porcelaine*' (*Fortescue Corr., Hist. MSS. Commission, 13th Rept., App.* iii. [1892], i, 153).

a secret ; and he also abstained from making any
overtures to Rousseau, whom, as he truly said,
he could scarcely have visited cordially, with a
letter in his pocket written to ridicule him.
But Hume had no sooner departed than Frederick's sham invitation went the round, ultimately
finding its way across the Channel, where it was
printed in the *St. James's Chronicle.* Rousseau,
always on the alert to pose as the victim of
plots and conspiracies, was naturally furious, and
wrote angrily from his retreat at Mr. Daven-
port's in Derbyshire to denounce the fabrication.
The worst of it was, that his morbid nature immediately suspected the innocent Hume of par-
ticipating in the trick. ' What rends and afflicts
my heart [is],' he told the *Chronicle,* ' that the
impostor hath his accomplices in England ; ' and
this delusion became one of the main elements
in that ' twice-told tale,' — the quarrel of Hume
and Rousseau. Walpole was called upon to
clear Hume from having any hand in the letter,
and several communications, all of which are
printed at length in the fourth volume of his
works, followed upon the same subject. Their
discussion would occupy too large a space in
this limited memoir.[1]   It is, however, worth

---

[1] Hume's narrative of the affair may be read in *A Con-
cise and Genuine Account of the Dispute between Mr. Hume*

Hume.

noticing that Walpole's instinct appears to have foreseen the trouble that fell upon Hume. ' I wish,' he wrote to Lady Hervey, in a letter which Hume carried to England when he accompanied his untunable *protégé* thither, ' I wish he may not repent having engaged with Rousseau. who contradicts and quarrels with all mankind, in order to obtain their admiration.'[1] He certainly, upon the present occasion, did not belie this uncomplimentary character.

Before the last stages of the Hume-Rousseau controversy had been reached, Hume was back again in Paris, and Walpole had returned to London. Upon the whole, he told Mann, he liked France so well that he should certainly go there again. In September, 1766, he was once

and *Mr. Rousseau: with the Letters that passed between them during their Controversy. As also, the Letters of the Hon. Mr. Walpole, and Mr. D'Alembert, relative to this extraordinary Affair. Translated from the French. London. Printed for T. Becket and P. A. De Hondt, near Surry-street, in the Strand, MDCCLXVI.*

[1] *Walpole to Lady Hervey*, 2 January, 1766. In a letter to Lady Mary Coke, dated two days later, he says : ' Rousseau set out this morning for England. As He loves to contradict a whole Nation, I suppose he will write for the present opposition. . . . As he is to live at Fulham, I hope his first quarrel will be with his neighbour the Bishop of London, who is an excellent subject for his ridicule ' (*Letters and Journals*, iii. 1892, xx).

more attacked with gout, and at the beginning
of October went to Bath, whose Avon (as compared with his favourite Thames) he considers
'paltry enough to be the Seine or Tyber.'
Nothing pleases him much at Bath, although it
contained such notabilities as Lord Chatham,
Lord Northington, and Lord Camden; but he
goes to hear Wesley, of whom he writes rather
flippantly to Chute. He describes him as 'a
lean, elderly man, fresh-coloured, his hair
smoothly combed, but with a *soupçon* of curl
at the ends.' ' Wondrous clean,' he adds, ' but
as evidently an actor as Garrick. He spoke
his sermon, but so fast, and with so little
accent, that I am sure he has often uttered it,
for it was like a lesson. There were parts and
eloquence in it; but towards the end he exalted
his voice, and acted very ugly enthusiasm; de-
cried learning, and told stories, like Latimer, of
the fool of his college, who said, ' I *thanks* God
for everything.' [1]   He returned to Strawberry
Hill in October. In August of the next year he
again went to Paris, going almost straight to
Madame du Deffand's, where he finds Mademoiselle Clairon (who had quitted the stage)
invited to declaim Corneille in his honour, and
he sups in a distinguished company. His visit

[1] *Walpole to Chute,* 10 October, 1766.

lasted two months ; but his letters for this period contain few interesting particulars, while those of the lady cease altogether, to be resumed again on the 9th October, a few hours after his departure. Two years later he travels once more to Paris and his blind friend, whom he finds in better health than ever, and with spirits so increased that he tells her she will go mad with age. ‘When they ask her how old she is, she answers, "*J'ai soixante et mille ans.*"’ Her septuagenarian activity might well have wearied a younger man. ‘She and I,’ he says, ‘went to the Boulevard last night after supper, and drove about there till two in the morning. We are going to sup in the country this evening, and are to go to-morrow night at eleven to the puppet-show.’ In a letter to George Montagu, which adds some details to her portrait, he writes : ‘ I have heard her dispute with all sorts of people, on all sorts of subjects, and never knew her in the wrong.[1] She humbles the learned, sets right their disciples, and finds conversation for everybody. Affectionate as

[1] Lady Mary Coke testifies to the charm of her conversation : ‘ In the evening I made a visit to Madame du Deffan [*sic*]. She talks so well that I wish'd to write down everything She said, as I thought I shou'd have liked to have read it afterwards’ (*Letters and Journals,* iii. [1892], 233).

Madame de Sévigné, she has none of her prejudices, but a more universal taste ; and, with
the most delicate frame, her spirits hurry her
through a life of fatigue that would kill me, if I
was to continue here. . . . I had great difficulty
last night to persuade her, though she was not
well, not to sit up till between two and three
for the comet ; for which purpose she had appointed an astronomer to bring his telescopes to
the President Hénault's, as she thought it would
amuse me.   In short, her goodness to me is so
excessive that I feel unashamed at producing
my withered person in a round of diversions.
which I have quitted at home.'[1]   One of the
other amusements which she procured for him
was the *entrée* of the famous convent of St. Cyr.
of which he gives an interesting account.   He
inspects the pensioners, and the numerous portraits of the foundress, Madame de Maintenon.
In one class-room he hears the young ladies
sing the choruses in *Athalie ;* in another sees
them dance minuets to the violin of a nun who
is not precisely St. Cecilia.   In the third room
they act *proverbes,* or conversations.   Finally, he
is enabled to enrich the archives of Strawberry
with a piece of paper containing a few sentences
of Madame de Maintenon's handwriting.

[1] *Walpole to Montagu,* 7 September, 1769.

Walpole's literary productions for this date (in addition to the letter from the King of Prussia to Rousseau) are scheduled in the *Short Notes* with his usual minuteness. In June, 1766, shortly after his return from Paris, he wrote a squib upon Captain Byron's description of the Patagonians, entitled, *An Account of the Giants lately discovered,* which was published on the 25th August. On 18 August he began his *Memoirs of the Reign of King George the Third;* and, in 1767, the detection of a work published at Paris in two volumes under the title of the *Testament du Chevalier Robert Walpole,* and ' stamped in that mint of forgeries, Holland.' This, which is printed in the second volume of his works, remained unpublished during his lifetime, as no English translation of the *Testament* was ever made. His next deliverance was a letter, subsequently printed in the *St. James's Chronicle* for 28 May, in which he announced to the Corporation of Lynn, in the person of their Mayor, Mr. Langley, that he did not intend to offer himself again as the representative in Parliament of that town. A wish to retire from all public business, and the declining state of his health, are assigned as the reasons for his thus breaking his Parliamentary connection, which had now lasted for five-and-twenty years. Following upon this comes the already mentioned account of his action in the Hume and Rousseau quarrel, and a couple of letters on *Political Abuse in Newspapers.* These appeared in the *Public Advertiser.* But the chief results of his leisure in 1766-8 are to be found in two efforts more ambitious than any of those above indicated, — the *Historic Doubts on Richard the Third,* and the tragedy of *The Mysterious Mother.* The *Historic Doubts* was begun in the winter of 1767, and published in February, 1768 ; the tragedy in December, 1766. and published in March, 1768.

The *Historic Doubts* was an attempt to vindicate Richard III. from his traditional character, which Walpole considered had been intentionally blackened in order to whiten that of Henry VII. ' *Vous seriez un excellent attornei général,* — wrote Voltaire to him, — ' *vous pesez toutes les probabilités.*' He might have added that they were all weighed on one side. Gray admits the clearness with which the principal part of the arguments was made out ; but he remained unconvinced, especially as regards the murder of Henry VI. Other objectors speedily appeared. who were neither so friendly nor so gentle. *The Critical Review* attacked him for not having referred to Guthrie's *His-*

tory of England, which had in some respects anticipated him ; and he was also criticised adversely
by the *London Chronicle.* Of these attacks
Walpole spoke and wrote very contemptuously ;
but he seems to have been considerably nettled
by the conduct of a Swiss named Deyverdun,
who, giving an account of the book in a work
called *Mémoires Littéraires de la Grande Bre-
tagne* for 1768, declared his preference for the
views which Hume had expressed in certain
notes to the said account. Deyverdun's action
appears to have stung Walpole into a supplementary defence of his theories, in which he dealt
with his critics generally. This he did not print,
but set aside to appear as a postscript in his
works. In 1770, however, his arguments were
contested by Dr. Milles, Dean of Exeter, to
whom he replied ; and later still, another antiquary, the Rev. Mr. Masters, came forward.
The last two assailants were members of the
Society of Antiquaries, from which body Walpole,
in consequence, withdrew. But he practically
abandoned his theories in a final postscript, written in February, 1793, which is to be found in
the second volume of his works.

Concerning the second performance above
referred to, *The Mysterious Mother*, most of
Walpole's biographers are content to abide in

generalities.   That the proprietor of Gothic
Strawberry should have produced *The Castle
of Otranto* has a certain congruity ; but one
scarcely expects to find the same person indulg-
ing in a blank-verse tragedy sombre enough to
have taxed the powers of Ford or Webster. It
is a curious example of literary reaction, and
his own words respecting it are doubtful-voiced.
To Montagu and to Madame du Deffand he
writes apologetically. ' *Il ne vous plairoit pas
assurément,*' he informs the lady ; ' *il n'y a
pas de beaux sentiments. Il n'y a que des passions sans envelope, des crimes, des repentis, et des
horreurs ;* '[1] and he lays his finger on one of its
gravest defects when he goes on to say that its
interest languishes from the first act to the last.
Yet he seems, too, to have thought of its being
played, for he tells Montagu a month later that
though he is not yet intoxicated enough with it
to think it would do for the stage, yet he wishes
to see it acted, — a wish which must have been
a real one, since he says further that he has
written an epilogue for Mrs. Clive to speak
in character. The postscript which is affixed to
the printed piece contradicts the above utterances considerably, or, at all events, shows that
fuller consideration has materially revised them.

[1] *Letters of Madame du Deffand,* 1810, i. 211 n.

He admits that *The Mysterious Mother* would not be proper to appear upon the boards. ' The subject is so horrid that I thought it would shock rather than give satisfaction to an audience. Still, I found it so truly tragic in the two essential springs of terror and pity that I could not resist the impulse of adapting it to the scene, though it should never be practicable to produce it there.' After his criticism to Madame du Deffand upon the plot, it is curious to find him later on claiming that ' every scene tends to bring on the catastrophe, and [that] the story is never interrupted or diverted from its course.' Notwithstanding its imaginative power, it is impossible to deny that the author's words as to the repulsiveness of the subject are just. But it is needless to linger longer upon a dramatic work which had such grave defects as to render its being acted impossible, and concerning the literary merit of which there will always be different opinions. Byron spoke of it as ' a tragedy of the highest order,' — a judgment which has been traversed by Macaulay and Scott; Miss Burney shuddered at its very name ; while Lady Di. Beauclerk illustrated it enthusiastically with a series of seven designs in ' sut-water,'[1] for

[1] *i. e.* Soot-water. There were two landscapes in soot-water by Mr. Bentley in the Green Closet at Strawberry.

which the enraptured author erected a special
gallery.[1]   Meanwhile, we may quote, from the
close of the above postscript, a passage where
Walpole is at his best.   It is a rapid and characteristic *aperçu* of tragedy in England :

‘The excellence of our dramatic writers is
by no means equal in number to the great men
we have produced in other walks. Theatric
genius lay dormant after Shakespeare ; waked
with some bold and glorious, but irregular and
often ridiculous, flights in Dryden ; revived in
Otway ; maintained a placid, pleasing kind of
dignity in Rowe, and even shone in his *Jane
Shore*. It trod in sublime and classic fetters
in *Cato*, but void of nature, or the power of
affecting the passions. In Southerne it seemed
a genuine ray of nature and Shakespeare ; but,
falling on an age still more Hottentot, was stifled
in those gross and barbarous productions, tra-
gi-comedies. It turned to tuneful nonsense in
the *Mourning Bride ;* grew stark mad in Lee,
whose cloak, a little the worse for wear, fell on
Young, yet in both was still a poet's cloak. It
recovered its senses in Hughes and Fenton, who
were afraid it should relapse, and accordingly
kept it down with a timid but amiable hand ;

[1] See chapter ix.

and then it languished. We have not mounted again above the two last.'[1]

The *Castle of Otranto* and the *Historic Doubts* were not printed by Mr. Robinson's latest successor, Mr. Kirgate. But the Strawberry Press had by this time resumed its functions, for *The Mysterious Mother*, of which 50 copies were struck off in 1768, was issued from it. Another book which it produced in the same year was *Cornélie*, a youthful tragedy by Madame du Deffand's friend, President Hénault. Walpole's sole reason for giving it the permanence of his type appears to have been gratitude to the venerable author, then fast hastening to the grave, for his kindness to himself in Paris. To Paris three-fourths of the impression went. More important reprints were Grammont's *Memoirs*, a small quarto, and a series of *Letters of Edward VI.;* both printed in 1772. The list for this period is completed by the loose sheets of *Hoyland's Poems*, 1769, and the well-known, but now rare, *Description of the Villa of Horace Walpole at Strawberry Hill*, 1774, 100 copies of which were printed, six being on large paper. To an account of this patchwork edifice, the ensuing chapter will be chiefly devoted. The present may fitly be

[1] *Works*, 1798, i. 129.

concluded with a brief statement of that always-debated passage in Walpole's life, his relations with the ill-starred Chatterton.

Towards the close of 1768, and early in 1769, Chatterton, fretting in Mr. Lambert's office at Bristol, and casting about eagerly for possible clues to a literary life, had offered some specimens of the pseudo-Rowley to James Dodsley of Pall-Mall, but apparently without success. His next appeal was made to Walpole, and mainly as the author of the *Anecdotes of Painting in England.* What documents he actually submitted to him, is not perfectly clear; but they manifestly included further fabrications of monkish verse, and hinted at, or referred to, a sequence of native artists in oil, hitherto wholly undreamed of by the distinguished virtuoso he addressed. The packet was handed to Walpole at Arlington Street by Mr. Bathoe, his bookseller (also notable as the keeper of the first circulating library in London); and. incredible to say, Walpole was instantly 'drawn.' He despatched without delay to his unknown Bristol correspondent such a courteous note as he might have addressed to Zouch or Ducarel, expressing interest, curiosity, and a desire for further particulars. Chatterton as promptly

rejoined, forwarding more extracts from the
Rowley poems. But he also, from Walpole's
recollection of his letter, in part unbosomed
himself, making revelation of his position as
a widow's son and lawyer's apprentice, who
had ‘ a taste and turn for more elegant studies,’
which inclinations, he suggested, his illustrious
correspondent might enable him to gratify.
Upon this, perhaps not unnaturally, Walpole's
suspicions were aroused, the more so that
Mason and Gray, to whom he showed the
papers, declared them to be forgeries. He
made, nevertheless, some private inquiry from
an aristocratic relative at Bath as to Chatterton's
antecedents, and found that, although his description of himself was accurate, no account
of his character was forthcoming. He accordingly — he tells us — wrote him a letter ‘ with
as much kindness and tenderness as if he had
been his guardian,’ recommending him to stick
to his profession, and adding, by way of postscript, that judges, to whom the manuscripts had
been submitted, were by no means thoroughly
convinced of their antiquity. Two letters from
Chatterton followed, — one (the first) dejected
and seemingly acquiescent ; the other, a week
later, curtly demanding the restoration of his
papers, the genuineness of which he re-affirmed.

These communications Walpole, by his own account, either neglected to notice, or overlooked.[1]   After an interval of some weeks arrived a final missive, the tone of which he regarded as ' singularly impertinent.'   Snapping up both poems and letters in a pet, he scribbled a hasty reply, but, upon reconsideration, enclosed them to their writer without comment, and thought no more of him or them. It was not until about a year and a half afterwards that Goldsmith told him, at the first Royal Academy dinner, that Chatterton had come to London and destroyed himself, — an announcement which seems to have filled him with unaffected pity.   ' Several persons of honour and veracity,' he says, ' were present when I first heard of his death, and will attest my surprise and concern. '[2]

[1] He says he 'was going to Paris in a day or two.' But his memory must have deceived him, for Chatterton's last letter is dated July 24th, 1769, and, according to Miss Berry, Walpole's visit to Paris lasted from the 18th August to the 5th October, 1769; and this is confirmed by his correspondence.

[2] *Works*, 1798, iv. 219.   In the above summary of the story we have relied by preference on the fairly established facts of the case, which is full of difficulties.   The most plausible version of it, as well as the most fair to Walpole, is given in Prof. D. Wilson's *Chatterton*, 1869.

The apologists of the gifted and precocious Bristol boy, reading the above occurrences by the light of his deplorable end, have attributed to Walpole a more material part in his misfortunes than can justly be ascribed to him ; and the first editor of Chatterton's *Miscellanies* did not scruple to emphasize the current gossip, which represented Walpole as ' the primary cause of his [Chatterton's] dismal catastrophe,'[1] — an aspersion which drew from the Abbot of Strawberry the lengthy letter on the subject which was afterwards reprinted in his *Works*.[2] So long a vindication, if needed then, is scarcely needed now. Walpole. it is obvious, acted very much as he might have been expected to act. He had been imposed upon, and he was as much annoyed with himself as with the impostor. But he was not harsh enough to speak his

---

[1] An example of this is furnished by Miss Seward's *Correspondence.* ' Do not expect [she writes] that I can learn to esteem that fastidious and unfeeling being, to whose insensibility we owe the extinction of the greatest poetic luminary [Chatterton], if we may judge from the brightness of its dawn, that ever rose in our, or perhaps in any other, hemisphere ' (*Seward to Hardinge*, 21 Nov., 1787).

[2] *Works*, 1798, iv. 205-45. See also Bibliographical Appendix to this volume.

mind frankly, nor benevolent enough to act the part of that rather rare personage, the ideal philanthropist. If he had behaved less like an ordinary man of the world ; if he had obtained Chatterton's confidence, instead of lecturing him ; if he had aided and counselled and protected him, — Walpole would have been different, and things might have been otherwise. As they were, upon the principle that 'two of a trade can ne'er agree,' it is difficult to conceive of any abiding alliance between the author of the fabricated *Tragedy of Ælla* and the author of the fabricated *Castle of Otranto*.

CHAPTER VIII.

Old Friends and New. — Walpole's Nieces. — Mrs. Damer. — Progress of Strawberry Hill. —Festivities and Later Improvements. — *A Description*, etc., 1774. — The House and Approaches. — Great Parlour, Waiting Room, China Room, and Yellow Bedchamber. — Breakfast Room. — Green Closet and Blue Bedchamber. — Armoury and Library. — Red Bedchamber, Holbein Chamber, and Star Chamber. — Gallery. — Round Drawing Room and Tribune. — Great North Bedchamber. — Great Cloister and Chapel. — Walpole on Strawberry. — Its Dampness. — A Drive from Twickenham to Piccadilly.

IN 1774, when, according to its title-page, the *Description of Strawberry Hill* was printed, Walpole was a man of fifty-seven. During the period covered by the last chapter, many changes had taken place in his circle of friends. Mann and George Montagu (until, in October, 1770, his correspondence with the latter mysteriously ceased) were still the most frequent recipients of his letters, and next to these, Conway, and Cole the antiquary. But three of his former correspondents, his deaf neighbour at Marble Hill, Lady Suffolk,[1] Lady Hervey

[1] Henrietta Hobart, Countess Dowager of Suffolk, died in July, 1767. Her portrait by Charles Jervas, with

(Pope's and Chesterfield's Molly Lepel, to whom he had written much from Paris), and Gray, were dead. On the other hand, he had opened what promised to be a lengthy series of letters with Gray's friend and biographer, the Rev. William Mason, Rector of Aston, in Yorkshire ; with Madame du Deffand ; and with the divorced Duchess of Grafton, who in 1769 had married his Paris friend, John Fitzpatrick, second Earl of Upper Ossory. There were changes, too, among his own relatives. By this time his eldest brother's widow, Lady Orford, had lost her second husband, Sewallis Shirley, and was again living, not very reputably, on the Continent. Her son George, who since 1751 had been third Earl of Orford, and was still unmarried, was eminently unsatisfactory. He was shamelessly selfish, and by way of complicating the family embarrassments, had taken to the turf. Ultimately he had periodical attacks of insanity, during which time it fell to Walpole's fate to look after his affairs. With Sir Edward Walpole, his second brother, he

Marble Hill in the background, hung in the Green Bedchamber in the Round Tower at Strawberry. It once belonged to Pope, who left it to Martha Blount ; and it is engraved as the frontispiece of vol. ii. of Cunningham's edition of the *Letters.*

seems never to have been on terms of real cordiality ; but he made no secret of his pride in his beautiful nieces, Edward Walpole's natural daughters, whose charms and amiability had victoriously triumphed over every prejudice which could have been entertained against their birth. Laura, the eldest, had married a brother of Lord Albemarle, subsequently created Bishop of Lichfield and Coventry ; Charlotte, the third, became Lady Huntingtower, and afterwards Countess of Dysart ; while Maria, the *belle* of the trio, was more fortunate still. After burying her first husband, Lord Waldegrave, she had succeeded in fascinating H. R. H. William Henry, Duke of Gloucester, the King's own brother. and so contributing to bring about the Royal Marriage Act of 1772. They were married in 1766 ; but the fact was not formally announced to His Majesty until September, 1772.[1] Another marriage which must have given Walpole almost as much pleasure was that of General Conway's daughter to Mr. Damer, Lord Milton's eldest son, which took

---

[1] 'The Duke of Gloucester '—wrote Gilly Williams to Selwyn, as far back as December, 1764 — 'has professed a passion for the Dowager Waldegrave. He is never from her elbow. This flatters Horry Walpole not a little, though he pretends to dislike it.'

place in 1767. After the unhappy death of her
husband, who shot himself in a tavern ten years
later, Mrs. Damer developed considerable talents
as a sculptor, and during the last years of Walpole's life was a frequent exhibitor at the Royal
Academy. *Non me Praxiteles finxit, at Anna
Damer*, wrote her admiring relative under
one of her works, a wounded eagle in terra-
cotta ;[1] and in the fourth volume of the *Anecdotes of Painting*, he likens 'her shock dog,
large as life,' to such masterpieces of antique
art as the Tuscan boar and the Barberini goat.

It is time, however, to return to the story of
Strawberry itself, as interrupted in Chapter V.
In the introduction to Walpole's *Description* of
1774, a considerable interval occurs between
the building of the Refectory and Library in
1753-4, and the subsequent erection of the
Gallery, Round Tower, Great Cloister, and
Cabinet, or Tribune, which, already in contem-
plation in 1759, were, according to the same
authority, erected in 1760 and 1761. But here,
as before, the date must rather be that of the
commencement than the completion of these
additions. In May, 1763, he tells Cole that

---

[1] The idea was borrowed from an inscription upon a
statue at Milan: ' Non me Praxiteles, sed Marcus finxit
Agrati !'

the Gallery is fast advancing, and in July it is almost ' in the critical minute of consummation.' In August, ' all the earth is begging to come to see it.' A month afterwards, he is ' keeping an inn ; the sign. " The Gothic Castle." ' His whole time is passed in giving tickets of admission to the Gallery, and hiding himself when it is on view. ' Take my advice,' he tells Montagu, ' never build a charming house for yourself between London and Hampton-court ; everybody will live in it but you.' A year later he is giving a great fête to the French and Spanish Ambassadors, March, Selwyn, Lady Waldegrave, and other distinguished guests, which finishes in the new room. ' During dinner there were French horns and clarionets in the cloister,' and after coffee the guests were treated ' with a syllabub milked under the cows that were brought to the brow of the terrace. Thence they went to the Printing-house, and saw a new fashionable French song printed. They drank tea in the Gallery, and at eight went away to Vauxhall.'

This last entertainment, the munificence of which, he says, the treasury of the Abbey will feel, took place in June, 1764 ; and it is not until four years later that we get tidings of any fresh improvements. In September, 1768, he tells Cole that he is going on with the Round Tower, or Chamber, at the end of the Gallery, which, in another letter, he says ' has stood still these five years,' and he is, besides, ' *play-ing* with the little garden on the other side of the road ' which had come into his hands by Francklin's death. In May of the following year he gives another magnificent *festino* at Strawberry, which will almost mortgage it, but the Round Tower still progresses. In October, 1770, he is building again, in the intervals of gout ; this time it is the Great Bedchamber, — a ' sort of room which he seems likely to in-habit much time together.' Next year the whole piecemeal structure is rapidly verging to completion. ' The Round Tower is finished, and magnificent ; and the State Bedchamber proceeds fast.' In June he is writing to Mann from the delicious bow window of the former, with Vasari's Bianca Capello (Mann's present) over against him, and the setting sun behind, ' throwing its golden rays all round.' Further on, he is building a tiny brick chapel in the garden, mainly for the purpose of receiving ' two valuable pieces of antiquity,' — one being a painted window from Bexhill of Henry III. and his Queen, given him by Lord Ashburnham ; the other Cavalini's Tomb of Capoccio from the Church of Santa Maria Maggiore at Rome, which had been sent to him by Sir William (then Mr.) Hamilton, the English Minister at Naples. In August, 1772, the Great Bedchamber is finished, the house is complete, and he has 'at last exhausted all his hoards and collections.' Nothing remains but to compile the *Description and Catalogue*, concerning which he had written to Cole as far back as 1768, and which, as already stated, he ultimately printed in 1774.

As time went on, his fresh acquisitions obliged him to add several *Appendices* to this issue ; and the copy before us, although dated 1774, has supplements which bring the record down to 1786. A fresh edition, in royal quarto, with twenty-seven plates, was printed in 1784 ;[1] and this, or an expansion of it, reappears in vol. ii. of his *Works*. With these later issues we have little to do ; but with the aid of that of 1774, may essay to give some brief account

[1] From a passage in a letter of 15 Sept., 1787, to Lady Ossory, it appears that this, though printed, was withheld, on account of certain difficulties caused by the over-ween-ing curiosity of Walpole's 'customers' (as he called them), the visitors to Strawberry. According to the sheet of regulations for visiting the house, it was to be seen between the 1st of May and the 1st of October. Children were not admitted ; and only one company of four on one day.

of the long, straggling, many-pinnacled building, with its round tower at the end, the east
and south fronts of which are figured in the
black-looking vignette upon the title-page. The
entrance was on the north side, from the Teddington and Twickenham road, here shaded by
lofty trees ; and once within the embattled
boundary wall, covered by this time with ivy,
the first thing that struck the spectator was a
small oratory inclosed by iron rails, with saint,
altar, niches, and holy-water basins designed
en suite by Mr. Chute. On the right hand —
its gaily-coloured patches of flower-bed glimmer-
ing through a screen of iron work copied from
the tomb of Roger Niger, Bishop of London,
in old St. Paul's — was the diminutive Abbot's,
or Prior's, Garden, which extended in front of
the offices to the right of the principal entrance.[1]
This was along a little cloister to the left,
beyond the oratory. The chief decoration of
this cloister was a marble *bas-relief*, inscribed
' Dia Helionora,' being, in fact, a portrait of
that Leonora D'Esté who turned the head of
Tasso. At the end was the door, which opened
into ' a small gloomy hall ' united with the staircase, the balustrades of which, designed by

---

[1] ' It is not much larger than an old lady's flower-knot
in Bloomsbury,' said Lady Morgan in 1826.

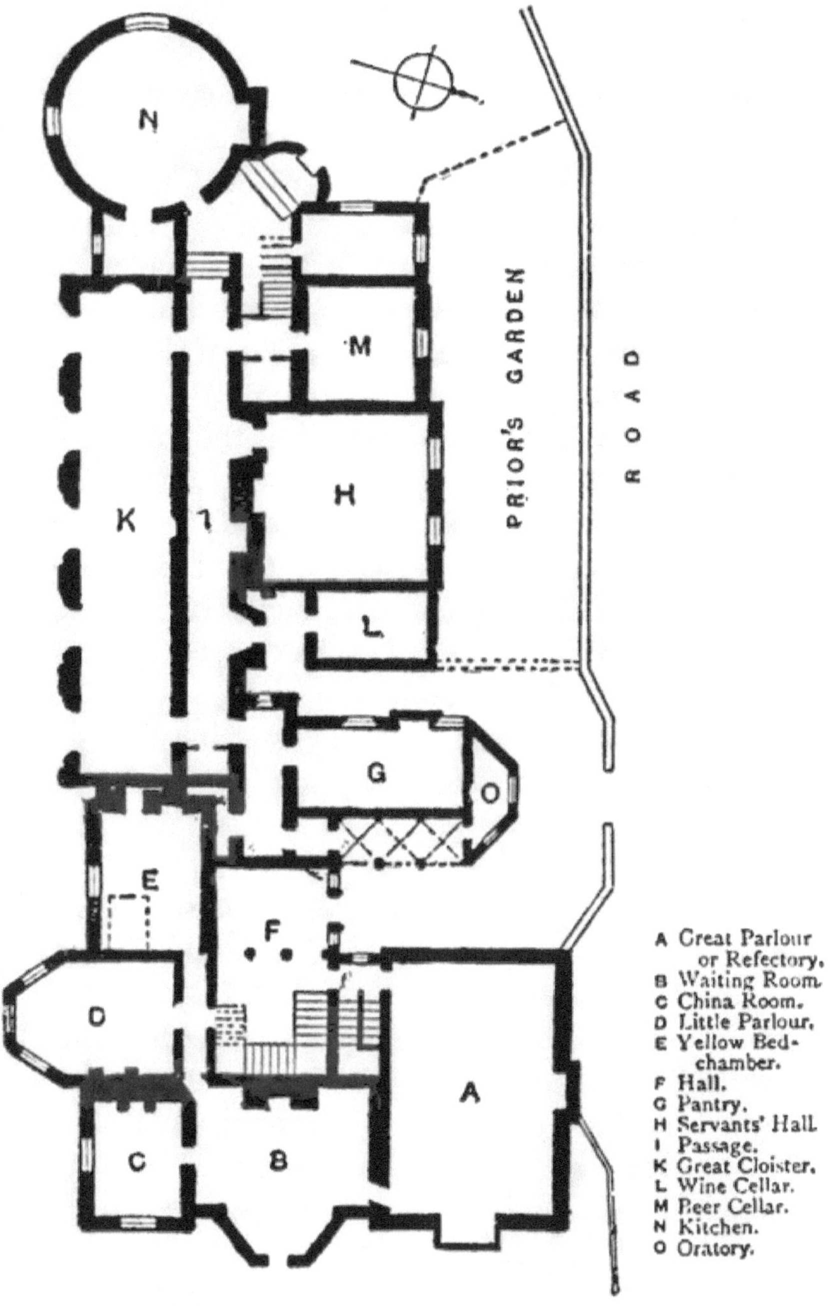

STRAWBERRY HILL: GROUND PLAN—1781.

Bentley, were decorated with antelopes, the Walpole supporters. In the well of the stair-case was a Gothic lantern of japanned tin, also due to Bentley's fertile invention. If, instead of climbing the stairs, you turned out of the hall into a little passage on your left, you found yourself in the Refectory, or Great Parlour, where were accumulated the family portraits. Here, over the chimney-piece, was the ' conversation,' by Sir Joshua Reynolds, representing the triumvirate of Selwyn, Williams, and Lord Edgcumbe, already referred to at p. 138; here also were Sir Robert Walpole and his two wives, Catherine Shorter and Maria Skerret; Robert Walpole the second, and his wife in a white riding-habit; Horace himself by Richardson; Dorothy Walpole, his aunt, who became Lady Townshend;[1] his sister, Lady Maria Churchill; and a number of others. In the Waiting Room, into which the Refectory opened, was a stone head of John Dryden, whom Catherine Shorter claimed as great-uncle; next to this again was the China Closet, neatly lined with blue and white Dutch tiles, and having its ceiling painted by Müntz, after a villa at Frascati, with convolvuluses on poles. In the China Room, among great stores of Sèvres and Chelsea, and

---

[1] See p. 6.

oriental china, perhaps the greatest curiosity
was a couple of Saxon tankards, exactly alike
in form and size, which had been presented to
Sir Robert Walpole at different times by the
mistresses of the first two Georges, the Duchess
of Kendal and the Countess of Yarmouth. To
the left of the China Closet, with a bow window
looking to the south, was the Little Parlour,
which was hung with stone-coloured 'gothic
paper' in imitation of mosaic, and decorated
with the 'wooden prints' already referred to,
the chiaroscuros of Jackson ;[1] and at the side
of this came the Yellow Bedchamber, known
later, from its numerous feminine portraits, as
the Beauty Room. The other spaces on the
ground floor were occupied, towards the Prior's
Garden, by the kitchen, cellars, and servants'
hall, and, at the back, by the Great Cloister.
which went under the Gallery.

Returning to the staircase, where, in later
years, hung Bunbury's original drawing[2] for his

---

[1] See p. 117 n.

[2] It was exhibited in the Royal Academy of 1781, and
was Bunbury's acknowledgment of the praise given him
by Walpole in the 'Advertisement' to the fourth volume
of the *Anecdotes of Painting*, 1 Oct., 1780. A copy of it
was shown at the Exhibition of English Humourists in
Art, June, 1889.

well-known caricature of ' Richmond Hill,' you entered the Breakfast Room on the first floor, the window of which looked towards the Thames. It was pleasantly furnished with blue paper, and blue and white linen, and contained many miniatures and portraits, notable among which were Carmontel's picture of Madame du Deffand and the Duchess de Choiseul ; [1] a print of Madame du Deffand's room and cats, given by the President Hénault ; and a view painted by Raguenet for Walpole in 1766 of the Hôtel de Carnavalet, the whilom residence of Madame de Sévigné.[2]

[1] In a note to Madame du Deffand's *Letters*, 1810, i. 201, the editor, Miss Berry, thus describes this picture: It was ' a washed drawing of Mad. la Duchesse de Choiseul and Mad. du Deffand, under their assumed characters of grandmother and granddaughter; Mad. de Choiseul giving Mad. du Deffand a doll. The scene the interior of Mad. du Deffand's sitting-room. It was done by M. de Carmontel, an amateur in the art of painting. He was reader to the Prince of Condé, and author of several little Theatrical pieces.' It is engraved as the frontispiece of vol. vii. of Walpole's *Letters*, by Cunningham, 1857–59. Mad. du Deffand's portrait was said to be extremely like; that of the Duchess was not good.

[2] ' It is now the Musée Carnavalet, and contains numberless souvenirs of the Revolution, notably a collection of china plates, bearing various dates, designs, and inscriptions applicable to the Reign of Terror ' (*Century*

The Breakfast Room opened into the Green Closet, over the door of which was a picture by Samuel Scott of Pope's house at Twickenham, showing the wings added after the poet's death by Sir William Stanhope. On the same side of the room hung Hogarth's portrait of Sarah Malcolm the murderess, painted at Newgate on the day preceding her execution in Fleet Street.[1] Here also was ' Mr. Thomas Gray ; etched from his shade [silhouette] ; by Mr. W. Mason.' There were many other portraits in this room, besides some water colours on ivory by Horace himself. In a line with the Green Closet, and looking east, was the Library ; and at the back of it, the Blue Bedchamber, the toilette of which was worked by Mrs. Clive, who, since her retirement from the stage in 1769, had lived wholly at Twickenham. The chief pictures in this room were Eckardt's portraits of Gray in a Vandyke dress

Magazine, Feb., 1890, p. 600). A washed drawing of Madame de Sévigné's country house at Les Rochers, ' done on the spot by Mr. Hinchcliffe, son of the Bishop of Peterborough, in 1786,' was afterwards added to this room.

[1] Both these pictures are in existence. The Scott belongs to Lady Freake, and was exhibited in the Pope Loan Museum of 1888.

and of Walpole himself in similar attire.[1]   There were also by the same artist pictures of Walpole's father and mother, and of General Conway and his wife, Lady Ailesbury.

Facing the Blue Bedchamber was the Armoury, a vestibule of three Gothic arches, in the left-hand corner of which was the door opening into the Library, a room twenty-eight feet by nineteen feet six, lighted by a large window looking to the east, and by two smaller rose-windows at the sides.   The books, arranged in Gothic arches of pierced work, went all round it.   The chimney-piece was imitated from the tomb of John of Eltham in Westminster Abbey, and the stone work from another tomb at Canterbury.   Over the chimney-piece was a picture (which is engraved in the *Anecdotes of Painting*) representing the marriage of Henry VI.   Walpole and Bentley had designed the ceiling, — a gorgeous heraldic medley surrounding a central Walpole shield.   Above the book-cases were pictures.   One of the greatest treasures of the room was a clock given by Henry VIII. to Anne Boleyn.   Of the books it is impossible to speak in detail.   Noticeable

---

[1] Both these are engraved in Cunningham's edition of the *Letters*, the former in vol. iv., p. 465, the latter in vol. ix., p. 529.

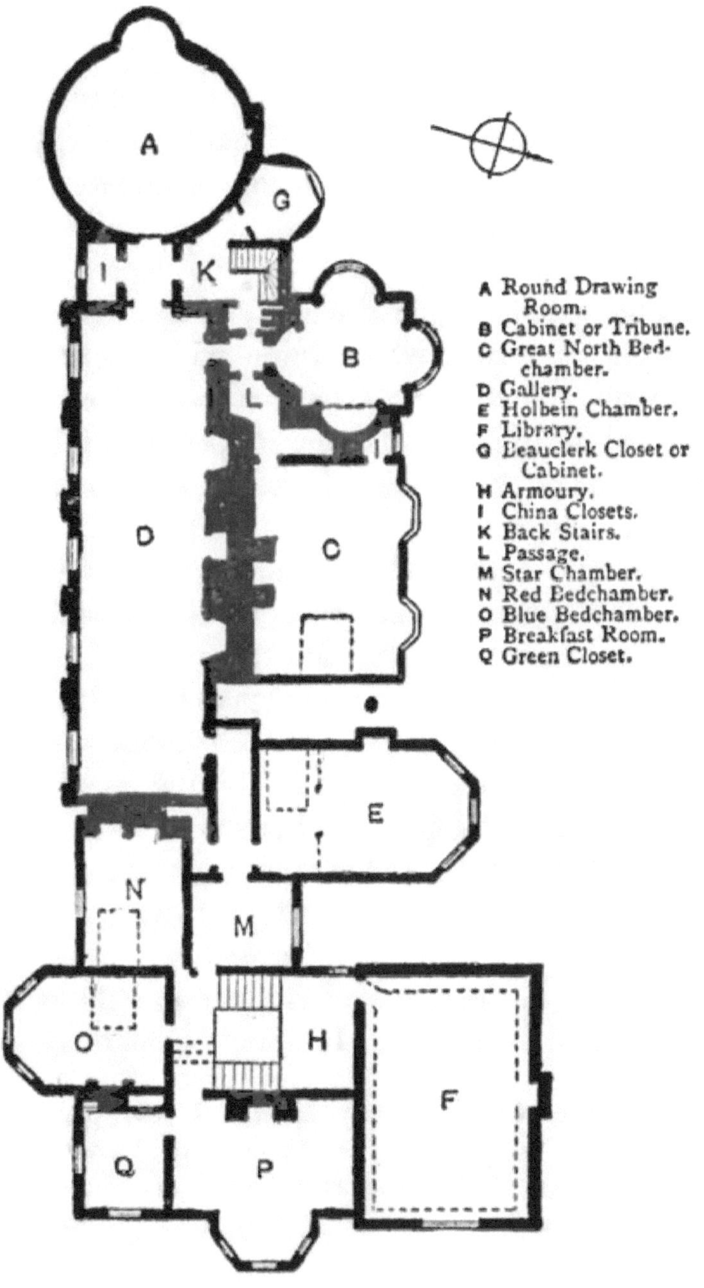

STRAWBERRY HILL: PRINCIPAL FLOOR—1781.

among them, however, was a Thuanus in
fourteen volumes, a very extensive set of
Hogarth's prints, and all the original drawings for the *Ædes Walpolianæ.* Vertue, Hollar.
and Faithorne were also largely represented.
Among special copies, were the identical *Iliad*
and *Odyssey* from which Pope made his transla-
tions of Homer,[1] a volume containing Bentley's
original designs for Gray's *Poems*, and a black
morocco pocket-book of sketches by Jacques
Callot.   In a rosewood case in this room was
also a fine collection of coins, which included
the rare silver medal struck by Gregory XIII.
on the Massacre of St. Bartholomew.

Concerning the Red Bedchamber, the Star
Chamber, and the Holbein Chamber, which
intervened between the rest of the first floor
and the latest additions, there is little to say.
In the Red Bedchamber, the most memorable
things (after the chintz bed on which Lord
Orford died) were some pencil sketches of
Pope and his parents by Cooper and the elder
Richardson.   In the Holbein Chamber, so

---

[1] This was the Amsterdam edition of 1707, in 2 vols.
12mo., inscribed 'E libris, A. Pope, 1714;' and lower
down, ' Finished ye translation in Feb. 1719-20, A. Pope.'
It also contained a pencil sketch by the poet of Twickenham Church.

Mrs. Clive.

called from a number of copies on oil-paper by
Vertue from the drawings of Holbein in Queen
Catherine's Closet at Kensington, were two of
those ' curiosities ' which represent the Don
Saltero, or Madame Tussaud, side of Strawberry, viz., a tortoise-shell comb studded with
silver hearts and roses which was said to have
belonged to Mary, Queen of Scots, and (later)
the red hat of Cardinal Wolsey. The pedigree
of the hat. it must, however, be admitted, was
unimpeachable. It had been found in the
great wardrobe by Bishop Burnet when Clerk
of the Closet. From him it passed to his son
the Judge (author of that curious squib on
Harley known as the *History of Robert Powel
the Puppet-Show-Man*). and thence to the
Countess Dowager of Albemarle, who gave it
to Walpole. A carpet in this room was worked
by Mrs. Clive, who seems to have been a most
industrious decorator of her friend's mansion
museum.[1] The Star Chamber was but an

---

[1] Walpole wrote an epilogue — not a very good one —
for Mrs. Clive when she quitted the stage ; and in the
same year, 1769, the *Town and Country Magazine* linked
their names in its ' *Tête-à-Têtes* ' as ' Mrs. Heildelberg '
(Clive's part in the *Clandestine Marriage*) and ' Baron
Otranto ' (a name under which Chatterton subsequently
satirized Walpole in this identical periodical). See
Memoirs of a Sad Dog, Pt. 2, July, 1770.

ante-room powdered with gold stars in mosaic,
the chief glory of which was a stone bust of
Henry VII. by Torregiano.

With these three rooms, the first floor of
Strawberry, as it existed previous to the erection of the addititions mentioned in the beginning of this chapter. — namely, the Gallery, the
Round Tower, the Tribune, and the Great
North Bedchamber, — came to an end.   But it
was in these newer parts of the house that
some of its rarest objects of art were assembled.
The Gallery, which was entered from a gloomy
little passage in front of the Holbein Chamber.
was a really spacious room, fifty-six feet by
thirteen, and lighted from the south by five high
windows.   Between these were tables laden
with busts, bronzes, and urns ; on the opposite side, fronting the windows, were recesses,
finished with gold network over looking-glass,
between which stood couch-seats. covered, like
the rest of the room, with crimson Norwich
damask.   The ceiling was copied from one of
the side aisles of Henry VII.'s Chapel ; the
great door at the western end, which led into
the Round Tower, was taken from the north
door of St. Albans.   A long carpet, made at
Moorfields, traversed the room from end to
end.   In one of the recesses — that to the left of

the chimney-piece, which was designed by Mr. Chute and Mr. Thomas Pitt of Boconnoc, — stood one of the finest surviving pieces of Greek sculpture, the Boccapadugli eagle, found in the precinct of the Baths of Caracalla, — a *chef-d' œuvre* from which Gray is said to have borrowed the ' ruffled plumes, and flagging wing' of the *Progress of Poesy*; to the right was a noble bust in basalt of Vespasian, which had been purchased from the Ottoboni collection. Of the pictures it is impossible to speak at large ; but two of the most notable were Sir George Villiers, the father of the Duke of Buckingham, and Mabuse's *Marriage of Henry VII. and Elizabeth of York.* Of Walpole's own relatives, there were portraits by Ramsay of his nieces, Mrs. Keppel (the Bishop's wife) and Lady Dysart, and of the Duchess of Gloucester (then Lady Waldegrave) by Reynolds. There were also portraits of Henry Fox, Lord Holland, of George Montagu, of Lord Waldegrave, and of Horace's uncle, Lord Walpole of Wolterton.[1]

Issuing through the great door of the Gallery, and passing on the left a glazed closet con-

---

[1] Horatio, brother of Sir Robert Walpole, created Baron Walpole of Wolterton in 1756. He died in 1757. His *Memoirs* were published by Coxe in 1802.

taining a quantity of china which had once belonged to Walpole's mother, a couple of steps
brought you into the pleasant Drawing Room in
the Round Tower, the bow window of which,
already mentioned, looked to the south-west.
Like the Gallery, this room was hung with
Norwich damask. Its chief glory was the picture of Bianca Capello, of which Walpole had
written to Mann. To the left of this room, at
the back of the Gallery, and consequently in the
front of the house, was the Cabinet, or Tribune,
a curious square chamber with semicircular recesses, in two of which, to the north and west,
were stained windows. In the roof, which was
modelled on the chapter house at York, was a
star of yellow glass throwing a soft golden glow
over all the room. Here Walpole had amassed
his choicest treasures, miniatures by Oliver and
Cooper, enamels by Petitot and Zincke,[1] bronzes
from Italy, ivory bas-reliefs, seal-rings and reli

---

[1] 'The chief boast of my collection,' he told Pinkerton,
'is the portraits of eminent and remarkable persons, particularly the miniatures and enamels; which, so far as I
can discover, are superior to any other collection whatever. The works I possess of Isaac and Peter Oliver are
the best extant; and those I bought in Wales for 300
guineas [*i.e.*, the Digby Family, in the Breakfast Room]
are as well preserved as when they came from the pencil'
(*Walpoliana*, ii. 157).

quaries, caskets and cameos and filigree work.
Here, with Madame du Deffand's letter inside
it,[1] was the 'round white snuff-box' with
Madame de Sévigné's portrait ; here, carven
with masks and flies and grasshoppers, was
Cellini's silver bell from the Leonati Collection,
at Parma, a masterpiece against which he had
exchanged all his collection of Roman coins
with the Marquis of Rockingham. A bronze
bust of Caligula with silver eyes ; a missal with
miniatures by Raphael ; a dagger of Henry VIII.,[2]
and a mourning ring given at the burial of
Charles I., — were among the other show objects
of the Tribune, the riches of which occupy more
space in their owner's Catalogue than any other
part of his collections.

With the Great North Bedchamber, which
adjoined the Tribune, and filled the remaining
space at the back of the Gallery, the account of
Strawberry Hill, as it existed in 1774, comes to
an end ; for the Green Chamber in the Round
Tower over the Drawing Room, and ' Mr. Walpole's Bedchamber, two pair of stairs ' (which

[1] It is printed in both the Catalogues.

[2] At the sale in 1842, King Henry's dagger was purchased for £54 12s. by Charles Kean the actor, who also
became the fortunate possessor, for £21, of Cardinal
Wolsey's hat.

contained the Warrant for beheading King Charles I., inscribed 'Major Charta,' so often referred to by Walpole's biographers),[1] may be dismissed without further notice. The Beauclerk Closet, a later addition, will be described in its proper place. Over the chimney-piece in the Great North Bedchamber was a large picture of Henry VIII. and his children, a recent purchase, afterwards remanded to the staircase to make room for a portrait of Catherine of Braganza, sent from Portugal previous to her marriage with Charles II. Fronting the bed was a head of Niobe, by Guido, which in its turn subsequently made way for *la belle Jennings.*[2] Among the pictures on the north or window side of the room was the original sketch by Hogarth of the *Beggar's Opera,* which Walpole had purchased at the sale of Rich, the fortunate manager who produced Gay's masterpiece at Lincoln's Inn Fields. It was exhibited at Manchester in

[1] Here is his own reference to this, in a letter to Montagu of 14 Oct., 1756: 'The only thing I have done that can compose a paragraph, and which I think you are Whig enough to forgive me, is, that on each side of my bed I have hung MAGNA CHARTA, and the Warrant for King Charles's execution, on which I have written Major Charta; as I believe, without the latter, the former by this time would be of very little importance.'

[2] See p. 7 n.

1857, being then the property of Mr. Willett, who had bought it at the Strawberry Hill sale of 1842. Another curious oil painting in this room was the *Rehearsal of an Opera* by the Riccis, which included caricature portraits of Nicolini (of *Spectator* celebrity), of the famous Mrs. Catherine Tofts, and of Margherita de l'Epine. In a nook by the window there was a glazed china closet, with a number of minor curiosities, among which were conspicuous the speculum of cannel coal with which Dr. Dee was in the habit of gulling his votaries,[1] and an agate puncheon with Gray's arms which his executors had presented to Walpole.

A few external objects claim a word. In the Great Cloister under the Gallery was the blue and white china tub in which had taken place that tragedy of the 'pensive Selima' referred to at p. 135 as having prompted the muse of Gray.[2] The Chapel in the Garden has already been

---

[1] 'Dr Dee's black stone was named in the catalogue of the collection of the Earls of Peterborough, whence it went to Lady Betty Germaine. She gave it to the last Duke of Argyle, and his son, Lord Frederic, to me' (*Walpole to Lady Ossory*, 12 Jan, 1782)

[2] This was afterwards moved to the Little Cloister at the entrance, where it appears in the later Catalogue. At the sale of 1842 the bowl, with its Gothic pedestal, was purchased by the Earl of Derby for £42.

sufficiently described.[1] In the Flower Garden across the road was a cottage which Walpole had erected upon the site of the building once occupied by Francklin the printer, and which he used as a place of refuge when the tide of sight-seers became overpowering. It included a Tea Room, containing a fair collection of china, and hung with green paper and engravings, and a little white and green Library, of which the principal ornament was a half-length portrait of Milton.[2] A portrait of Lady Hervey, by Allan Ramsay, was afterwards added to its decorations.[3]

Many objects of interest, as must be obvious, have remained undescribed in the foregoing account, and those who seek for further infor-

---

[1] Not far from the Chapel was 'a large seat in the form of a shell, carved in oak from a design by Mr. Bentley.' It must have been roomy, for in 1759 the Duchesses of Hamilton and Richmond, and Lady Ailesbury (the last two, daughter and mother), occupied it together. 'There never was so pretty a sight as to see them all three sitting in the shell,' says the delighted Abbot of Strawberry. (*Walpole to Montagu,* 2 June.)

[2] In a note to the obituary notice of Walpole in the *Gentleman's Magazine* for March, 1797, p. 260, it is stated that this library was 'formed of all the publications during the reigns of the three Georges, or Mr. W.'s own time.'

[3] This was exhibited at South Kensington in 1867 by Viscount Lifford, and is now (1892) at Austin House, Broadway, Worcester.

mation concerning what its owner called his
' paper fabric and assemblage of curious trifles '
must consult either the Catalogue of 1774 itself,
or that later and definitive version of it which is
reprinted in Volume II. of the *Works* (pp. 393–
516).   The intention in the main has here been
to lay stress upon those articles which bear most
directly upon Walpole's biography.   It will also
be observed that, during the prolonged progress
of the house towards completion, his experience
and his views considerably enlarged, and the
pettiness and artificiality of his first improvements disappeared.   The house never lost, and
never could lose, its invertebrate character ; but
the Gallery, the Round Tower, and the North
Bedchamber were certainly conceived in a more
serious and even spacious spirit of Gothicism
than any of the early additions.   That it must,
still, have been confined and needlessly gloomy,
may be allowed ; but as a set-off to some of
those accounts which insist so pertinaciously
upon its ' paltriness,' its ' architectural solecisms,'
and its lack of beauty and sublimity, it is only
fair to recall a few sentences from the preface
which its owner prefixed to the *Description* of
1784. It was designed, he says of the Catalogue,
to exhibit ' specimens of Gothic architecture, as
collected from standards in cathedrals and chapel-

tombs,' and to show ' how they may be applied
to chimney-pieces, ceilings, windows, balustrades, loggias, etc.'   Elsewhere he charac-
terizes the building itself as candidly as any of
its critics.   He admits its diminutive scale and
its unsubstantial character (he calls it himself,
as we have seen, a ' paper fabric '), and he confesses to the incongruities arising from an antique
design and modern decorations.   ' In truth,' he
concludes, ' I did not mean to make my house so
Gothic as to exclude convenience, and modern
refinements in luxury. . . . It was built to please
my own taste, and in some degree to realize my
own visions.   I have specified what it contains ;
could I describe the gay but tranquil scene
where it stands, and add the beauty of the landscape to the romantic cast of the mansion, it
would raise more pleasing sensations than a dry
list of curiosities can excite, — at least the prospect would recall the good humour of those who
might be disposed to condemn the fantastic fabric,
and to think it a very proper habitation of, as it
was the scene that inspired, the author of the
Castle of Otranto.'[1]   As one of his censors has
remarked, this tone disarms criticism ; and it
is needless to accumulate proofs of peculiarities which are not denied by the person most
concerned.

[1] *Works,* 1798, ii. 395-98.

In spite of its charming situation, Strawberry Hill was emphatically a summer residence ; and there is more than one account in Walpole's letters of the sudden floods which, when Thames flowed with a fuller tide than now, occasionally surprised the inhabitants of the pleasant-looking villas along its banks.   It was decidedly damp, and its gouty owner had sometimes to quit it precipitately for Arlington Street, where, he says, 'after an hour,' he revives, 'like a member of parliament's wife.' His best editor, Mr. Peter Cunningham, whose knowledge as an antiquary was unrivalled, — for was he not the author of the *Handbook of London?* — has amused himself, in an odd corner of one of his prefaces, by retracing the route taken in these townward flights.   The extract is so packed with suggestive memories that no excuse is needed for reproducing it (with a few now necessary notes) as the tail-piece of the present chapter.

'At twelve his [Walpole's] light bodied chariot was at the door, with his English coachman and his Swiss valet [Philip Colomb] . . . In a few minutes he left Lord Radnor's villa to the right, rolled over the grotto of Pope, saw on his left Whitton, rich with recollections of Kneller and Argyll, passed Gumley House,

one of the country seats of his father's oppo-
nent and his own friend, Pulteney, Earl of
Bath, and Kendal House,[1] the retreat of the
mistress of George I., Ermengard de Schulen-
burg, Duchess of Kendal. At Sion, the princely
seat of the Percys, the Seymours, and the
Smithsons, he turned into the Hounslow
Road, left Sion on his right, and Osterly, not
unlike Houghton, on his left, and rolled through
Brentford, —

" Brentford, the Bishopric of Parson Horne,"[2]

then, as now, infamous for its dirty streets, and
famous for its white-legged chickens.[3] Quitting Brentford, he approached the woods that
concealed the stately mansion of Gunnersbury.
built by Inigo Jones and Webb, and then in-
habited by the Princess Amelia, the last surviving child of King George II.[4] Here he was
often a visitor, and seldom returned without
being a winner at silver loo. At the Pack

---

[1] Kendal House now no longer exists.

[2] *An Heroic Epistle to Sir William Chambers, Knight,*
1773.

[3]   ' —— *Brandford's* tedious town,
For dirty streets, and white-leg'd chickens known.'
                              Gay's *Journey to Exeter.*

[4] Gunnersbury House (or Park), a new structure, now
belongs to Lord Rothschild.

Horse [1] on Turnham Green he would, when the roads were heavy, draw up for a brief bait. Starting anew, he would pass a few red brick houses on both sides, then the suburban villas of men well to do in the Strand and Charing Cross. At Hammersmith, he would leave the church [2] on his right, call on Mr. Fox at Holland House, look at Campden House, with recollections of Sir Baptist Hickes, [3] and not without an ill-suppressed wish to transfer some little part of it to his beloved Strawberry. He was now at Kensington Church, then, as it still is, an ungraceful structure, [4] but rife with associations which he would at times relate to the

[1] The Old Pack Horse, somewhat modernized by red-brick additions, still (1892) stands at the corner of Turnham Green. It is mentioned in the *London Gazette* as far back as 1697. The sign, a common one for posting inns in former days, is on the opposite side of the road.

[2] Hammersmith church was rebuilt in 1882–3.

[3] Sir Baptist Hickes, once a mercer in Cheapside, and afterwards Viscount Campden, erected it *circa* 1612. At the time to which Mr. Cunningham is supposed to refer, it was a famous ladies' boarding-school, kept by a Mrs. Terry, and patronized by Selwyn and Lady Di. Beauclerk.

[4] The (with all due deference to the writer) quaint and picturesque old church of St. Mary the Virgin, in Kensington High Street, at which Macaulay, in his later days, was a regular attendant, gave way, in 1869, to a larger and more modern edifice by Sir Gilbert Scott, R.A.

friend he had with him. On his left he would leave the gates of Kensington Palace, rich with reminiscences connected with his father and the first Hanoverian kings of this country. On his right he would quit the red brick house in which the Duchess of Portsmouth lived,[1] and after a drive of half a mile (skirting a heavy brick wall), reach Kingston House,[2] replete with stories of Elizabeth Chudleigh, the bigamist maid of honour, and Duchess-Countess of Kingston and Bristol. At Knightsbridge (even then the haunt of highwaymen less gallant than Maclean) he passed on his left the little chapel [3] in which his father was married. At Hyde Park Corner he saw the Hercules Pillars ale-house of Fielding and Tom Jones,[4] and at one door from Park Lane

[1] Old Kensington House, as it was called, has also been pulled down. One of its inmates, long after the days of ' Madam Carwell,' was Elizabeth Inchbald, the author of *A Simple Story*, who died there in 1821.

[2] Now Lord Listowel's. It stands near the Prince's Gate into Hyde Park.

[3] Restored and remodelled in 1861, and now the Church of the Holy Trinity.

[4] The Hercules Pillars, where Squire Western put up his horses when he came to town, stood just east of Apsley House, ' on the site of what is now the pavement opposite Lord Willoughby's.'

would occasionally call on old " Q " for the
sake of Selwyn, who was often there.[1] The
trees which now grace Piccadilly were in the
Green Park in Walpole's day ; they can recollect Walpole, and that is something. On his
left, the sight of Coventry House[2] would remind
him of the Gunnings, and he would tell his
friend the story of the " beauties," with which
(short story-teller as he was) he had not completed when the chariot turned into Arlington
Street on the right, or down Berkeley Street
into Berkeley Square, on the left.'[3] In these
last lines Mr. Cunningham anticipates our story,
for in 1774, Walpole had not yet taken up his
residence in Berkeley Square.

[1] The Duke of Queensberry's house afterwards became
138 and 139 Piccadilly.

[2] This is No. 106, — the present St. James's Club. It
was built in 1764 by George, sixth Earl of Coventry, some
years after the death of his first wife, the elder Miss
Gunning.

[3] *Letters*, by Cunningham, 1857-9, ix. xx.-xxi.

CHAPTER IX.

AFTER the completion of Strawberry Hill
and the printing of the *Catalogue*, Walpole's
life grows comparatively barren of events.
There are still four volumes of his *Correspondence*, but they take upon them imperceptibly
the nature of *nouvelles à la main*, and are less
fruitful in personal traits. Between his books
and his prints, his time passes agreeably, ' but
will not do to relate.' Indeed, from this period
until his death, in 1797, the most notable occurrences in his history are his friendship with the

Miss Berrys in 1787–8, and his belated accession to the Earldom of Orford. Both at Strawberry and Arlington Street, his increasing years and his persistent malady condemn him more and more to seclusion and retirement. He is most at Strawberry, despite its dampness, for in the country he holds 'old, useless people ought to live.' 'If you were not to be in London,' he tells Lady Ossory in April, 1774, 'the spring advances so charmingly, I think I should scarce go thither. One is frightened with the inundation of breakfasts and balls that are coming on. Every one is engaged to everybody for the next three weeks, and if one must hunt for a needle, I had rather look for it in a bottle of hay in the country than in a crowd.' 'By age and situation,' he writes from Strawberry in September, 'at this time of the year I live with nothing but old women. They do very well for me, who have little choice left, and who rather prefer common nonsense to wise nonsense, — the only difference I know between old women and old men. I am out of all politics, and never think of elections, which I think I should hate even if I loved politics, — just as, if I loved tapestry I do not think I could talk over the manufacture of worsteds. Books I have almost done with too, — at least, read only such

as nobody else would read. In short, my way
of life is too insipid to entertain anybody but
myself; and though I am always employed, I
must own I think I have given up every thing
in the world, only to be busy about the most
arrant trifles.' His London life was not greatly
different. 'How should I see or know anything?' he says a year later, apologizing for his
dearth of news. 'I seldom stir out of my
house [at Arlington Street] before seven in the
evening, see very few persons, and go to fewer
places, make no new acquaintance, and have
seen most of my old wear out. Loo at Princess Amelie's, loo at Lady Hertford's, are the
capital events of my history, and a Sunday alone,
at Strawberry, my chief entertainment. All this
is far from gay ; but as it neither gives me *ennui*,
nor lowers my spirits, it is not uncomfortable,
and I prefer it to being *déplacé* in younger company.' Such is his account of his life in 1774-5,
when he is nearing sixty, and it probably represents it with sufficient accuracy. But a trifling
incident easily stirs him into unwonted vivacity.
While he is protesting that he has nothing to
say, his letters grow under his pen, and, almost
as a necessary consequence of his leisure, they
become more frequent and more copious. In
the edition of Cunningham, up to September,

1774, they number fourteen hundred and fifty. Speaking roughly, this represents a period of nearly forty years. During the two-and-twenty years that remained to him, he managed to swell them by what was, proportionately, a far greater number. The last letter given by Cunningham is marked 2665 ; and this enumeration does not include a good many letters and fragments of letters belonging to this later period, which were published in 1865 in Miss Berry's *Journals and Correspondence*. Nevertheless, as stated above, they more and more assume what he somewhere calls ' their proper character of newspapers.'

During the remainder of his life, they were his chief occupation, and his gout was seldom so severe but that he could make shift to scribble a line to his favourite correspondents, calling in his printer Kirgate as secretary in cases of extremity.[1] Of literature generally he pro-

---

[1] Kirgate, who will not be again mentioned, fared but ill at his master's decease, receiving no more than a legacy of £100, — a circumstance which Pinkerton darkly attributes to 'his modest merit' having been 'supplanted by intriguing impudence' (*Walpoliana*, i. xxiv). There is a portrait of him, engraved by William Collard, after Septimus Harding, the Pall Mall miniature painter, who also wrote in 1797 for Kirgate some verses in which he is made to speak of himself as ' forlorn, neglected, and forgot.' He

fessed to have taken final leave. 'I no longer care about fame,' he tells Mason in 1774; 'I have done being an author.' Nevertheless, the *Short Notes* piously chronicle the production of more than one trifle, which are reprinted in his *Works.* When, in the above year, Lord Chesterfield's letters to his son were published, Walpole began a parody of that famous performance in a *Series of Letters from a Mother to a Daughter*, with the general title of the *New Whole Duty of Woman.* He grew tired of the idea too soon to enable us to judge what his success might have been with a subject which, in his hands, should have been diverting as a satire ; for, although he was a warm admirer of Chesterfield's parts, as he had shown in his character of him in the *Royal and Noble Authors*, he was thoroughly alive to the assailable side of what he styles his 'impertinent institutes of education.'[1]   Another work of this year was a

had an unique collection of the Strawberry Press issues, which was dispersed at his death, in 1810.

[1] It was his good sense rather than his inclination that made him condemn one with whom he had many points of sympathy. Speaking of the quarrel of Johnson and Chesterfield, he says, 'The friendly patronage [*i. e.* of the earl] was returned with ungrateful rudeness by the proud pedant ; and men smiled, without being surprised, at seeing a bear worry his dancing-master.'

reply to some remarks by Mr. Masters in the *Archæologia* upon the old subject of the *Historic Doubts*, which calls for no further notice. But early in 1775 he was persuaded into writing an epilogue for the *Braganza* of Captain Robert Jephson, a maiden tragedy of the *Venice Preserved* order, which was produced at Drury Lane in February of that year, with considerable success. In a correspondence which ensued with the author, Walpole delivered himself of his views on tragedy for the benefit of Mr. Jephson, who acted upon them, but not (as his Mentor thought) with conspicuous success, in his next attempt, the *Law of Lombardy*. Jephson's third play, however, the *Count of Narbonne*, which was well received in 1781, had a natural claim upon Walpole's good opinion, since it was based upon the *Castle of Otranto*.[1] Besides the above letters on tragedy, Walpole wrote, 'in 1775 and 1776,' a rather longer paper on comedy, which is printed with them in the second volume of his works (pp. 315–22). He held, as he

---

[1] 'Jephson's *Count of Narbonne* has been more admired than any play I remember to have appeared these many years. It is still [Jan., 1782] acted with success to very full houses' (*Malone to Charlemont, Hist. MSS. Commission*, 12th *Rept., App.*, Pt. x., 1891, p. 395). Malone wrote the epilogue.

says, 'a good comedy the *chef-d'œuvre* of human genius;' and it is manifest that his keenest sympathies were on the side of comic art. His remarks upon Congreve are full of just appreciation. Yet, although he mentions the *School for Scandal* (which, by the way, shows that he must have written rather later than the dates given above), he makes no reference to the most recent development, in *She Stoops to Conquer*, of the school of humour and character, and he seems rather to pose as the advocate of that genteel or sentimental comedy which Foote and Goldsmith and Sheridan had striven to drive from the English stage. When his prejudices are aroused, he is seldom a safe guide, and in addition to his personal contempt for Goldsmith,[1] that writer had irritated him by his reference to the Albemarle Street Club, to which many of his friends belonged. It was an additional offence that the 'Miss Biddy [originally Miss Rachael] Buckskin' of the comedy was said to stand for Miss Rachael Lloyd, long housekeeper at Kensington Palace.

---

[1] 'Silly Dr. Goldsmith,' he calls him to Cole in April, 1773. 'Goldsmith was an idiot, with once or twice a fit of parts,' he says again to Mason in October, 1776.

and a member of the club well known both to himself and to Madame du Deffand.[1]

In the second of the letters to Mr. Jephson, Walpole refers to his own efforts at comedy, and implies that he had made attempts in this direction even before the tragedy of *The Mysterious Mother*. He had certainly the wit, and much of the gift of direct expression, which comedy requires. But nothing of these earlier essays appears to have survived, and the only dramatic effort included among his *Works* (his tragedy excepted) is the little piece entitled *Nature will Prevail*, which, with its fairy machinery, has something of the character of such earlier productions of Mr. W. S. Gilbert as the *Palace of Truth*. This he wrote in 1773, and, according to the *Short Notes*, sent it anonymously to the elder Colman, then manager of Covent Garden. Colman (he says) was much pleased with it, but regarding it as too short for a farce, wished to have it enlarged. This, however, its author thought

[1] The rules of the so-called *Female Coterie* in Albemarle Street, together with the names of the members, are given in the *Gentleman's Magazine* for 1770, pp. 414-5. Besides Walpole and Miss Lloyd, Fox, Conway, Selwyn, the Waldegraves, the Damers, and many other 'persons of quality' belonged to it.

too much trouble ' for so slight and extempore a performance.' Five years after, it was produced at the little theatre in the Haymarket, and, being admirably acted, — says the *Biographia Dramatica,* — met with considerable applause. But it is obviously one of those works to which the verdict of Goldsmith's critic, that it would have been better if the author had taken more pains, may judiciously be applied. It is more like a sketch for a farce than a farce itself ; and it is not finished enough for a *proverbe.* Yet the dialogue is in parts so good that one almost regrets the inability of the author to nerve himself for an enterprise *de longue haleine.*

Between 1774 and 1780 the Strawberry Hill Press still now and then showed signs of vitality. In 1775, it printed as a loose sheet some verses by Charles James Fox, — celebrating, as Amoret, that lover of the Whigs, the beautiful Mrs. Crewe, — and three hundred copies of an Eclogue by Mr. Fitzpatrick,[1] entitled *Dorinda,* which contains the couplet, —

' And oh ! what Bliss, when each alike is pleas'd,
The Hand that squeezes, and the Hand that 's squeez'd.'

These were followed, in 1778, by the *Sleep Walker,* a comedy from the French of Madame

---

[1] The Hon. Richard Fitzpatrick, Lord Ossory's brother. He afterwards became a General, and Secretary

du Deffand's friend Pont de Veyle, translated
by Lady Craven, afterwards Margravine of
Anspach, and played for a charitable purpose
at Newbury. A year later came the vindication
of his conduct to Chatterton, already mentioned
at pp. 196–200 ; and after this a sheet of verse
by Mr. Charles Miller to Lady Horatia Waldegrave,[1] a daughter of the Duchess of Gloucester
by her first husband. The last work of any
importance was the fourth volume of the *Anecdotes of Painting*, which had been printed as far
back as 1770, but was not issued until Oct.,
1780. This delay, the Advertisement informs

at War. At this time he was a captain in the Grenadier
Guards. As a *littérateur* he had written *The Bath Picture ; or, a Slight Sketch of its Beauties;* and he was later
one of the chief contributors to the *Rolliad.* Besides
being the life-long friend of Fox, he was a highly popular
wit and man-of-fashion. Lord Ossory put him above
Walpole and Selwyn ; and Lady Holland is said to have
thought him the most agreeable person she had ever
known. He died in 1813.

[1] One of the three beautiful sisters painted by Reynolds, — Elizabeth Laura, afterwards Viscountess Chew-
ton ; Charlotte Maria, afterwards Countess of Euston ;
and Anne Horatia, who married Captain Hugh Conway.
'Sir Joshua Reynolds gets avaricious in his old age. My
picture of the young ladies Waldegrave is doubtless very
fine and graceful, but it cost me 800 guineas ' (*Walpoliana*, ii. 157).

us, arose 'from motives of tenderness.' The
author was 'unwilling [he says] to utter even
gentle censures, which might wound the affec-
tions, or offend the prejudices, of those related
to the persons whom truth forbad him to com-
mend beyond their merits.'[1]   But despite his
unwillingness to 'dispense universal panegyric,'
and the limitation of his theme to living pro-
fessors, he manages, in the same Advertisement,
to distribute a fair amount of praise to some of
his particular favourites.   Of H. W. Bunbury,
the husband of Goldsmith's ' Little Comedy,' he
says that he is the ' second Hogarth,' and the
' first imitator who ever fully equalled his original,' — which is sheer extravagance.   He lauds
the miniature copying of Lady Lucan, as almost
depreciating the ' exquisite works ' of the artists
she follows, — to wit, Cooper and the Olivers ;
and he speaks of Lady Di. Beauclerk's drawings as 'not only inspired by Shakespeare's
insight into nature, but by the graces and taste
of Grecian artists.'   After this, the comparison
of Mrs. Damer with Bernini seems almost tame.

[1] He was not successful as regards Hogarth, whose
widow was sorely and justly wounded by his coarse
treatment of *Sigismunda,* which is said to have been a
portrait of herself. The picture is now in the National
Gallery.

Yet her works ' from the life are not inferior to the antique, and those . . . were not more like.' One can scarcely blame Walpole severely for this hearty backing of the friends who had added so much to the attractions of his Gothic castle ; but the value of his criticisms, in many other instances sound enough, is certainly impaired by his loyalty to the old-new practice of ' log-rolling.'

Lady Di. Beauclerk, whose illustrations to Dryden's *Fables* are still a frequent item in second-hand catalogues, has a personal connection with Strawberry through the curious little closet bearing her name, which, with the assistance of Mr. Essex, a Gothic architect from Cambridge, Walpole in 1776-8 managed to tuck in between the Cabinet and the Round Tower. It was built on purpose to hold the ' seven incomparable drawings,' executed in a fortnight, which her Ladyship prepared, to illustrate *The Mysterious Mother.* These were the designs to which he refers in the *Anecdotes of Painting*, and, in a letter to Mann, says could not be surpassed by Guido and Salvator Rosa. They were hung on Indian blue damask, in frames of black and gold ; and Clive's friend, Miss Pope, the actress, when she dined at Strawberry, was affected by them to such a degree that she shed tears, although she did not know the story, — an anecdote which may be regarded either as a genuine compliment to Lady Di., or a merely histrionic tribute to her entertainer. 'The drawings,' Walpole says, 'do not shock and disgust, like their original, the tragedy ;' but they were not to be shown to the profane. They were, nevertheless, probably exhibited pretty freely, as a copy of the play, carefully annotated in MS. by the author, and bound in blue leather to match the hangings, was always kept in a drawer of one of the tables, for the purpose of explaining them.[1]   Walpole afterwards added one or two curiosities to this closet. It contained, according to the last edition of the *Catalogue*, a head in basalt of Jupiter Serapis, and a book of Psalms illuminated by Giulio Clovio, the latter purchased for £168 at the Duchess of Portland's sale in May, 1786. There was also a portrait by Powell, after Reynolds, of Lady Di. herself, who lived for some time

---

[1] Miss Hawkins (*Anecdotes*, etc., 1822, p. 103) did not think highly of these performances : 'Unless the proportions of the human figure are of no importance in drawing it, these ' Beauclerk drawings ' can be looked on only with disgust and contempt.' But she praises the gipsies hereafter mentioned (p. 260 n.) as having been copied by Agnes Berry.

at Twickenham in a house now known as
Little Marble Hill, many of the rooms of
which she decorated with her own performances. These were apparently the efforts
which prompted the already mentioned postscript to the *Parish Register of Twickenham* :

> " Here Genius in a later hour
>   Selected its sequester'd bow'r,
>   And threw around the verdant room
>   The blushing lilac's chill perfume.
>   So loose is flung each bold festoon,
>   Each bough so breathes the touch of noon,
>   The happy pencil so deceives,
>   That Flora, doubly jealous, cries,
>   ' The work 's not mine, — yet, trust these eyes,
>   'T is my own Zephyr waves the leaves.' " [1]

Mention has been made of the intermittent
attacks of insanity to which Walpole's nephew,
the third Earl of Orford, was subject. At the
beginning of 1774, he had returned to his senses,
and his uncle, on whom fell the chief care
of his affairs during his illnesses, was, for a
brief period, freed from the irksome strain of an
uncongenial and a thankless duty. In April,
1777, however, Lord Orford's malady broke
out again, with redoubled severity. In August.
he was still fluctuating ' between violence and

-----
[1] See pp. 158, 159.

stupidity ;' but in March, 1778, a lucid interval had once more been reached, and Walpole was relieved of the care of his person. Of his affairs he had declined to take care, as his Lordship had employed a lawyer of whom Walpole had a bad opinion. 'He has resumed the entire dominion of himself,' says a letter to Mann in April, 'and is gone into the country, and intends to command the militia.' One of the earliest results of this 'entire dominion' was a step which filled his relative with the keenest distress. He offered the famous Houghton collection of pictures to Catherine of Russia, — 'the most signal mortification to my idolatry for my father's memory that it could receive,' says Walpole to Lady Ossory. By August, 1779, the sale was completed. 'The sum stipulated,' he tells Mann, 'is forty or forty-five thousand pounds,[1] I neither know nor care which ; nor whether the picture merchant ever receives the whole sum, which probably he will not do, as I hear it is to be discharged at three payments, — a miserable

[1] The exact sum was £40,555. Cipriani and West were the valuers. Most of the family portraits were reserved ; but so many of the pictures were presents that it is not easy to estimate the actual profit over their first cost to the original owner.

bargain for a mighty empress! . . . Well! adieu to Houghton! about its mad master I shall never trouble myself more. . . . Since he has stript Houghton of its glory, I do not care a straw what he does with the stone or the acres!'[1]

Not very long after the date of the above letter Walpole made what was, for him, an important change of residence. The lease of his house in Arlington Street running out, he fixed upon a larger one in the then very fashionable district of Berkeley Square. The house he selected, now (1892) numbered 11, was then 40,[2] and he had commenced negotiations for its purchase as early as November, 1777, when, he tells Lady Ossory, he had come to town to take possession. But difficulties arose over the sale, and he found himself involved in a Chancery suit. He was too adroit, however, to allow this to degenerate into an additional annoyance, and managed (by his own account) to turn what promised to be a tedious course of litigation into a combat of courtesy. Ultimately, in July, 1779, he

---

[1] *Walpole to Mann*, 4 Aug., 1779.

[2] This, according to Harrison's *Memorable Houses*, 3rd ed., 1890, p. 62, is Lord Orford's number as given in *Boyle's Court Guide* for 1796.

had won his cause, and was hurrying from Strawberry to pay his purchase money and close the bargain. Two months later, he is moving in, and is delighted with his acquisition. He would not change his two pretty mansions for any in England, he says. On the 14th October, he took formal possession, upon which day — his ' inauguration day ' — he dates his first letter ' Berkeley Square.' ' It is seeming to take a new lease of life,' he tells Mason. ' I was born in Arlington Street, lived there about fourteen years, returned thither, and passed thirty-seven more ; but I have sober monitors that warn me not to delude myself.' He had still a decade and a half before him.

Little more than twelve months after he had settled down in his new abode, he lost the faithful friend at Paris, to whom, for the space of fifteen years, he had written nearly once a week. By 1774, he had become somewhat nervous about this accumulated correspondence in a language not his own. For an Englishman, his French was good, and, as might be expected of anything he wrote, characteristic and vivacious. But, almost of necessity, it contained many minor faults of phraseology and arrangement, besides abounding in personal anecdote ;

and he became apprehensive lest, after Madame du Deffand's death, his utterances should fall into alien hands. General Conway, who visited Paris in October, 1774, had therefore been charged to beg for their return, — a request which seems at first to have been met by the reply on the lady's part that sufficient precautions had already been taken for ensuring their restoration. Ultimately, however, they were handed to Conway.[1] It was in all probability under a sense of this concession that Walpole once more risked a tedious journey to visit his blind friend. In the following year he went to Paris, to find her, as usual, impatiently expecting his arrival. She sat with him until half-past two, and before his eyes were open again, he had a letter from her. ' Her soul is immortal, and forces her body to keep it company.' A little later he complains that he never gets to bed from her suppers before two or three o'clock. ' In short,' he says, ' I need have the activity

---

[1] According to a note in the selection from Madame du Deffand's Correspondence with Walpole, published in 1810, iii. 44, these letters were at that date extant. But all the subsequent letters were burnt by her at Walpole's earnest desire, — those only excepted which she received during the last year of her life, and these, also, were sent back when she died.

of a squirrel, and the strength of a Hercules, to go through my labours, — not to count how many *démêlés* I have had to *raccommode* and how many *mémoires* to present against Tonton,[1] who grows the greater favourite the more people he devours.' But Tonton's mistress is more worth visiting than ever, he tells Selwyn, and she is apparently as tireless as of yore. ' Madame du Deffand and I [says another letter] set out last Sunday at seven in the evening, to go fifteen miles to a ball, and came back after supper ; and another night, because it was but

---

[1] Tonton was a snappish little dog belonging to Madame du Deffand, which, when in its mistress's company, must have been extremely objectionable. In January, 1778, the Maréchale de Luxembourg presented her old friend with Tonton's portrait in wax on a gold snuff-box, together with the last six volumes of Madame du Deffand's favourite, Voltaire, adding the following epigram by the Chevalier de Boufflers : —

> ' Vous les trouvez tous deux charmans,
> Nous les trouvons tous deux mordans :
>   Voilà la ressemblance ;
> L'un ne mord que ses ennemis,
> Et l'autre mord tous vos amis :
>   Voilà la différence.'

At Madame du Deffand's death, both dog and box passed to Walpole, the latter finding an honoured place among the treasures of the Tribune. (See *A Description of the Villa*, etc., 1774, p. 137, *Appendix of Additions*.)

one in the morning when she brought me home, she ordered the coachman to make the tour of the Quais, and drive gently because it was so early.' At last, early in October, he tears himself away, to be followed almost immediately by a letter of farewell.   Here it is : —

' Adieu, ce mot est bien triste ; souvenez-vous que vous laissez ici la personne dont vous êtes le plus aimé, et dont le bonheur et le malheur consistent dans ce que vous pensez pour elle. Donnez-moi de vos nouvelles le plus tôt qu'il sera possible.

' Je me porte bien, j'ai un peu dormi, ma nuit n'est pas finie ; je serai très-exacte au régime, et j'aurai soin de moi puisque vous vous y intéressez.'

The correspondence thus resumed was continued for five years more. Walpole does not seem to have visited Paris again, and the references to Madame du Deffand in his general correspondence are not very frequent. Towards the middle of 1780, her life was plainly closing in. In July and August, she complained of being more than usually languid, and in a letter of the 22nd of the latter month intimates that it may be her last, as dictation grows painful to her. ' Ne vous devant revoir de ma vie,' — she says pathetically, — ' je n'ai rien à regretter.'

From this time she kept her bed, and in September Walpole tells Lady Ossory that he is trembling at every letter he gets from Paris. 'My dear old friend, I fear, is going ! . . . To have struggled twenty days at eighty-four shows such stamina that I have not totally lost hopes.' On the 24th, however, after a lethargy of several days, she died quietly, ' without effort or struggle.' ' Elle a eu la mort la plus douce,' — says her faithful and attached secretary, Wiart, — ' quoique la maladie ait été longue.' She was buried, at her own wish, in the parish church of St. Sulpice. By her will she made her nephew, the Marquis d'Aulan, her heir. Long since, she had wished Walpole to accept this character. Thereupon he had threatened that he would never set foot in Paris again if she carried out her intention ; and it was abandoned. But she left him the whole of her manuscripts[1] and books.

As his own letters to her have not been printed, her death makes no difference in the amount of his correspondence. The war with the American Colonies, of which he foresaw the disastrous results, and the course of

---

[1] The MSS., which included eight hundred of Madame du Deffand's letters, were sold in the Strawberry Hill sale of 1842 for £157 10*s.*

which he follows to Mann with the greatest keenness, fully absorbs as much of his time as he can spare from the vagaries of the Duchess of Kingston and the doings of the Duchess of Gloucester. Not many months before Madame du Deffand died had occurred the famous Gordon Riots, which, as he was in London most of the time, naturally occupy his pen. It was General Conway who, as the author of *Barnaby Rudge* has not forgotten, so effectively remonstrated with Lord George upon the occasion of the visit of the mob to the House of Commons; and four days later Walpole chronicles from Berkeley Square the events of the terrible ‘ Black Wednesday.’ From the roof of Gloucester House he sees the blazing prisons, — a sight he shall not soon forget. Other subjects for which one dips in the lucky bag of his records are the defence of Gibraltar, the trial of Warren Hastings, the loss of the *Royal George*. But it is generally in the minor chronicle that he is most diverting. The last *bon mot* of George Selwyn or Lady Townshend, the newest ‘ royal pregnancy,’ the details of court ceremonial, the most recent addition to Strawberry, the endless stream of anecdote and tittle-tattle which runs dimpling all the way, — these are the themes he loves best ; this is the element in which his easy persiflage delights to disport itself. He is, above all, a *rieur*. About his serious passages there is generally a false ring, but never when he pours out the gossip that he loves, and of which he has so inexhaustible a supply. 'I can sit and amuse myself with my own memory,' he says to Mann in February, 1785, 'and yet find new stores at every audience that I give to it. Then, for private episodes [he has been speaking of his knowledge of public events], varieties of characters, political intrigues, literary anecdotes, etc., the profusion that I remember is endless ; in short, when I reflect on all I have seen, heard, read, written, the many idle hours I have passed, the nights I have wasted playing at faro, the weeks, nay months, I have spent in pain, you will not wonder that I almost think I have, like Pythagoras, been Panthoides Euphorbus, and have retained one memory in at least two bodies.'

He was sixty-eight when he wrote the above letter. Mann was eighty-four, and the long correspondence — a correspondence 'not to be paralleled in the annals of the Post Office ' — was drawing to a close. 'What Orestes and Pylades ever wrote to each other for four-and-

forty years without meeting?' Walpole asks.
In June. 1786, however. the last letter of the
eight hundred and nine specimens printed by
Cunningham was despatched to Florence.[1]   In
the following November, Mann died, after a
prolonged illness.   He had never visited England. nor had Walpole set eyes upon him since
he had left him at Florence in May, 1741.
His death followed hard upon that of another
faithful friend (whose gifts, perhaps, hardly
lay in the epistolary line),—bustling, kindly
Kitty Clive.   Her cheerful, ruddy face, 'all
sun and vermilion,' set peacefully in December, 1785, leaving Cliveden vacant, not, as we
shall see, for long.[2]   Earlier still had departed

[1] Walpole, as in the case of Madame du Deffand, had
taken the precaution of getting back his letters, and at
his friend's death not more than a dozen of them were
still in Mann's possession.   According to Cunningham
(*Corr.*, ix. xv), Mann's letters to Walpole are 'absolutely
unreadable.'   An attempt to skim the cream of them
(such as it is) was made by Dr. Doran in two volumes
entitled '*Mann' and Manners at the Court of Florence,*
1740-1786, Bentley, 1876.

[2] Mrs. Clive is buried at Twickenham, where a mural
slab was erected to her in the parish church by her
protégée and successor, Miss Jane Pope, the clever actress
who shed tears over the Beauclerk drawings (see p. 244).
Her portrait by Davison, which is engraved as the frontispiece to Cunningham's fourth volume, hung in the

another old ally, Cole, the antiquary, and the
lapse of time had in other ways contracted
Walpole's circle.   In 1781, Lady Orford had
ended her erratic career at Pisa, leaving her
son a fortune so considerable as to make his
uncle regret vaguely that the sale of the
Houghton pictures had not been delayed for
a few months longer.   Three years later, she
was followed by her brother-in-law, Sir Edward
Walpole, — an occurrence which had the effect
of leaving between Horace Walpole and his
father's title nothing but his lunatic and child-
less nephew.

If his relatives and friends were falling
away, however, their places — the places of the
friends, at least — were speedily filled again ;
and, as a general rule, most of his male favourites were replaced by women.   Pinkerton,
the antiquary, who afterwards published the
Walpoliana, is one of the exceptions ; and
several of Walpole's letters to him are contained in that book, and in the volumes of
Pinkerton's own correspondence published by
Dawson Turner in 1830.   But Walpole's appe-
tite for correspondence of the purely literary
kind had somewhat slackened in his old age,

Round Bedchamber at Strawberry.   It was given to
Walpole by her brother, James Raftor.

and it was to the other sex that he turned for sympathy and solace. He liked them best ; his style suited them ; and he wrote to them with most ease. In July, 1785, he was visited at Strawberry by Madame de Genlis, who arrived with her friend Miss Wilkes and the famous Pamela,[1] afterwards Lady Edward Fitzgerald. Madame de Genlis at this date was nearing forty, and had lost much of her good looks. But Walpole seems to have found her less *précieuse* and affected than he had anticipated, and she was, on this occasion, unaccompanied by the inevitable harp. A later visit was from Dr. Burney and his daughter Fanny, — ' Evelina-Cecilia ' Walpole calls her, — a young lady for whose good sense and modesty he expresses a genuine admiration. Miss Burney had not as yet entered upon that court bondage which was to be so little to her advantage. Another and more intimate

---

[1] ' Whom she [Madame de Genlis] has educated to be very like herself in the face,' says Walpole, referring to a then current scandal. At this date, however, it is but just to add that the recent investigations of Mr. J. G. Alger, as embodied in vol. xix. of the *Dictionary of National Biography*, tend to show that it is by no means certain that Pamela was the daughter of the accomplished lady whom Philippe *Egalité* entrusted with the education of his sons.

acquaintanceship of this period was with Miss Burney's friend, Hannah More. Hannah More ultimately became one of Walpole's correspondents, although scarcely ' so corresponding' as he wished ; and they met frequently in society when she visited London. On her side, she seems to have been wholly fascinated by his wit and conversational powers ; he, on his, was attracted by her mingled puritanism and vivacity. He writes to her as ' St. Hannah ; ' and she, in return, sighs plaintively over his lack of religion. Yet (she adds) she ' must do him the justice to say, that except the delight he has in teasing me for what he calls over-strictness, I have never heard a sentence from him which savoured of infidelity.'[1]   He evidently took a great interest in her works, and indeed in 1789 printed at his press one of her poems, *Bonner's Ghost.*[2]

[1] He is not explicit as to his creed. 'Atheism I dislike,' he said to Pinkerton. ' It is gloomy, uncomfortable ; and, in my eye, unnatural and irrational. It certainly requires more credulity to believe that there is no God, than to believe that there is ' (*Walpoliana*, i. 75-6). But Pinkerton must be taken with caution. (Cf. *Quarterly Review*, 1843, lxxii. 551.)

[2] In 1786 she had dedicated to him her *Florio, A Tale*, etc., with a highly complimentary Preface, in which she says : 'I should be unjust to your very engaging and

Hannah More.

His friendship for her endured for the remainder of his life ; and not long before his death he presented her with a richly bound copy of Bishop Wilson's *Bible*, with a complimentary inscription which may be read in the second volume of her Life and Correspondence.

It was, however, neither the author of *Evelina* nor the author of *The Manners of the Great* who was destined to fill the void created by the death of Madame du Deffand. In the winter of 1787–8, he had first seen, and a year later he made the formal acquaintance of, 'two young ladies of the name of Berry.' They had a story. Their father, at this time a widower, had married for love, and had afterwards been supplanted in the good graces of a rich uncle by a younger brother who had the generosity to allow him an annuity of a thousand a year. In 1783, Mr. Berry had taken his daughters abroad to Holland, Switzerland, and Italy, whence, in June, 1785, they had returned, being then highly cultivated and attractive young women of two-and-twenty and one-and-twenty respectively. Three years later, Walpole met

well-bred turn of wit, if I did not declare that, among all the lively and brilliant things I have heard from you, I do not remember ever to have heard an unkind or an ungenerous one.'

them for the second time at the house of a Lady
Herries, the wife of a banker in St. James's
Street.   The first time he saw them he ' would
not be acquainted with them, having heard so
much in their praise that he concluded they
would be all pretension.'   But on the second
occasion, ' in a very small company,' he sat next
the elder, Mary, ' and found her an angel both
inside and out.'   ' Her face ' — he tells Lady
Ossory — ' is formed for a sentimental novel,
but it is ten times fitter for a fifty times better
thing, genteel comedy.'   The other sister was
speedily discovered to be nearly as charming.
· They are exceedingly sensible, entirely natural
and unaffected, frank, and, being qualified to
talk on any subject, nothing is so easy and agreeable as their conversation, nor more apposite
than their answers and observations.   The eldest,
I discovered by chance, understands Latin, and
is a perfect Frenchwoman in her language.   The
younger draws charmingly, and has copied
admirably Lady Di.'s gipsies,[1] which I lent,
though for the first time of her attempting
colours.   They are of pleasing figures : Mary,

<hr>

[1] This (we are told) was Lady Di.'s *chef-d'œuvre*.   It
was a water-colour drawing representing ' Gipsies telling
a country-maiden her fortune at the entrance of a beech-
wood,' and hung in the Red Bedchamber at Strawberry.

the eldest, sweet, with fine dark eyes that are very lively when she speaks, with a symmetry of face that is the more interesting from being pale ; Agnes, the younger, has an agreeable, sensible countenance, hardly to be called handsome, but almost. She is less animated than Mary, but seems, out of deference to her sister, to speak seldomer ; for they dote on each other, and Mary is always praising her sister's talents. I must even tell you they dress within the bounds of fashion, though fashionably ; but without the excrescences and balconies with which modern hoydens overwhelm and barricade their persons. In short, good sense, information, simplicity, and ease characterize the Berrys ; and this is not particularly mine, who am apt to be prejudiced, but the universal voice of all who know them.'[1]

'This delightful family,' he goes on to say. 'comes to me almost every Sunday evening. [They were at the time living on Twickenham Common.] Of the father not much is recorded beyond the fact that he was 'a little merry man with a round face,' and (as his eldest daughter reports) 'an odd inherent easiness in his disposition,' who seems to have been perfectly contented in his modest and unobtrusive char-

[1] *Walpole to Lady Ossory*, 11 Oct., 1788.

acter of paternal appendage to the favourites. Walpole's attachment to his new friends grew rapidly. Only a few days after the date of the foregoing letter, Mr. Kirgate's press was versifying in their honour, and they themselves were already ' his two Straw Berries,' whose praises he sang to all his friends. He delighted in devising new titles for them, — they were his ' twin wives,' his ' dear Both,' his ' Amours.' For them in this year he began writing the charming little volume of *Reminiscences of the Courts of George the 1st and 2nd*, and in December, 1789, he dedicated to them his *Catalogue of Strawberry Hill*. It was not long before he had secured them a home at Teddington and finally, when, in 1791, Cliveden became vacant, he prevailed upon them to become his neighbours. He afterwards bequeathed the house to them, and for many years after his death, it was their summer residence. On either side the acquaintance was advantageous. His friendship at once introduced them to the best and most accomplished fashionable society of their day, while the charm of their ' company, conversation and talents ' must have inexpressibly sweetened and softened what, on his part, had begun to grow more and more a solitary, joyless, and painful old age.

Miss Berry.

His establishment of his 'wives' in his immediate vicinity was not, however, accomplished without difficulty. For a moment some ill-natured newspaper gossip, which attributed the attachment of the Berry family to interested motives, so justly aroused the indignation of the elder sister that the whole arrangement threatened to collapse. But the slight estrangement thus caused soon passed away; and at the close of 1791, they took up their abode in Mrs. Clive's old house, now doubly honoured. On the 5th of the December in the same year, after a fresh fit of frenzy, Walpole's nephew died, and he became fourth Earl of Orford. The new dignity was by no means a welcome one, and scarcely compensated for the cares which it entailed. 'A small estate, loaded with debt, and of which I do not understand the management, and am too old to learn; a source of law suits amongst my near relations, though not affecting me; endless conversations with lawyers, and packets of letters to read every day and answer,—all this weight of new business is too much for the rag of life that yet hangs about me. and was preceded by three weeks of anxiety about my unfortunate nephew, and a daily correspondence with physicians and mad-doctors, falling upon me when I had been out

of order ever since July.'[1] 'For the other
empty metamorphosis,' he writes to Hannah
More, ' that has happened to the outward man.
you do me justice in concluding that it can do
nothing but tease me ; it is being called names
in one's old age. I had rather be my Lord
Mayor, for then I should keep the nickname
but a year ; and mine I may retain a little
longer, — not that at seventy-five I reckon on
becoming my Lord Methusalem.'   For some
time he could scarcely bring himself to use his
new signature, and occasionally varied it by
describing himself as ' The uncle of the late
Earl of Orford.'   In 1792, he delivered himself,
after the fashion of Cowley, of the following
Epitaphium vivi Auctoris : —

' An estate and an earldom at seventy-four !
  Had I sought them or wished them, 't would add one
    fear more, —
  That of making a countess when almost four-score.
  But Fortune, who scatters her gifts out of season,
  Though unkind to my limbs, has still left me my reason ;
  And whether she lowers or lifts me, I 'll try,
  In the plain simple style I have lived in, to die :
  For ambition too humble, for manners too high.'

The last line seems like another of the many
echoes of Goldsmith's *Retaliation.* As for the

___

[1] *Walpole to Pinkerton,* 26 Dec., 1791.

fear indicated in the third, it is hinted that this at one time bade fair to be something more than a poetical apprehension. If we are to credit a tradition handed down by Lord Lansdowne, he had been willing to go through the form of marriage with either of the Berrys, merely to secure their society, and to enrich them, as he had the power of charging the Orford estate with a jointure of £2000 per annum. But this can only have been a passing thought at some moment when their absence, in Italy or elsewhere, left him more sensitive to the loss of their gracious and stimulating presence. He himself was far too keenly alive to ridicule, and too much in bondage to *les bienséances*, to take a step which could scarcely escape ill-natured comment ; and Mary Berry, who would certainly have been his preference, was not only as fully alive as was he to the shafts of the censorious, but, during the greater part of her acquaintanceship with him, was, apparently with his knowledge, warmly attached to a certain good-looking General O'Hara, who, a year before Walpole's death, in November, 1796, definitely proposed. He had just been appointed Governor of Gibraltar, and he wished Miss Berry to marry him at once, and go out with him. This, ' out of con-

sideration for others,' she declined to do. A
few months later the engagement was broken
off, and she never again saw her soldier admirer.
Whether Lord Orford's comfort went for anything in this adjournment of her happiness, does
not clearly **appear**; but it is only reasonable to
suppose that his tenacious desire **for** her com-
panionship had its influence in a decision which,
however much it may have been for the best
(and there were those of her friends who regarded it as a providential escape), was nevertheless a lifelong source of regret to herself.
When, in 1802, she heard suddenly at the
Opera of O'Hara's death, she fell senseless to
the floor.

The 'late Horace Walpole' never took his
seat in the House of Lords. He continued,
as before, to divide his time between Berkeley
Square and Strawberry, to eulogize his 'wives'
to Lady Ossory, and to watch life from his
beloved Blue Room. Now and then he did
the rare honours of his home to a distinguished
guest, — in 1793, it was the Duchess of York;
in 1795, Queen Charlotte herself. In the
latter year died his old friend Conway, by
this time a Field-Marshal; and it was evident
at the close of 1796 that his faithful correspondent would not long survive him. His

ailments had increased, and in the following January, he wrote his last letter to Lady Ossory : —

Jan. 15, 1797.

MY DEAR MADAM. —

You distress me infinitely by showing my idle notes, which I cannot conceive can amuse anybody. My old-fashioned breeding impels me every now and then to reply to the letters you honour me with writing, but in truth very unwillingly, for I seldom can have anything particular to say ; I scarce go out of my own house, and then only to two or three very private places, where I see nobody that really knows anything. and what I learn comes from Newspapers, that collect intelligence from coffee-houses, consequently what I neither believe nor report. At home I see only a few charitable elders, except about four-score nephews and nieces of various ages, who are each brought to me about once a-year. to stare at me as the Methusalem of the family. and they can only speak of their own contemporaries, which interest me no more than if they talked of their dolls. or bats and balls. Must not the result of all this, Madam, make me a very entertaining correspondent ? And can such letters be worth showing ? or can I have any spirit when so old, and reduced to dictate?

Oh! my good Madam, dispense with me from such a task, and think how it must add to it to apprehend such letters being shown. Pray send me no more such laurels, which I desire no more than their leaves when decked with a scrap of tinsel, and stuck on twelfth-cakes that lie on the shop-boards of pastry-cooks at Christmas. I shall be quite content with a sprig of rosemary thrown after me, when the parson of the parish commits my dust to dust. Till then, pray, Madam, accept the resignation of your

Ancient servant,

ORFORD.

Six weeks after the date of the above letter, he died at his house in Berkeley Square, to which he had been moved at the close of the previous year. During the latter days of his life, he suffered from a cruel lapse of memory, which led him to suppose himself neglected even by those who had but just quitted him. He sank gradually, and expired without pain on the 2nd of March, 1797, being then in his eightieth year. He was buried at the family seat of Houghton.

His fortune, over and above his leases, amounted to ninety-one thousand pounds. To each of the Miss Berrys he left the sum of £4000 for their lives, together with the house and garden of ' Little Strawberry ' (Cliveden), the long meadow in front of it, and all the furniture. He also bequeathed to them and to their father his printed works and his manuscripts, with discretionary power to publish. It was understood that the real editorship was to fall on the elder sister, who forthwith devoted herself to her task. The result was the edition, in five quarto volumes, of Lord Orford's *Works*, which has been so often referred to during the progress of these pages, and which appeared in 1798. It was entirely due to Mary Berry's unremitting care, her father's share being confined to a final paragraph in the preface, in which she is eulogized.[1]

[1] Mary Berry died 20th Nov., 1852; Agnes Berry, Jan., 1852. They were buried in one grave in Petersham churchyard, ' amidst scenes ' — says Lord Carlisle's inscription — ' which in life they had frequented & loved.' H. F. Chorley (*Autobiography*, etc., 1873, vol. i., p. 276) describes them as ' more like one's notion of ancient Frenchwomen than anything I have ever seen ; rouged, with the remains of some beauty, managing large fans like the Flirtillas, etc., etc., of Ranelagh.' See also *Extracts from Miss Berry's Journals and Correspondence*, 1783-1852, edited by Lady Theresa Lewis, 1865.

Strawberry Hill passed to Mrs. Damer for life, together with £2000 to keep it in repair. After living in it for some years, she resigned it, in 1811, to the Countess Dowager of Waldegrave, in whom the remainder in fee was vested. It subsequently passed to George, seventh Earl of Waldegrave, who sold its contents in 1842. At his death, in 1846, he left it to his widow, Frances, Countess of Waldegrave, who subsequently married the Rt. Hon. Chichester S. Parkinson-Fortescue, now Lord Carlingford. Lady Waldegrave died in 1879 ; but she had greatly added to and extended the original building, besides restoring many of the objects by which it had been decorated in Walpole's day.

CHAPTER X.

Macaulay on Walpole. — Effect of the *Edinburgh* Essay. — Macaulay and Mary Berry. — Portraits of Walpole. — Miss Hawkins's Description. — Pinkerton's Rainy Day at Strawberry. — Walpole's Character as a Man ; as a Virtuoso ; as a Politician ; as an Author and Letter-writer.

WHEN, in October, 1833, Lord (then Mr.) Macaulay completed for the *Edinburgh* his review of Lord Dover's edition of Walpole's letters to Sir Horace Mann, he had apparently performed to his entire satisfaction the operation known, in the workmanlike vocabulary of the time, as ' dusting the jacket ' of his unfortunate reviewee. ' I was up at four this morning to put the last touch to it,' he tells his sister Hannah. ' I often differ with the majority about other people's writings, and still oftener about my own ; and therefore I may very likely be mistaken ; but I think that this article will be a hit. . . . Nothing ever cost me more pains than the first half ; I never wrote anything so flowingly as the latter half ; and I like the latter half the best. [The latter half, it should

be stated, was a rapid and very brilliant sketch
of Sir Robert Walpole ; the earlier, which
involved so much labour, was the portrait of
Sir Robert's youngest son.] I have laid it on
Walpole [*i. e.*, Horace Walpole] so unsparingly,' he goes on to say, ' that I shall not be
surprised if Miss Berry should cut me. . . .
Neither am I sure that Lord and Lady Holland
will be well pleased.' [1]

His later letters show him to have been a
true prophet. Macvey Napier, then the editor
of the ' Blue and Yellow,' was enthusiastic,
praising the article ' in terms absolutely extravagant.' ' He says that it is the best that I
ever wrote,' the critic tells his favourite correspondent. — a statement which at this date must
be qualified by the fact that he penned some
of his most famous essays subsequent to its
appearance. On the other hand, Miss Berry
resented the review so much that Sir Stratford
Canning advised its author not to go near her.
But apparently her anger was soon dispelled.
for the same letter which makes this announcement relates that she was already appeased.
Lady Holland, too, was ' in a rage,' though
with what part of the article does not transpire,
while her good-natured husband told Macaulay

[1] Trevelyan's *Life and Letters of Lord Macaulay*, ch. v.

privately that he quite agreed with him. but that they had better not discuss the subject. Lady Holland's irritation was probably prompted by her intimacy with the Waldegrave family, to whom the letters edited by Lord Dover belonged, and for whose benefit they were published. But, as Macaulay said justly, his article was surely not calculated to injure the sale of the book. Her imperious ladyship's displeasure, however, like that of Miss Berry, was of brief duration. Macaulay was too necessary to her *réunions* to be long exiled from her little court.

Among those who occupy themselves in such enquiries, it has been matter for speculation what particular grudge Macaulay could have cherished against Horace Walpole when, to use his own expression, he laid it on him ' so unsparingly.' To this his correspondence affords no clue. Mr. Cunningham holds that he did it ' to revenge the dislike which Walpole bore to the Bedford faction, the followers of Fox and the Shelburne school.' It is possible, as another authority has suggested, that ' in the Whig circles of Macaulay's time, there existed a traditional grudge against Horace Walpole,' owing to obscure political causes connected with his influence over his friend

Conway. But these reasons do not seem relevant enough to make Macaulay's famous onslaught a mere *vendetta.* It is more reasonable to suppose that between his avowed delight in Walpole as a letter-writer, and his robust contempt for him as an individual, he found a subject to his hand, which admitted of all the brilliant antithesis and sparkle of epigram which he lavished upon it. Walpole's trivialities and eccentricities, his whims and affectations, are seized with remorseless skill, and presented with all the rhetorical advantages with which the writer so well knew how to invest them. As regards his literary estimate, the truth of the picture can scarcely be gainsaid ; but the personal character, as Walpole's surviving friends felt, is certainly too much *en noir.* Miss Berry, indeed, in her ' Advertisement ' to vol. vi. of Wright's edition of the *Letters,* raised a gentle cry of expostulation against the entire representation. She laid stress upon the fact that Macaulay had not known Walpole in the flesh (a disqualification to which too much weight may easily be assigned) ; she dwelt upon the warmth of Walpole's attachments ; she contested the charge of affectation ; and, in short, made such a gallant attempt at a defence as her loyalty

Lord Macaulay.

to her old friend enabled her to offer. Yet, if Macaulay had never known Walpole at all, she herself, it might be urged, had only known him in his old age. Upon the whole, 'with due allowance for a spice of critical pepper on one hand, and a handful of friendly rosemary on the other,' as Croker says, both characters are 'substantially true.' Under Macaulay's brush Walpole is depicted as he appeared to that critic's masculine and (for the nonce) unsympathetic spirit ; in Miss Berry's picture, the likeness is touched with a pencil at once grateful, affectionate, and indulgent. The biographer of to-day who is neither endeavouring to portray Walpole in his most favourable aspect, nor preoccupied (as Cunningham supposed the great Whig essayist to have been) with what would be thought of his work ' at Woburn, at Kensington, and in Berkeley Square,' may safely borrow details from the delineation of either artist.

Of portraits of Walpole (not in words) there is no lack. Besides that belonging to Mrs. Bedford, described at p. 11, there is the enamel by Zincke painted in 1745, which is reproduced at p. 71 of vol. i. of Cunningham's edition of the letters. There is another portrait of him by Nathaniel Hone, R.A., in the National

Portrait Gallery.   A more characteristic present-
ment than any of these is the little drawing by
Müntz which shows his patron sitting in the
Library at Strawberry, with the Thames and a
passing barge seen through the open window.
But his most interesting portraits are two which
exhibit him in manhood and old age.   One is
the half-length by J. G. Eckardt which once
hung in its black-and-gold frame in the Blue
Bedchamber, near the companion pictures of
Gray and Bentley.[1]   Like these, it was 'from
Vandyck,' that is to say, it was in a costume
copied from that painter, and depicts the sitter
in a laced collar and ruffles, leaning upon a copy
of the *Ædes Walpolianæ*, with a view of part
of the Gothic castle in the distance.   The
canvas bears at the back the date of 1754, so
that it represents him at the age of seven-and-
thirty.   The shaven face is rather lean than thin,
the forehead high, the brown hair brushed back
and slightly curled.   The eyes are dark, bright,
and intelligent, and the small mouth wears a
slight smile.   The other, a drawing made for
Samuel Lysons by Sir Thomas Lawrence, is that
of a much older man, having been executed in

---

[1] This is engraved in vol. ix. of Cunningham, facing
the Index; while the Müntz, above referred to, forms the
frontispiece to vol. viii.

1796. The eyelids droop wearily, the thin lips have a pinched, mechanical urbanity, and the features are worn by years and ill-health. It was reproduced by T. Evans as a frontispiece for vol. i. of his works. There are other portraits by Reynolds, 1757 (which McArdell and Reading engraved), by Rosalba, Falconet, and Dance ;[1] but it is sufficient to have indicated those mentioned above.

Of the Walpole of later years there are more descriptions than one, and among these, that given by Miss Hawkins, the daughter of the pompous author of the *History of Music*, is, if the most familiar, also the most graphic. Sir John Hawkins was Walpole's neighbour at Twickenham House, and the *History* is said to have been undertaken at Walpole's instance. Miss Hawkins's description is of Walpole as she recalled him before 1772. ' His figure,' she says, ' . . . was not merely tall, but more properly *long* and slender to excess ; his complexion, and particularly his hands, of a most

---

[1] The writer of the obituary notice in the *Gentleman's Magazine* for March, 1797, says that Dance's portrait is 'the only faithful representation of him [Walpole].' Against this must be set the fact that it was not selected by the editor of his works ; and, besides being in profile, it is certainly far less pleasing than the Lawrence.

unhealthy paleness. . . . His eyes were remark-
ably bright and penetrating, very dark and
lively ; his voice was not strong, but his tones
were extremely pleasant, and, if I may so say,
highly gentlemanly.   I do not remember his
common gait ;[1] he always entered a room in
that style of affected delicacy, which fashion
had then made almost natural, — *chapeau bras*
between his hands as if he wished to compress
it, or under his arm, knees bent, and feet on
tip-toe, as if afraid of a wet floor.   His dress
in visiting was most usually, in summer when I
most saw him, a lavender suit, the waistcoat
embroidered with a little silver, or of white silk
worked in the tambour, partridge silk stockings,
and gold buckles, ruffles and frill generally lace.
I remember when a child, thinking him very
much under-dressed if at any time, except in
mourning, he wore hemmed cambric.   In summer no powder, but his wig combed straight,
and showing his very smooth pale forehead, and
queued behind ; in winter powder.'[2]

[1] It must, by his own account, have been peculiar.
' Walking is not one of my excellences,' he writes.   ' In my
best days Mr. Winnington said I tripped like a peewit ;
and if I do not flatter myself, my march at present is more
like a dabchick's ' (*Walpole to Lady Ossory*, 18 August,
1775).
[2] *Anecdotes, etc.*, by L. M. Hawkins, 1822, pp. 105-6.

Pinkerton, who knew Walpole from 1784 until his death, and whose disappointment of a legacy is supposed, in places, to have mingled a more than justifiable amount of gall with his ink, has nevertheless left a number of interesting particulars respecting his habits and personal characteristics. They are too long to quote entire, but are, at the same time, too picturesque to be greatly compressed. He contradicts Miss Hawkins in one respect, for he says Walpole was 'short and slender,' but 'compact and neatly formed,'—an account which is confirmed by Müntz's full-length. 'When viewed from behind, he had somewhat of a boyish appearance, owing to the form of his person, and the simplicity of his dress.' None of his pictures, says Pinkerton, 'express the placid goodness of his eyes,[1] which would often sparkle with sudden rays of wit, or dart forth flashes of the most keen and intuitive intelligence. His laugh was forced and uncouth, and even his smile not the most pleasing.'

[1] 'I have lately become acquainted with your friend Mr. Walpole, and am quite charmed with him,'—writes Malone to Lord Charlemont in 1782. 'There is an unaffected benignity and good nature in his manner that is, I think, irresistibly engaging' (*Hist. MSS. Commission, 12th Rept., App.*, Pt. x., 1891, p. 395).

'His walk was enfeebled by the gout; which, if the editor's memory do not deceive, he mentioned that he had been tormented with since the age of twenty-five; adding, at the same time, that it was no hereditary complaint, his father, Sir Robert Walpole, who always drank ale, never having known that disorder, and far less his other parent. This painful complaint not only affected his feet, but attacked his hands to such a degree that his fingers were always swelled and deformed, and discharged large chalk-stones once or twice a year; upon which occasions he would observe, with a smile, that he must set up an inn, for he could chalk up a score with more ease and rapidity than any man in England.'

After referring to the strict temperance of his life, Pinkerton goes on : —

'Though he sat up very late, either writing or conversing, he generally rose about nine o'clock, and appeared in the breakfast room, his constant and chosen apartment, with fine vistos towards the Thames. His approach was proclaimed, and attended, by a favourite little dog, the legacy of the Marquise du Deffand,[1] and which ease and attention had

[1] Tonton. See note to p. 250.

rendered so fat that it could hardly move. This was placed beside him on a small sofa; the tea-kettle, stand, and heater were brought in, and he drank two or three cups of that liquor out of most rare and precious ancient procelain of Japan, of a fine white, embossed with large leaves. The account of his china cabinet, in his description of his villa, will show how rich he was in that elegant luxury. . . . The loaf and butter were not spared, . . . and the dog and the squirrels had a liberal share of his repast.[1]

'Dinner [his hour for which was four] was served up in the small parlour, or large dining room, as it happened : in winter generally the former. His valet supported him downstairs;[2] and he ate most moderately of chicken, pheasant, or any light food. Pastry he disliked, as difficult of digestion, though he would taste a morsel of venison pye. Never, but once that

[1] Another passage in the *Walpoliana* (i. 71-2) explains this : ' Regularly after breakfast, in the summer season, at least, Mr. Walpole used to mix bread and milk in a large bason, and throw it out at the window of the sitting-room, for the squirrels ; who, soon after, came down from the high trees, to enjoy their allowance.'

[2] ' I cannot go up or down stairs without being led by a servant. It is *tempus abire* for me : *lusi satis* ' (*Walpole to Pinkerton*, 15 May, 1794).

he drank two glasses of white-wine, did the editor see him taste any liquor, except ice-water. A pail of ice was placed under the table, in which stood a decanter of water, from which he supplied himself with his favourite beverage. . . .

'If his guest liked even a moderate quantity of wine, he must have called for it during dinner, for almost instantly after he rang the bell to order coffee upstairs. Thither he would pass about five o'clock ; and generally resuming his place on the sofa, would sit till two o'clock in the morning, in miscellaneous chit-chat, full of singular anecdotes, strokes of wit, and acute observations, occasionally sending for books or curiosities, or passing to the library, as any reference happened to arise in conversation. After his coffee he tasted nothing ; but the snuff box of *tabac d'étrennes* from Fribourg's was not forgotten, and was replenished from a canister lodged in an ancient marble urn of great thickness, which stood in the window seat, and served to secure its moisture and rich flavour.

'Such was a private rainy day of Horace Walpole. The forenoon quickly passed in roaming through the numerous apartments of the house, in which, after twenty visits, still something new would occur ; and he was indeed constantly adding fresh acquisitions. Sometimes a walk in the grounds would intervene, on which occasions he would go out in his slippers through a thick dew ; and he never wore a hat. He said that, on his first visit to Paris, he was ashamed of his effeminacy, when he saw every little meagre Frenchman, whom even he could have thrown down with a breath, walking without a hat, which he could not do, without a certainty of that disease, which the Germans say is endemial in England, and is termed by the natives *le-catch-cold.*[1] The first trial cost him a slight fever, but he got over it, and never caught cold afterwards : draughts of air, damp rooms, windows open at his back, all situations were alike to him in this respect. He would even show some little offence at any solicitude, expressed by his guests on such an occasion, as an idea arising from the seeming tenderness of his frame ; and would say, with a half smile of good-humoured crossness, " My back is the same with my face, and my neck is like my

---

[1] 'I have persisted'— he tells Gray from Paris in January, 1766 —'through this Siberian winter in not adding a grain to my clothes and in going open-breasted without an under waistcoat.'

nose." [1]   His iced water he not only regarded as a preservative from such an accident, but he would sometimes observe that he thought his stomach and bowels would last longer than his bones ; such conscious vigour and strength in those parts did he feel from the use of that beverage.' [2]

The only particular that Cunningham adds to this chronicle of his habits is one too characteristic of the man to be omitted.   After dinner at Strawberry, he says, the smell was removed by ' a censer or pot of frankincense.'   According to the *Description*, etc., there was a tripod of ormoulu kept in the Breakfast Room for this purpose.   It is difficult to identify the ' ancient marble urn of great thickness ' in which the snuff was stored ; but it may have been that ' of granite, brought from one of the Greek Islands, and given to Sir Robert Walpole by Sir Charles Wager,' which also figures in the Catalogue.

Walpole's character may be considered in a

[1] He was probably thinking of *Spectator*, No. 228 : ' The *Indian* answered very well to an *European*, who asked him how he could go naked : I am all Face.' Lord Chesterfield wished his little godson to have the same advantage.   ' I am very willing that he should be *all face*,' he says in a letter to Arthur Stanhope of 19th October, 1762.

[2] *Walpoliana*, i. xi-xiv.

fourfold aspect, as a man, a virtuoso, a politician, and an author. The first is the least easy to describe. What strikes one most forcibly is, that he was primarily and before all an aristocrat, or, as in his own day he would have been called, a ' person of quality,' whose warmest sympathies were reserved for those of his own rank. Out of the charmed circle of the peerage and baronetage, he had few strong connections ; and although in middle life he corresponded voluminously with antiquaries such as Cole and Zouch, and in the languor of his old age turned eagerly to the renovating society of young women such as Hannah More and the Miss Berrys, however high his heart may have placed them, it may be doubted whether his head ever quite exalted them to the level of Lady Caroline Petersham, or Lady Ossory, or Her Grace of Gloucester. In a measure, this would also account for his unsympathetic attitude to some of the great *literati* of his day. With Gray he had been at school and college, which made a difference ; but he no doubt regarded Fielding and Hogarth and Goldsmith and Johnson, apart from their confessed hostility to ' high life ' and his beloved ' genteel comedy,' as gifted but undesirable outsiders, — ' horn-handed breakers of the glebe ' in Art and Letters, — with whom it

would be impossible to be as intimately familiar
as one could be with such glorified amateurs as
Bunbury and Lady Lucan and Lady Di. Beauclerk, who were all more or less born in the
purple. To the friends of his own class he was
constant and considerate. and he seems to have
cherished a genuine affection for Conway,
George Montagu, and Sir Horace Mann. With
regard to Gray, his relations, it would seem,
were rather those of intellectual affinity and
esteem than downright affection. But his closest
friends were women. In them, that is, in the
women of his time, he found just that atmos-
phere of sunshine and *insouciance*, — those conversational ' lilacs and nightingales,' — in which
his soul delighted, and which were most congenial to his restless intelligence and easily
fatigued temperament. To have seen him at
his best, one should have listened to him, not
when he was playing the antiquary with Ducarel
or Conyers Middleton, but gossipping of ancient
green-room scandals at Cliveden, or explaining
the mysteries of the ' Officina Arbuteana ' to
Madame de Boufflers or Lady Townshend, or
delighting Mary and Agnes Berry. in the half-
light of the Round Drawing Room at Strawberry, with his old stories of Lady Suffolk and
Lady Hervey, and of the monstrous raven, under

guise of which the disembodied spirit of His Majesty King George the First was supposed to have revisited the disconsolate Duchess of Kendal. Comprehending thoroughly that cardinal precept of conversation, — ' never to weary your hearer,' — he was an admirable *raconteur;* and his excellent memory, shrewd perceptions, and volatile wit — all the more piquant for its never-failing mixture of well-bred malice — must have made him a most captivating companion. If, as Scott says, his temper was ' precarious,' it is more charitable to remember that in middle and later life he was nearly always tormented with a malady seldom favourable to good humour, than to explain the less amiable details of his conduct (as does Mr. Croker) by the hereditary taint of insanity. In a life of eighty years many hot friendships cool, even with tempers not ' precarious.' As regards the charges sometimes made against him of coldness and want of generosity, very good evidence would be required before they could be held to be established ; and a man is not necessarily niggardly because his benefactions do not come up to the standard of all the predatory members of the community. It is besides clear, as Conway and Madame du Deffand would have testified, that he could be royally generous when necessity required. That he was careful rather than lavish in his expenditure must be admitted. It may be added that he was very much in bondage to public opinion, and morbidly sensitive to ridicule.

As a virtuoso and amateur, his position is a mixed one. He was certainly widely different from that typical art connoisseur of his day,— the butt of Goldsmith and of Reynolds, — who travelled the Grand Tour to litter a gallery at home with broken-nosed busts and the rubbish of the Roman picture-factories. As the preface to the *Ædes Walpolianæ* showed, he really knew something about painting, in fact was a capable draughtsman himself; and besides, through Mann and others, had enjoyed exceptional opportunities for procuring genuine antiques. But his collection was not so rich in this way as might have been anticipated ; and his portraits, his china, and his miniatures were probably his best possessions. For the rest, he was an indiscriminate rather than an eclectic collector ; and there was also considerable truth in that strange ' attraction from the great to the little, and from the useful to the odd,' which Macaulay has noted. Many of the marvels at Strawberry would never have found a place in the treasure-houses — say of Beckford or Samuel Rogers.

It is difficult to fancy Bermingham's fables in paper on looking-glass, or Hubert's cardcuttings, or the fragile mosaics of Mrs. Delany either at Fonthill or St. James's Place. At the same time, it should be remembered that several of the most trivial or least defensible objects were presents which possibly reflected rather the charity of the recipient than the good taste of the giver. All the articles over which Macaulay lingers — Wolsey's hat, Van Tromp's pipe-case, and King William's spurs — were obtained in this way ; and (with a laugher) Horace Walpole, who laughed a good deal himself, would probably have made as merry as the most mirth-loving spectator could have desired. But such items gave a heterogeneous character to the gathering, and turned what might have been a model museum into an old curiosity-shop. In any case, however, it was a memorable curiosity-shop, and in this modern era of *bric-à-brac* would probably attract far more serious attention than it did in those practical and pre-æsthetic days of 1842, when it fell under the hammer of George Robins.[1]

[1] See Mr. Robins's *Catalogue of the Classic Contents of Strawberry Hill*, etc. (1842), 4to. It is compiled in his well-known grandiloquent manner ; but includes an account of the Castle by Harrison Ainsworth, together with

Walpole's record as a politician is a brief one, and if his influence upon the questions of his time was of any importance, it must have been exercised unobtrusively. During the period of the 'great Walpolean battle,' as Junius styled the struggle that culminated in the downfall of Lord Orford, he was a fairly regular attendant in the House of Commons ; and, as we have seen, spoke in his father's behalf when the motion was made for an enquiry into his conduct. Nine years later, he moved the address, and a few years later still, delivered a speech upon the employment of Swiss Regiments in the Colonies. Finally he resigned his ' senatorial dignity,' quitting the scene with the valediction of those who depreciate what they no longer desire to retain. ' What could I see but sons and grandsons playing over the same knaveries, that I have seen their fathers and grandfathers act ? Could I hear oratory beyond my Lord Chatham's ? Will there ever be parts equal to Charles Townshend's ? Will George Grenville cease to be the most tiresome of beings ?'[1] In his earlier days he was a violent Whig, — ' at

many interesting details. It gave rise to a humorous squib by Crofton Croker, entitled *Gooseberry Hall*, with ' Puffatory Remarks,' and cuts.

[1] *Walpole to Montagu*, 12 March, 1768.

times almost a Republican' (to which latter phase of his opinions must be attributed the transformation of King Charles's death-warrant into ' Major Charta ') ; ' in his old and enfeebled age,' says Miss Berry, ' the horrors of the first French Revolution made him a Tory ; while he always lamented, as one of the worst effects of its excesses, that they must necessarily retard to a distant period the progress and establishment of religious liberty.' He deplored the American War, and disapproved the Slave Trade ; but, in sum, it is to be suspected that his main interest in politics, after his father's death, and apart from the preservation throughout an ' age of small factions ' of his own uncertain sinecures, was the good and ill fortune of the handsome and amiable, but moderately eminent statesman, General Conway. It was for Conway that he took his most active steps in the direction of political intrigue ; and perhaps his most important political utterance is the *Counter Address to the Public on the late Dismission of a General Officer*, which was prompted by Conway's deprivation of his command for voting in the opposition with himself in the debate upon the illegality of general warrants. Whether he would have taken office if it had been offered to him, may be a question :

but his attitude, as disclosed by his letters, is a rather hesitating *nolo episcopari.* The most interesting result of his connection with public affairs is the series of sketches of political men dispersed through his correspondence, and through the posthumous *Memoirs* published by Lord Holland and Sir Denis Le Marchant. Making every allowance for his prejudices and partisanship (and of neither can Walpole be acquitted), it is impossible not to regard these latter as highly important contributions to historical literature. Even Mr. Croker admits that they contain ' a considerable portion of voluntary or involuntary truth ; ' and such an admission, when extorted from Lord Beaconsfield's ' Rigby,' of whom no one can justly say that he was ignorant of the politics of Walpole's day, has all the weight which attaches to a testimonial from the enemy.[1]

---

[1] The full titles of these memoirs are *Memoires of the last Ten Years of the Reign of King George II.* Edited by Lord Holland. 2 vols. 4to., 1822 ; and *Memoirs of the Reign of King George III.* Edited, with Notes, by Sir Denis Le Marchant, Bart. 4 vols. 8vo., 1845. Both were reviewed, *more suo*, by Mr. Croker in the *Quarterly*, with the main intention of proving that all Walpole's pictures of his contemporaries were coloured and distorted by successive disappointments arising out of his solicitude concerning the patent places from which he derived his

This mention of the *Memoirs* naturally leads us to that final consideration, the position of Walpole as an author. Most of the productions which fill the five bulky volumes given to the world in 1798 by Miss Berry's pious care have been referred to in the course of the foregoing pages, and it is not necessary to recapitulate them here. The place which they occupy in English literature was never a large one, and it has grown smaller with lapse of time. Walpole, in truth, never took letters with sufficient seriousness. He was willing enough to obtain repute, but upon condition that he should be allowed to despise his calling and

income,— in other words (Mr. Croker's words !), that 'the whole is "a copious polyglot of spleen."' Such an investigation was in the favourite line of the critic, and might be expected to result in a formidable indictment. But the best judges hold it to have been exaggerated, and to-day the method of Mr. Croker is more or less discredited. Indeed, it is an instance of those quaint revenges of the whirligig of Time, that some of his utterances are really more applicable to himself than to Walpole. 'His [Walpole's] natural inclination [says Croker] was to grope an obscure way through mazes and *souterrains* rather than walk the high road by daylight. He is never satisfied with the plain and obvious cause of any effect, and is for ever striving after some tortuous solution.' This is precisely what unkind modern critics affirm of the Rt. Honourable John Wilson Croker.

laugh at 'thoroughness.' If masterpieces could have been dashed off at a hand-gallop; if antiquarian studies could have been made of permanent value by the exercise of mere elegant facility; if a dramatic reputation could have been secured by the simple accumulation of horrors upon Horror's head, — his might have been a great literary name. But it is not thus the severer Muses are cultivated ; and Walpole's mood was too variable, his indstry too intermittent, his fine-gentleman self-consciousness too inveterate, to admit of his producing anything that (as one of his critics has said) deserves a higher title than '*opuscula*.' His essays in the *World* lead one to think that he might have made a more than respectable essayist, if he had not fallen upon days in which that form of writing was practically outworn ; and it is manifest that he would have been an admirable writer of familiar poetry if he could have forgotten the fallacy (exposed by Johnson)[1] that easy verse is easy to write. Nevertheless, in the Gothic romance which was suggested by his Gothic castle — for, to speak paradoxically, Strawberry Hill is almost as much as Walpole the author of the *Castle of Otranto* — he managed to initiate a

[1] *Idler*, No. lxxvii. (6 Oct., 1759).

new form of fiction ; and by decorating 'with gay strings the gatherings of Vertue' he preserved serviceably, in the *Anecdotes of Painting*, a mass of curious, if sometimes uncritical, information which, in other circumstances, must have been hopelessly lost. If anything else of his professed literary work is worthy of recollection, it must be a happy squib such as the *Letter of Xo Ho*, a fable such as *The Entail*, or an essay such as the pamphlet on Landscape Gardening, which even Croker allows to be 'a very elegant history and happy elucidation of that charming art.'[1]

But it is not by his professedly literary work that he has acquired the reputation which he

[1] See Appendix, p. 320. To the advocates of the rival school Walpole's utterance, perhaps inevitably, appears in a less favourable light. 'Horace Walpole published an *Essay on Modern Gardening* in 1785, in which he repeated what other writers had said on the subject. This was at once translated, and had a great circulation on the Continent. The *jardin à l'Anglaise* became the rage; many beautiful old gardens were destroyed in France and elsewhere ; and Scotch and English gardeners were in demand all over Europe to renovate gardens in the English manner. It is not an exhilarating thought that in the one instance in which English taste in a matter of design has taken hold on the Continent, it has done so with such disastrous results' (*The Formal Garden in England*, 2nd edn., 1892, p. 86).

retains and must continue to retain. It is
as a letter-writer that he survives ; and it is
upon the vast correspondence, of which, even
now, we seem scarcely to have reached the
limits, that is based his surest claim *volitare
per ora virum.* The qualities which are his
defects in more serious productions become
merits in his correspondence ; or, rather, they
cease to be defects. No one looks for prolonged effort in a gossipping epistle ; a weighty
reasoning is less important than a light hand ;
and variety pleases more surely than symmetry of structure. Among the little band of
those who have distinguished themselves in
this way, Walpole is in the foremost rank, —
nay, if wit and brilliancy, without gravity or
pathos, are to rank highest, he is first. It
matters nothing whether he wrote easily or
with difficulty ; whether he did, or did not,
make minutes of apt illustrations or descrip-
tive incidents : the result is delightful. For
diversity of interest and perpetual entertainment, for the constant surprises of an unique
species of wit, for happy and unexpected turns
of phrase, for graphic characterization and
clever anecdote, for playfulness, pungency,
irony, persiflage, there is nothing in English
like his correspondence. And when one re-

members that, in addition, this correspondence constitutes a sixty-years' social chronicle of a specially picturesque epoch by one of the most picturesque of picturesque chroniclers, there can be no need to bespeak any further suffrage for Horace Walpole's ' incomparable letters.'

APPENDIX.

BOOKS PRINTED AT THE STRAW-BERRY HILL PRESS.

.*. The following list contains all the books mentioned in the *Description of the Villa of Mr. Horace Walpole*, etc., 1784, together with those issued between that date and Walpole's death. It does *not* include the several title-pages and labels which he printed from time to time, or the quatrains and verses purporting to be addressed by the Press to Lady Rochford, Lady Townshend, Madame de Boufflers, the Miss Berrys, and others. Nor does it comprise the pieces struck off by Mr. Kirgate, the printer, for the benefit of himself and his friends. On the other hand, all the works enumerated here are, with three exceptions, described from copies either in the possession of the present writer, or to be found in the British Museum and the Dyce and Forster Libraries at South Kensington.

1757.

Odes by Mr. Gray. Φωνάντα συνετοῖσι — Pin-
dar, Olymp. II. [Strawberry Hill Bookplate.] *Printed at Strawberry Hill, for R.
and J. Dodsley in Pall-Mall, MDCCLVII.*

> Half-title, 'Odes by Mr. Gray. [Price one Shil-
> ling.]'; Title as above; Text, pp. 5-21. 4to. 1,000
> copies printed. 'June 25th [1757], I erected a
> printing-press at my house at Strawberry Hill.'
> 'Aug. 8th, I published two Odes by Mr. Gray, the
> first production of my press' (*Short Notes*). 'And
> with what do you think we open? *Cedite, Romani
> Impressores,* — with nothing under *Graii Carmina.*
> I found him [Gray] in town last week: he had
> brought his two Odes to be printed. I snatched
> them out of Dodsley's hands' . . . (*Walpole to
> Chute*, 12 July, 1757). 'I send you two copies (one
> for Dr. Cocchi) of a very honourable opening of
> my press, — two amazing Odes of Mr. Gray; they
> are Greek, they are Pindaric, they are sublime!
> consequently, I fear, a little obscure' (*Walpole to
> Mann*, 4 Aug., 1757). 'You are very particular, I
> can tell you, in liking Gray's Odes; but you must
> remember that the age likes Akenside, and did like
> Thomson! Can the same people like both?' (*Wal-
> pole to Montagu*, 25 Aug., 1757).

To Mr. Gray, on his Odes. [By David Garrick.]

> Single leaf, containing six quatrains (24 lines).
> 4to. Only six copies are said to have been printed;

but it is not improbable that there were more.
There is a copy in the Dyce Collection at South
Kensington.

A Journey into England. By Paul Hentzner,
in the year M.D.XC.VIII. [Strawberry
Hill Bookplate.] *Printed at Strawberry-Hill,
MDCCLVII.*

> Title, Dedication (2 leaves); 'Advertisement,'
> i-x; half-title; Latin and English Text on opposite
> pages, 1 to 103 (double numbers). Sm. 8vo. 220
> copies printed. 'In Oct., 1757, was finished at my
> press an edition of Hentznerus, translated by Mr.
> Bentley, to which I wrote an advertisement. I
> dedicated it to the Society of Antiquaries, of which
> I am a member' (*Short Notes*). 'An edition of
> Hentznerus, with a version by Mr. Bentley, and a
> little preface of mine, were prepared [*i. e.*, as the
> first issue of the press], but are to wait [for Gray's
> *Odes*]' (*Walpole to Chute*, 12 July, 1757).

1758.

A Catalogue of the Royal and Noble Authors of
England, with Lists of their Works. *Dove,
diavolo! Messer Ludovico, avete pigliato tante
coglionerie?* Card. d'Este, to Ariosto. Vol. i.
[Strawberry Hill Bookplate.] *Printed at
Strawberry-Hill. MDCCLVIII.*

—— Vol. ii. [Strawberry Hill Bookplate.]
Printed at Strawberry-Hill. MDCCLVIII.

Vol. i., — Title; Dedication of 2 leaves to Lord Hertford; Advertisement, pp. i-viii; half-title; Text, pp. 1-219, and unpaged Index. There is also a frontispiece engraved by Grignion. Vol. ii., — Half-title; Title; Text, pp. 1-215, and unpaged Index. 8vo. 300 copies issued. A second edition, 'corrected and enlarged,' was printed in 1758 (but dated 1759), in two vols. 8vo., 'for R. and J. Dodsley, in Pallmall; and J. Graham in the Strand.' According to Baker (*Catalogue of Books, etc., printed at the Press at Strawberry Hill* [1810]), 40 copies of a supplement or Postscript to the *Royal and Noble Authors* were printed by Kirgate in 1786. 'In April, 1758, was finished the first impression of my "Catalogue of Royal and Noble Authors," which I had written the preceding year in less than five months' (*Short Notes*). 'My book is marvellously in fashion, to my great astonishment. I did not expect so much truth and such notions of liberty would have made their fortune in this our day' (*Walpole to Montagu*, 4 May, 1758). 'Dec. 5th [1758] was published the second edition of my "Catalogue of Royal and Noble Authors." Two thousand were printed, but *not* at Strawberry Hill' (*Short Notes*). 'I have but two motives for offering you the accompanying trifle [*i. e.*, the Postscript above referred to]. . . . Coming from my press, I wish it may be added to your Strawberry editions. It is so far from being designed for the public that I have printed but forty copies' (*Walpole to Hannah More*, 1 Jan., 1787).

An Account of Russia as it was in the Year 1710. By Charles Lord Whitworth. [Straw-

berry Hill Bookplate.] *Printed at Strawberry-
Hill. MDCCLVIII.*

Title, ' Advertisement,' pp. i-xxiv; Text, pp.
1-158; Errata, one page. Sm. 8vo. 700 copies
printed. 'The beginning of October [1758] I published Lord Whitworth's account of Russia, to
which I wrote the advertisement' (*Short Notes*).
'A book has been left at your ladyship's house ;
it is Lord Whitworth's Account of Russia' (*Walpole to Lady Hervey*, 17 Oct., 1758). Mr. (afterwards Lord) Whitworth was Ambassador to St.
Petersburg in the reign of Peter the Great.

The Mistakes ; or, the Happy Resentment.
A Comedy. By the late Lord * * * *
[Henry Hyde, Lord Hyde and Cornbury.]
*London : Printed by S. Richardson, in the
Year 1758.*

Title ; List of Subscribers, pp. xvi ; Advertisement, Prologue, and *Dramatis Personæ*, 2 leaves ;
Text, 1-83 ; Epilogue unpaged. Baker gives the
following particulars from the *Biographia Dramatica* as to this book : 'The Author of this Piece
was the learned, ingenious, and witty LORD CORN-
BURY, but it was never acted. He made a present
of it to that great Actress, Mrs. PORTER, to make
what Emolument she could by it. And that Lady,
after his Death, published it by Subscription, at
Five Shillings, each Book, which was so much
patronized by the Nobility and Gentry that Three
Thousand Copies were disposed of. Prefixed to it
is a Preface, by Mr. HORACE WALPOLE, at whose

Press at Strawberry-Hill it was printed.' Baker
adds, ' Mr. Yardley, who when living, kept a Bookseller's Shop in New-Inn-Passage, confirmed this
account, by asserting, that he assisted in printing
it at that Press.' But Baker nevertheless prefixes
an asterisk to the title, which implies that it was
' not printed for Mr. Walpole,' and this probably
accounts for Richardson's name on the title-page.
By the subscription list, the Hon. Horace Walpole
took 21 copies, David Garrick, 38, and Mr. Samuel
Richardson, of Salisbury Court, 4. All Walpole
says is, ' About the same time [1758] Mrs. Porter
published [for her benefit] Lord Hyde's play, to
which I had written the advertisement ' (*Short
Notes*).

A Parallel ; in the Manner of Plutarch : between a most celebrated Man of Florence ;
and One, scarce ever heard of, in England.
By the Reverend Mr. Spence. ' — *Parvis com-
ponere magna* ' — Virgil. [Portrait in circle
of Magliabecchi.] *Printed at Strawberry-
Hill, by William Robinson ; and Sold by Mes-
sieurs Dodsley, at Tully's-Head, Pall-Mall ;
for the Benefit of Mr. Hill. M.DCC.LVIII.*

Title ; Text, pp. 4-104. Sm. 8vo. 700 copies
printed. ' 1759. Feb. 2nd. I published Mr.
Spence's Parallel of Magliabecchi and Mr. Hill, a
tailor of Buckingham ; calculated to raise a little
sum of money for the latter poor man. Six hundred
copies were sold in a fortnight, and it was reprinted
in London ' (*Short Notes*). ' Mr. Spence's Magliabecchi is published to-day from Strawberry ; I be-

lieve you saw it, and shall have it ; but 't is not worth sending you on purpose ' (*Walpole to Chute,* 2 Feb., 1759).

Fugitive Pieces in Verse and Prose. *Pereunt et imputantur.* [Strawberry Hill Bookplate.] *Printed at Strawberry-Hill, MDCCLVIII.*

Title ; Dedication and 'Table of Contents,' iii–vi ; Text, 1–219. Sm. 8vo. 200 copies printed. ' In the summer of 1758, I printed some of my own Fugitive Pieces, and dedicated them to my cousin, General Conway' (*Short Notes*). 'March 17 [1759]. I began to distribute some copies of my " Fugitive Pieces," collected and printed together at Strawberry Hill, and dedicated to General Conway ' (*ibid.*). One of these, which is in the Forster Collection at South Kensington, went to Gray. ' This Book [says a MS. inscription] once belonged to Gray the Poet, and has his autograph on the Titlepage. I [*i. e.,* George Daniel, of Canonbury] bought it at Messrs. Sotheby and Wilkinson's Sale Rooms for £1. 19 on Thursday, 28 Augt. 1851, from the valuable collection of Mr. Penn of Stoke.'

1760.

Catalogue of the Pictures and Drawings in the Holbein Chamber at Strawberry Hill. *Strawberry-Hill,* 1760.

Pp. 8. 8vo. [Lowndes.]

Catalogue of the Collection, of Pictures of the Duke of Devonshire, General Guise, and the

late Sir Paul Methuen.　*Strawberry-Hill,*
1760.

> Pp. 44. 8vo. 12 copies, printed on one side
> only. [Lowndes.]

M. Annæi Lucani Pharsalia cum Notis Hugonis
Grotii, et Richardi Bentleii.　*Multa sunt con-
donanda in opere postumo.*　In Librum iv,
Nota 641.　[Emblematical vignette.]　*Strawberry-Hill, MDCCLX.*

> Title, Dedication (by Richard Cumberland to
> Halifax), and Advertisement (*Ad Lectorem*), 3
> leaves ; Text, pp. 1–525. 4to. 500 copies printed.
> Cumberland took up the editing when Bentley the
> younger resigned it. ‘I am just undertaking an
> edition of Lucan, my friend Mr. Bentley having in
> his possession his father’s notes and emendations
> on the first seven books ’ (*Walpole to Zouch*, 9 Dec.,
> 1758). ‘I would not *alone* undertake to correct the
> press ; but I am so lucky as to live in the strictest
> friendship with Dr. Bentley’s only son, who, to all
> the ornament of learning, has the amiable turn of
> mind, disposition, and easy wit ’ (*Walpole to Zouch*,
> 12 Jan., 1759). ‘Lucan is in poor forwardness. I
> have been plagued with a succession of bad printers,
> and am not got beyond the fourth book. It will
> scarce appear before next winter ’ (*Walpole to
> Zouch*, 23 Dec., 1759). ‘My Lucan is finished, but
> will not be published till after Christmas ’ (*Walpole
> to Zouch*, 27 Nov., 1760). ‘I have delivered to
> your brother . . . a Lucan, printed at Strawberry,
> which, I trust, you will think a handsome edition ’
> (*Walpole to Mann*, 27 Jan., 1761).

1762.

Anecdotes of Painting in England; with some Account of the principal Artists; and incidental Notes on other Arts; collected by the late Mr. George Vertue; and now digested and published from his original MSS. By Mr. Horace Walpole. *Multa renascentur quæ jam cecidere.* Vol. I. [Device with Walpole's crest.] *Printed by Thomas Farmer at Strawberry-Hill, MDCCLXII.*

—— *Le sachant Anglois, je crus qu'il m'alloit parler d'edifices et de peintures.* Nouvelle Eloise, vol. i. p. 245. Vol. II. [Device with Walpole's crest.] *Printed by Thomas Farmer at Strawberry-Hill, MDCCLXII.*

—— Vol. III. (Motto of six lines from Prior's *Protogenes and Apelles.*) *Strawberry-Hill : Printed in the Year MDCCLXIII.*

—— To which is added the History of the Modern Taste in Gardening. *The Glory of* Lebanon *shall come unto thee, the Fir-tree, the Pine-tree, and the Box together, to beautify the Place of my Sanctuary, and I will make the Place of my Feet glorious.* Isaiah, lx. 13. Volume the Fourth and last. *Strawberry-Hill : Printed by Thomas Kirgate, MDCCLXXI.*

Vol. i., — Title, Dedication, Preface, pp. i–xiii ; Contents ; Text, pp. 1–168, with Appendix and

Index unpaged.   Vol. ii., — Title; Text, pp. 1–158, with Appendix, Index, and 'Errata' unpaged; and 'Additional Lives to the First Edition of Anecdotes of Painting in England,' pp. 1–12.   Vol. iii., — Title; pp. 1–155, with Appendix and Index unpaged; and ' Additional Lives to the First Edition of Anecdotes of Painting in England,' pp. 1–4.   Vol. iv., — Title, Dedication, Advertisement (dated October 1, 1780), pp. i-x; Contents; Text, pp. 1–151 (dated August 12, 1770); ' Errata; ' pp. x-52; Appendix of one leaf (' Prints by or after Hogarth, discovered since the Catalogue was finished '), and Index unpaged. The volumes are 4to., with many portraits and plates. 600 copies were printed. The fourth volume was in type in 1770, but not issued until Oct., 1780. It was dedicated to the Duke of Richmond, — Lady Hervey, to whom the three earlier volumes had been inscribed, having died in 1768. A second edition of the first three volumes was printed by Thomas Kirgate at Strawberry Hill in 1765. ' Sept. 1st [1759]. I began to look over Mr. Vertue's MSS., which I bought last year for one hundred pounds, in order to compose the Lives of English Painters ' (*Short Notes*). ' 1760, Jan. 1st. I began the Lives of English Artists, from Vertue's MSS. (that is, " Anecdotes of Painting," etc.) ' (*ibid.*). 'Aug. 14th. Finished the first volume of my " Anecdotes of Painting in England." Sept. 5th, began the second volume.   Oct. 23d, finished the second volume ' (*ibid.*). ' 1761. Jan. 4th, began the third volume ' (*ibid.*). ' June 29th, resumed the third volume of my " Anecdotes of Painting," which I had laid aside after the first day ' (*ibid.*). ' Aug. 22nd, finished the third volume of my " Anecdotes of Painting " ' (*ibid.*). ' The " Anecdotes of Painting " have succeeded to the press : I have finished two volumes; but as there will at least be a third, I am not determined whether I shall not wait to publish the whole together. You will be surprised, I think, to see what a quantity of materials the industry of one man [Vertue] could amass!' (*Walpole to Zouch*, 27 Nov., 1760.) 'You drive your expectations much too fast, in thinking my "Anecdotes of Painting" are ready to appear, in demanding three volumes. You will see but *two*, and it will be February first' (*Walpole to Montagu*, 30 Dec., 1761). 'I am now publishing the third volume, and another of Engravers' (*Walpole to Dalrymple*, 31 Jan., 1764). 'I have advertised my long-delayed last volume of "Painters" to come out, and must be in town to distribute it' (*Walpole to Lady Ossory*, 23 Sept., 1780). 'I have left with Lord Harcourt for you my new old last volume of "Painters"' (*Walpole to Mason*, 13 Oct., 1780).

1763.

A Catalogue of Engravers, who have been born, or resided in England ; digested by Mr. Horace Walpole from the MSS. of Mr. George Vertue ; to which is added an Account of the Life and Works of the latter. *And Art reflected Images to Art. . . . * Pope. *Strawberry-Hill : Printed in the Year MDCCLXIII.*

Title; pp. 1-128, last page dated 'Oct. 10th, 1762;' 'Life of Mr. George Vertue,' pp. 1-14; 'List of Vertue's Works,' pp. 1-20, last page dated 'Oct. 22d, 1762;' Index of Names of Engravers,

unpaged. 4to. There are several portraits, includ-
ing one of Vertue after Richardson. 'Aug. 2nd
[1762], began the "Catalogue of Engravers." October 10th, finished it' (*Short Notes*). 'The volume of Engravers is printed off, and has been some
time; I only wait for some of the plates' (*Walpole
to Cole*, 8 Oct., 1763). 'I am now publishing the
third volume [of the 'Anecdotes of Painting'], and
another of "Engravers"' (*Walpole to Dalrymple*,
31 Jan., 1764).

1764.

Poems by Anna Chamber Countess Temple. [Plate of Strawberry Hill.] *Strawberry-Hill: Printed in the Year MDCCLXIV.*

Title, Verses signed 'Horace Walpole, January
26th, 1764,' Text, 1-34 in all. 4to. 100 copies
printed by Prat. 'I shall send you, too, Lady
Temple's Poems' (*Walpole to Montagu*, 16 July,
1764).

The Magpie and her Brood, a Fable, from the Tales of Bonaventure des Periers, Valet de Chambre to the Queen of Navarre; addressed to Miss Hotham.

4 pp., containing 72 lines, — initialed 'H. W.'
4to. 'Oct. 15th, [1764] wrote the fable of "The
Magpie and her Brood" for Miss [Henrietta]
Hotham, then near eleven years old, great niece of
Henrietta Hobart, Countess Dowager of Suffolk.
It was taken from *Les Nouvelles Récréations de
Bonaventure des Periers*, Valet-de-Chambre to the
Queen of Navarre' (*Short Notes*).

The Life of Edward Lord Herbert of Cherbury,
written by Himself. [Plate of Strawberry
Hill.] *Strawberry-Hill: Printed by Prat in
the Year MDCCLXIV.*

> Title, Dedication, and Advertisement, 5 leaves;
> Text, pp. 1-171. Folding plate portrait. 4to. 200
> copies printed. '1763. Beginning of September
> wrote the Dedication and Preface to Lord Herbert's
> Life' (*Short Notes*). 'I have got a most delect-
> able work to print, which I had great difficulty to
> obtain, and which I must use while I can have it.
> It is the life of the famous Lord Herbert of Cher-
> bury' (*Letter to the Bishop of Carlisle*, 10 July,
> 1763). 'It will not be long before I have the pleasure
> of sending you by far the most curious and enter-
> taining book that my press has produced. . . . It is
> the life of the famous Lord Herbert of Cherbury,
> and written by himself, — of the contents I will not
> anticipate one word' (*Letter to Mason*, 29 Dec.,
> 1763). 'The thing most in fashion is my edition
> of Lord Herbert's Life; people are mad after it, I
> believe because only two hundred were printed'
> (*Letter to Montagu*, 16 Dec., 1764). 'This singular
> work was printed from the original MS. in 1764, at
> Strawberry-hill, and is perhaps the most extraor-
> dinary account that ever was given seriously by a
> wise man of himself' (Walpole, *Works*, 1798,
> i. 363).

1768.

Cornélie, Vestale. Tragédie. [By the President Hénault.] *Imprimée à Strawberry-Hill,
MDCCLXVIII.*

Title; Dedication '*à Mons. Horace Walpole,*' dated '*Paris ce 27 Novembre,* 1767,' pp. iii-iv; 'Acteurs;' Text, 1-91. 8vo. 200 copies printed; 150 went to Paris. Kirgate printed it. 'My press is revived, and is printing a French play written by the old President Hénault. It was damned many years ago at Paris, and yet I think is better than some that have succeeded, and much better than any of *our* modern tragedies. I print it to please the old man, as he was exceedingly kind to me at Paris; but I doubt whether he will live till it is finished. He is to have a hundred copies, and there are to be but an hundred more, of which you shall have one' (*Letter to Montagu,* 15 April, 1768). President Hénault died November, 1770, aged eighty-six.

The Mysterious Mother. A Tragedy. By Mr. Horace Walpole. *Sit mihi fas audita loqui!* Virgil. *Printed at Strawberry-Hill:* MDCCLXVIII.

Title, 'Errata,' 'Persons' (2 leaves); Text, pp. 1-120, with Postscript, pp. 1-10 (which see for origin of play). Sm. 8vo. 50 copies issued. *The Mysterious Mother* is reprinted in Walpole's *Works,* 1798, i., pp. 37-129. 'March 15 [1768]. I finished a tragedy called "The Mysterious Mother," which I had begun Dec. 25, 1766' (*Short Notes*). 'I thank you for myself, not for my Play. . . . I accept with great thankfulness what you have voluntarily been so good as to do for me; and should the Mysterious Mother ever be performed when I am dead, it will owe to you its presentation' (*Walpole to Mason,* 11 May, 1769).

1769.

Poems by the Reverend Mr. Hoyland. *Printed at Strawberry-Hill : MDCCLXIX.*

> Title, Advertisement [by Walpole], pp. i-iv ; Text, 1-19. 8vo. 300 copies printed. In the British Museum is a copy which simply has ' Printed in the Year 1769.' ' I enclose a short Advertisement for Mr. Hoyland's poems. I mean by it to tempt people to a little more charity, and to soften to him, as much as I can, the humiliation of its being asked for him ; if you approve it, it shall be prefixed to the edition ' (*Walpole to Mason*, 5 April, 1769).

1770.

Reply to the Observations of the Rev. Dr. Milles, Dean of Exeter, and President of the Society of Antiquaries, on the Ward Robe Account.

> Pp. 24 Six copies printed, dated 28 August, 1770 [Baker]. ' In the summer of this year [1770] wrote an answer to Dr. Milles' remarks on my " Richard the Third " ' (*Short Notes*).

1772.

Copies of Seven Original Letters from King Edward VI. to Barnaby Fitzpatrick. *Strawberry-Hill. Printed* in the Year *M.DCC.LXXII.*

> Pp. viii-14. 4to. 200 copies printed. ' 1771. End of September, wrote the Advertisement to the

> "Letters of King Edward the Sixth"' (*Short Notes*). 'I have printed "King Edward's Letters," and will bring you a copy' (*Walpole to Mason*, 6 July, 1772).

Miscellaneous Antiquities ; or, a Collection of Curious Papers : either republished from *scarce Tracts*, or now first printed from *origi-nal* MSS.   Number I.   To be continued occasionally.   *Invenies illic et festa domestica vobis.   Sæpe tibi Pater est, sæpe legendus Avus.*   Ovid. Fast. Lib. 1.   *Strawberry-Hill : Printed by Thomas Kirgate*, M.DCC.LXXII.

> Title, 'Advertisement,' pp. i-iv ; Text, 1-48. 4to.   500 copies printed.   'I have since begun a kind of Desiderata Curiosa, and intend to publish it in numbers, as I get materials ; it is to be an Hospital of Foundlings ; and though I shall not take in all that offer, there will be no enquiry into the nobility of the parents ; nor shall I care how heterogeneous the brats are' (*Walpole to Mason*, 6 July, 1772).   'By that time too I shall have the first number of my " Miscellaneous Antiquities " ready.   The first essay is only a republication of some tilts and tournaments' (*Walpole to Mason*, 21 July, 1772).

Miscellaneous Antiquities ; or, a Collection of Curious Papers : either republished from *scarce Tracts*, or now first printed from *ori-ginal* MSS.   Number II.   To be continued occasionally.   *Invenies illic et festa domestica*

vobis. Sæpe tibi Pater est, sæpe legen-
dus Avus. Ovid. Fast. Lib. 1. *Straw-*
berry-Hill: Printed by Thomas Kirgate,
M.DCC.LXXII.

> Title and Text, pp. 1-62. 500 copies printed.
> 'In July [1772] wrote the "Life of Sir Thomas
> Wyat [the Elder]," No. II. of my edition of " Mis-
> cellaneous Antiquities " ' (*Short Notes*).

Memoires du Comte de Grammont, par Mon-
sieur le Comte Antoine Hamilton. Nouvelle
Edition, augmentée de Notes & d'Eclaircis-
semens, necessaires, par M. Horace Walpole.
Des gens qui écrivent pour le Comte de Gram-
mont, peuvent compter sur quelque indulgence.
V. l'Epitre prelim. p. xviii. *Imprimée à*
Strawberry-Hill, M.DCC.LXXII.

> Title, Dedication, ' Avis de L'Editeur,' 'Avertis-
> sement,' 'Epitre à Monsieur le Comte de Gram-
> mont,' ' Table des Chapitres,' 'Errata,' pp. xxiv ;
> Text, pp. 1-290: ' Table des personnes,' 3 pp. Por-
> traits of Hamilton, Mdlle. d'Hamilton, and Philibert
> Comte de Grammont. 4to. 100 copies printed ; 30
> went to Paris. It was dedicated to Madame du
> Deffand, as follows : *' L'Editeur vous consacre*
> *cette Edition, comme un monument de son Amitié, de*
> *son Admiration, & de son Respect ; à Vous, dont les*
> *Grâces, l'Esprit, & le Goût retracent au siecle présent*
> *le siecle de Louis quatorze & les agremens de*
> *l'Auteur de ces Mémoires.'* 'I want to send you
> these [the *Miscellaneous Antiquities*] . . . and a
> "Grammont," of which I have printed only a

hundred copies, and which will be extremely scarce, as twenty-five copies are gone to France' (*Walpole to Cole*, 8 Jan., 1773).

1774.

A Description of the Villa of Horace Walpole. [Plate of Strawberry Hill.] A Description of the Villa of Horace Walpole, youngest son of Sir Robert Walpole Earl of Orford, at Strawberry-Hill, near Twickenham. With an Inventory of the Furniture, Pictures, Curiosities, &c. *Strawberry-Hill : Printed by Thomas Kirgate*, M.DCC.LXXIV.

Two titles; Text, pp. 1-119. 4to. 100 copies printed, 6 on large paper. Many copies have the following: 'Appendix. Pictures and Curiosities added since the Catalogue was printed,' pp. 121-145; 'List of the Books printed at Strawberry-Hill,' unpaged; 'Additions since the Appendix,' pp. 149–152; 'More Additions,' pp. 153-158. Baker speaks of an earlier issue of 65 pp. which we have not met with. Lowndes (*Appendix to Bibliographer's Manual*, 1864, p. 239) states that it was said by Kirgate to have been used by the servants in showing the house, and differed entirely from the editions of 1774 and 1784.

1775.

To Mrs. Crewe. [Verses by Charles James Fox.] N.D.

Pp. 2. Single leaf. 4to. 300 copies printed. Walpole speaks of these in a letter to Mason dated 12
June, 1774; and he sends a copy of them to him,
27 May, 1775. Mrs. Crewe, the Amoret addressed,
was the daughter of Fulke Greville, and the wife
of J. Crewe. She was painted by Reynolds as an
Alpine shepherdess.

Dorinda, a Town Eclogue. [By the Hon.
Richard Fitzpatrick, brother of the Earl of
Ossory.] [Plate of Strawberry Hill.] *Straw-
berry-Hill : Printed by Thomas Kirgate.
M.DCC.LXXV.*

Title ; Text, 3-8. 4to. 300 copies printed. ‘I
shall send you soon Fitzpatrick’s “Town Eclogue,”
from my own furnace. The verses are charmingly
smooth and easy. . . .’ ‘P. S. Here is the
Eclogue ’ (*Letter to Mason*, 12 June, 1774).

1778.

The Sleep-Walker, a Comedy : in two Acts.
Translated from the French [of Antoine de
Ferriol, Comte de Pont de Veyle], in March,
M.DCC.LXXVIII. [By Elizabeth Lady
Craven, afterwards Margravine of Anspach.]
*Strawberry-Hill : Printed by T. Kirgate,
M.DCC.LXXVIII.*

Title, Quatrain, Prologue, Epilogue, Persons, pp.
i-viii ; Text, 1-56. 8vo. 75 copies printed. The
quatrain is by Walpole to Lady Craven, ‘on her
Translation of the Somnambule.’ ‘ I will send . . .
for yourself a translation of a French play. . . . It

is not for your reading, but as one of the Strawberry editions, and one of the rarest; for I have
printed but seventy-five copies. It was to oblige
Lady Craven, the translatress . . .' (*Walpole to
Cole*, 22 Aug., 1778).

1779.

A Letter to the Editor of the Miscellanies of
Thomas Chatterton. *Strawberry-Hill: Printed
by T. Kirgate*, M.DCC.LXXIX.

Half-title ; Title ; Text, pp. 1-55. The letter is
dated at end : 'May 23, 1778.' 8vo. 200 copies
printed. '1779. In the preceding autumn had
written a defence of myself against the unjust
aspersions in the Preface to the Miscellanies of
Chatterton. Printed 200 copies at Strawberry
Hill this January, and gave them away. It was
much enlarged from what I had written in July'
(*Short Notes*).

1780.

To the Lady Horatia Waldegrave, on the
Death of the Duke of Ancaster. [Verses by
Mr. Charles Miller.] N. D.

Pp. 3, dated at end ' A. D. 1779.' 4to. 150 copies
printed. ' I enclose a copy of verses, which I have
just printed at Strawberry, only a few copies, and
which I hope you will think pretty. They were
written three months ago by Mr. Charles Miller,
brother of Sir John, on seeing Lady Horatia at
Nuneham. The poor girl is better' (*Walpole to
Lady Ossory*, 29 Jan., 1780). Lady Horatia

Waldegrave was to have been married to the Duke of Ancaster, who died in 1779.

1781.

The Muse recalled, an Ode, occasioned by the Nuptials of Lord Viscount Althorp and Miss Lavinia Bingham, eldest daughter of Charles Lord Lucan, March vi., M.DCC.LXXXI. By William Jones, Esq. [afterwards Sir William Jones]. *Strawberry-Hill : Printed by Thomas Kirgate, M.DCC.LXXXI.*

> Title ; pp. 1-8. 4to. 250 copies printed. There is a well-known portrait of Lavinia Bingham by Reynolds, in which she wears a straw hat with a blue ribbon.

A Letter from the Honourable Thomas Walpole, to the Governor and Committee of the Treasury of the Bank of England. *Strawberry-Hill : Printed by Thomas Kirgate, M.DCC.LXXXI.*

> Title, and pp. 16 (last blank). 4to. 120 copies printed.

1784.

A Description of the Villa of Mr. Horace Walpole, youngest son of Sir Robert Walpole Earl of Orford, at Strawberry-Hill near Twickenham, Middlesex. With an Inventory of the Furniture, Pictures, Curiosities, &c. *Strawberry-Hill : Printed by Thomas Kirgate, M.DCC.LXXXIV.*

Title ; ' Preface.' i-iv ; Text, pp. 1-88. 'Errata, etc,' 'Appendix,' pp. 89-92 ; 'Curiosities added,' etc., 93-4 ; 'More Additions,' 95-6. 27 plates. 4to. 200 copies printed. 'The next time he [Sir Horace Mann's nephew] visits you, I may be able to send you a description of my *Galleria*, — I have long been preparing it, and it is almost finished, — with some prints, which, however, I doubt, will convey no very adequate idea of it' (*Walpole to Mann*, 30 Sept., 1784). 'In the list for which Lord Ossory asks, is the Description of this place ; now, though printed, I have entirely kept it up [i. e., *held it back*], and mean to do so while I live' (*Walpole to Lady Ossory*, 15 Sept., 1787).

1785.

Hieroglyphic Tales.　*Schah Baham ne compre-noit jamais bien que les choses absurdes & hors de toute vraisemblance.　Le Sopha, p. 5. Strawberry-Hill : Printed by T. Kirgate, M.DCC.LXXXV.*

Title ; 'Preface,' iii–ix ; Text, pp. 50 ; 'Postscript.' 8vo. Walpole's own MS. note in the Dyce example says, 'Only six copies of this were printed, besides the revised copy.' '1772. This year, the last, and sometime before, wrote some Hieroglyphic Tales. There are only five' (*Short Notes*). 'I have some strange things in my drawer, even wilder than the 'Castle of Otranto,' and called 'Hieroglyphic Tales ;' but they were not written lately, nor in the gout, nor, whatever they may seem, written when I was out of my senses' (*Wal-*

pole to Cole, 28 Jan., 1779). 'This [he is speaking of Darwin's *Botanic Garden*] is only the Second Part; for, like my King's eldest daughter in the 'Hieroglyphic Tales,' the First Part is not born yet: no matter ' (*Walpole to the Miss Berrys*, 28 April, 1789). In 1822, the *Hieroglyphic Tales* were reprinted at Newcastle for Emerson Charnley.

Essay on Modern Gardening, by Mr. Horace Walpole. [Strawberry Hill Bookplate.] Essai sur l'Art des Jardins Modernes, par M. Horace Walpole, traduit en François by M. le Duc de Nivernois, en MDCCLXXXIV. *Imprimé à Strawberry-Hill, par T. Kirgate,* MDCCLXXXV.

Two titles; English and French Text on opposite pages, 1-94. 4to. 400 copies printed. 'How may I send you a new book printed here? . . . It is the translation of my ' Essay on Modern Gardens ' by the Duc de Nivernois. . . . You will find it a most beautiful piece of French, of the genuine French spoken by the Duc de la Rochefoucault and Madame de Sévigné, and not the metaphysical galimatias of La Harpe and Thomas, &c., which Madame du Deffand protested she did not understand. The versions of Milton and Pope are wonderfully exact and poetic and elegant, and the fidelity of the whole translation, extraordinary' (*Walpole to Lady Ossory*, 17 Sept., 1785). The original MS. of the Duc de Nivernois — ' a most exquisite specimen of penmanship ' — was among the papers at Strawberry.

1789.

Bishop Bonner's Ghost. [By Hannah More.]
[Plate of Strawberry Hill.] *Strawberry-
Hill: Printed by Thomas Kirgate,
MDCCLXXXIX.*

> Title and argument, 2 leaves; Text, pp. 1-4.
> 4to. 96 copies printed, 2 on brown paper, one of
> which was at Strawberry. It was written when
> Hannah More ('my *imprimée*,' as Walpole calls
> her) was on a visit to Dr. Beilby Porteus, Bishop
> of London, at his palace at Fulham, June, 1789.
> 'I will forgive all your enormities if you will let
> me print your poem. I like to filch a little immor-
> tality out of others, and the Strawberry press could
> never have a better opportunity' (*Walpole to
> Hannah More*, 23 June, 1789). 'The enclosed
> copy of verses pleased me so much, that, though
> not intended for publication, I prevailed on the
> authoress, Miss Hannah More, to allow me to take
> off a small number.' . . . 'I have been disap-
> pointed of the completion of "Bonner's Ghost,"
> by my rolling press being out of order, and was
> forced to send the whole impression to town to
> have the copper-plate taken off. . . . Kirgate has
> brought the whole impression, and I shall have the
> pleasure of sending your Ladyship this with a
> "Bonner's Ghost" to-morrow morning ' (*Walpole
> to Lady Ossory*, 16-18 July, 1789).

The History of Alcidalis and Zelida. A tale of
the Fourteenth Century. [By Vincent
de Voiture.] *Printed at Strawberry-Hill.
MDCCLXXXIX.*

Title; Text, pp. 3-96. 8vo. This is a translation of Voiture's unfinished *Histoire d'Alcidalis et de Zelide.* (See *Nouvelles Œuvres de Monsieur de Voiture. Nouvelle Edition. A Paris, Chez Louis Bilaine, au Palais, au second Pilier de la grand' Salle, à la Palme & au Grand Cesar,* MDCLXXII.) There is a copy in the Dyce Collection. Another was sold in 1823 with the books of John Trotter Brockett, in whose catalogue it was said to be 'surreptitiously printed.' Kirgate had a copy, although Baker does not mention it.

Doubtful Date.

Verses sent to Lady Charles Spencer [Mary Beauclerc, daughter of Lord Vere, and wife of Lord Charles Spencer] with a painted Taffety, occasioned by saying she was low in Pocket and could not buy a new Gown.

Single leaf. Baker says these were by Anna Chamber, Countess Temple.

Besides the above, Walpole printed at his press in 1770 vols. i. and ii. of a 4to edition of his works.

INDEX.

* 9 7 8 3 3 3 7 0 8 7 4 6 3 *